All for You

All for You

by LAURA FLORAND

Chapter 1

Paris, near Rêpublique

Célie worked in heaven. Every day she ran up the stairs to it, into the light that reached down to her, shining through the great casement windows as she came into the *laboratoire*, gleaming in soft dark tones off the marble counters. She hung up her helmet and black leather jacket and pulled on her black chef's jacket instead and ran her fingers through her hair to perk it back out into its current wild pixie cut. She washed her hands and stroked one palm all down the length of one long marble counter as she headed to check on her chocolates from the day before.

Oh, the beauties. There they were, the flat, perfect squares with their little prints, subtle but adamant, the way her boss liked them. Perfect. There were the ganaches and the pralinés setting up in their metal frames. Day three on the mint ganache. Time to slice it into squares with the *guitare* and send them to the enrober.

She called teasing hellos to everyone. "What, you here already, Amand? I didn't expect you until noon." Totally unfair to the hardworking caramellier, but he had slept in once, after a birthday bash, arriving to work so late and so horrified at himself that no one had ever let him forget it.

"Dom, when's the wedding again?" Dominique Richard, their boss, was diligently trying to resist marrying his girlfriend until he had given her enough time to figure out what a bad bet he was, and the only way to handle that was tease him. Otherwise Célie's heart might squeeze too much in this warm, fuzzy, mushy urge to give the man a big hug—and then a very hard shove into the arms of his happiness.

Guys who screwed over a woman's chance at happiness because they were so convinced they weren't good enough did *not* earn any points in her book.

"Can somebody work around here besides me?" Dom asked in complete exasperation, totally unmerited, just because the guy had no idea how to deal with all the teasing that came his way. It was why they couldn't resist. He was so big, and he got all ruffled and grouchy and adorable.

"I want to have time to pick out my dress!" Célie protested, hauling down the *guitare*. "I know exactly what you two are going to do. You'll put it off until all of a sudden you wander in some Monday with a stunned, scared look on your face, and we'll find out you eloped over the weekend to some village in Papua New Guinea. And we'll have missed the whole thing!"

Dom growled desperately, like a persecuted bear, and bent his head over his éclairs.

Célie grinned and started slicing her mint ganache into squares, the guitar wires cutting through it effortlessly. *There you go.* She tasted one. Soft, dissolving in her mouth, delicately infused with fresh mint. *Mmm. Perfect. Time to get it all dressed up.* Enrobing time.

She got to spend her days like this. In one of the top chocolate *laboratoires* in Paris. Okay, the top, but some people over in the Sixth like a certain Sylvain Marquis persisted in disputing that point. What*ever.* He was such a classicist. *Bo*ring. And *everyone* knew that cinnamon did not marry well with dark chocolate, so that latest Cade Marquis bar of his was just ridiculous.

And she didn't even want to think about Simon Casset with his stupid sculptures. So he could do fancy sculptures. Was that real chocolate? Did people eat that stuff? No. So. *She* did important chocolate. Chocolate that adventured. Chocolate people wanted to sink their teeth into. Chocolate that opened a whole world up in front of a person, right there in her mouth.

Chocolate that was so much beyond anything she had ever dreamed her life would be as a teenager. *God,* she loved her day. She stretched out her arms, nearly bopped their apprentice Zoe, who was carrying a bowl of chocolate to the scale, grinned at her in apology, and carried her mint ganaches over to the enrober.

She'd been loving her day for a little over three hours and was getting kind of ready to take a little break from doing so and let her back muscles relax for fifteen minutes when Guillemette showed up at the top of the stairs. Célie cocked her eyebrows at the other woman hopefully. Time for a little not-smoke break, perhaps? Were things quiet enough downstairs? Célie didn't smoke anymore, not since some stupid guy she once knew made her quit and she found out how many *flavors* there were out there when they weren't being hidden by tobacco. But sometimes she'd give just about anything to be able to hold a cigarette between her fingers and blow smoke out with a sexy purse of her lips and truly believe that was all it took to make her cool.

Because the double ear piercings and the spiky pixie hair were a lot less expensive over the long-term, but they could be misinterpreted as bravado, whereas—

A teenager slouching against a wall and blowing smoke from her mouth was *always* clearly genuine coolness, no bravado about it, of course. Célie rolled her eyes at herself, and Guillemette, instead of gesturing for her to come join her for the not-smoke break, instead came up to her counter where she was working and stole a little chocolate. "There's a guy here to see you," Guillemette said a little doubtfully. "And we're getting low on the Arabica."

Célie glanced at the trolley full of trays where the Arabica chocolates had finished and were ready to be transferred to metal flats. "I'll bring some down with me. Who's the guy?" Maybe that guy she had met Saturday, Danny and Tiare's friend? She tried to figure out if she felt any excitement about that, but adrenaline ran pretty high in her on a normal day in the *laboratoire*, so it was hard to tell.

"He didn't say."

And Guillemette hadn't asked? Maybe there had been several customers at once or something.

"I'll be down in a second," Célie said, and Guillemette headed back while Célie loaded up a couple of the metal flats they used in the display cases with the Arabica, with its subtle texture, no prints on this one. Dark and exotic and touched with coffee.

She ran down the spiral metal stairs with her usual happy energy, and halfway down, the face of the big man waiting with his hands in his pockets by the pastry display counter came into view, and she—

Tripped.

The trays flew out of her hands as her foot caught on one of the metal steps, and she grabbed after them even as they sailed away. Her knuckles knocked against one tray, and chocolates shot off it, raining down everywhere just as she started to realize she was falling, too.

Oh, *fuck*, that instant flashing realization of how much this was going to hurt and how much too late it was to save herself, even as she tried to grab the banister, and—

Hard hands caught her, and she *oofed* into them and right up against a big body, caught like a rugby ball, except it was raining chocolates during this game, and—

She gasped for breath, post impact, and pulled herself upright, staring up at the person who still held her in steadying hands.

Wary, hard, intense hazel green eyes stared back down at her. He looked caught, instead of her, his lips parted, as if maybe he had meant to say something. But, looking down at her, he didn't say anything at all.

Strong eyebrows, strong stubborn forehead and cheekbones and chin—every single damn bone in his body stubborn—and skin so much more tanned and weathered than when she had last seen it. Brown hair cropped military-close to his head and sanded by sun.

Célie wrenched back out of his hands, her own flying to her face as she burst into tears.

Just—burst. Right there in public, with all her colleagues and their customers around her. She backed up a step and then another, tears flooding down her cheeks, chocolate crushing under her feet.

"Célie," he said, and even his voice sounded rougher and tougher. And wary.

She turned and ran back up the staircase, dashing at her eyes to try to see the steps through the tears, and burst back up through the glass doors into the *laboratoire*. Dom looked up immediately, and then straightened. "Célie? *What's wrong?*"

Big, bad Dom, yeah, right, with the heart of gold. He came forward while she shook her head, having nothing she could tell him, scrubbing at her eyes in vain.

The glass door behind her opened. "Célie," that rough, half-familiar voice said. "I—"

She darted toward the other end of the *laboratoire* and her ganache cooling room.

"Get the fuck out of my kitchen," Dom said behind her, flat, and she paused, half turning.

Dom Richard, big and dark, stood blocking the other man in the glass doorway. Joss locked eyes with him, these two big dangerous men, one who wanted in and one who wasn't about to let him. Célie bit a finger, on sudden fear, and started back toward them.

Joss Castel looked past Dom to her. Their eyes held.

"Célie, go in the other room," Dom said without turning around. And to Joss: "You. *Get out.*"

Joss thrust his hands in his pockets. Out of combat. Sheathing his weapons. He nodded once, a jerk of his head at Célie, and turned and made his way down the stairs.

Dom followed. Célie went to the casement window above the store's entrance and watched as Joss left the store, crossed the street, and turned to look up at the window. She started crying again, just at that look, and when she lifted her hand to swipe her eyes, he must have caught the movement through the reflection off the glass, because his gaze focused on her.

"What was that all about?" Dom asked behind her. She turned, but she couldn't quite get herself to leave the window. She couldn't quite get herself to walk out of sight. "Célie, who is that guy and what did he do?"

She shook her head.

"Célie."

She slashed a hand through the air, wishing she could shut things down like a *man* could, make her hand say, *This subject is closed.* When *Dom* slashed a subject closed with one move of his hand like that, no one messed with *him.* Well, except for her, of course. "Just someone I knew before. Years ago. Before I worked here."

"When you lived in Tarterets?" Their old, bad *banlieue.* "And he was bad? Did he hit you? Was he dealing? What was it?"

She gazed at Dom uneasily. For all that he was so big and bad and dark, always seeming to have that threat of violence in him, it was the first time she had ever seen him about to commit violence.

"No," she said quickly. "No. He didn't."

"Célie."

"No, he really didn't, damn it, Dom! *Merde.* Do you think I would *let* him?"

"You couldn't have been over eighteen."

"Yeah, well—he didn't."

Dom's teeth showed, like a man who didn't believe her and was about to reach out and rip the truth out of her. "Then *what—*"

"He left me! That's all. He fucking left me there, so that he could go make himself into a better person. Yeah. So *fuck you,* Dom. Go marry your girlfriend instead of playing around with this *I-need-to-be-good-enough* shit and leave me alone!"

And she sank down on her butt, right there in the cooling room, between the trolleys full of chocolate and the marble island, in the slanting light from the casement window, and cried.

Just cried and cried and cried.

It sure as hell put a damper on chocolate production for a while, but for as long as she needed it, people did leave her alone.

Chapter 2

Les Tarterets, five years before

"Always smiling," said Louis, the old, gray-haired baker who had taken Célie on as an apprentice three years ago, at fifteen, when she had first made the choice to pursue a practical career instead of the university track. Girls like her, with no father, a sometimes-there mother, and a brother and cousins who made their money off drugs and dog fights, well ... university in the distant future seemed a very tenuous way of giving her life possibilities. Baking and pastry, though—a fifteen-year-old girl could start *that* career, could give herself something that *mattered*. That had value. That she could count on, when she could count on nothing else.

Plus she loved it. As she opened the oven to slide out fresh croissants, the vivid, happy smell of that fresh flakiness washed over her, and she grinned at Louis. Outside, the world might weigh heavy and gray, but a baker could always gather all these scents around her, sink her hands into dough, and stick her tongue out at that nasty world. *You can't get me. Nah, nah, nah, nah, nah, nah.*

Louis shook his head at her. "I suppose that boyfriend of yours is waiting out there?"

Célie checked, and yes, Joss *was*. That big rugby body of his leaning against the wall up there a little to the right, on the opposite side of the street, where he always waited, his brown hair a little tousled. He held something in his hand that was too small to see, his hand fisting over it and relaxing, then fisting tight again, his expression somber, his head bent.

She bounced on her toes and had to flip her braid back off her shoulder. The thing was a pure pain in baking—she should really cut her hair off—but Joss liked to tug it sometimes. Recently, she'd dyed it burgundy, just to make it catch the eye more. More tugs that way, maybe.

"He's not my boyfriend," she forced herself to say.

Because ... he wasn't.

Never had been.

Never shown the slightest interest in taking on that role.

Louis rolled his eyes.

"He's just ... a friend," she said. She'd almost said "a friend of my brother," but nobody liked her brother anymore.

"He's a good friend," Louis said dryly.

"I know," Célie said smugly. It wasn't every girl in their *banlieue* of graffiti and concrete and burned cars who had a *good* friend, a guy she could trust, a guy she could count on. Célie was lucky. Or Joss was just that good a guy. Or maybe she was even ... worth it, a little bit? The friendship of a good guy? Maybe there was something about her that was *likable* and good and deserved it?

Of course there was. She stuck her chin up, determined to believe it.

"You'd better go," Louis said with half-pretend exasperation. "You don't want to keep him waiting."

"He'll wait," Célie said confidently. Steady and patient, he would wait as long as it took for her to get off. But she was already unbuttoning her chef's jacket.

Because no matter how bad the world outside this bakery, when Joss showed up, Célie couldn't wait to get off work.

She boxed up her favorite thing she had done that day, a fig tart with balsamic caramel gleaming so prettily over its brown-red fruit and pale custard cream, and ran across the street to him with it.

Joss shoved whatever he'd had in his hand into his pocket as soon as he saw her and straightened from the wall as she got closer to him, so that he was so big, and she was so small, and a girl definitely felt *protected*. Safe. She loved it when she could walk home with him. No one ever messed with her at all. Maybe it was the size of him, or maybe it was the way he carried himself, or maybe it was the way that stubborn jaw made your fist feel fragile, as if it would break if you tried to punch it.

She grinned at him and bounced up on her toes for kisses on each cheek. Damn. He didn't smell of motor oil again today. Meaning still no new job after association with her brother had gotten him fired from his last one. That probably explained the tension in him, too.

A kiss on each cheek and a tug of her braid. "Célie."

Just her name. He had a way of saying it that made her come true.

"Hey, Joss," she said sassily, so he would know that she was just the kid sister who teased and taunted him. So he wouldn't know how those steady hazel green eyes of his caught at her heart every time and how she had to keep squashing her unruly crush down into the bottom of her stomach where it wiggled nonstop whenever he was around. All her friends had crushes on him, too, it wasn't like she was weird. But he was *her* brother's friend, so she got to keep him. Even if not in a crush way.

"Hungry?" She held up her box to him. She liked to keep the reward system going: *If you stop by when I'm getting off work, I'll feed you something yummy. So ... stop by.*

He smiled a little. "I'm always hungry when you're around, Célie."

She grinned in triumph. Pavlov had nothing on her. "Wait until you see this!" She opened the box.

He looked at the fig tart and then at her face. Joss's face was always a hard read—he kept such an adamant control over his expression—but something moved across it, intense almost to pain. "Célie," he said, with unexpected roughness, "you're the best part of my day."

Damn it. Joss was having such a hard time. And all because of her damn brother. That his friend's brat sister had become the best part of his day was proof enough of how shitty the rest of his life must seem.

But at least it was nice to know she helped make it better. She was having a hard time, too, and Joss helped make her better.

She hugged herself proudly as he lifted the tart to his mouth. As his teeth sank into it, she bounced on her toes again and made a little humming sound at the flavors and textures that must be bursting in his mouth.

"Mmm," he said, his voice deepening, his eyes warm on her.

It was looks like those that made her crush squirm so much she couldn't stand still. So she pivoted out and back and took a step in the direction of their HLM, the giant tower of broken-windowed concrete and rarely functioning elevators that housed all the people the Paris government had wanted to keep around as a workforce, but not badly enough to let them live in actual Paris. Well, that was its immigration history anyway. Back in the sixties, Parisian government officials had actually patted themselves on the back for building those HLMs. After all, they'd been such a step up from disease-ridden shantytowns where workers had lived among rats and mud and rubbish.

The problem was, you could make a giant step up from rats and mud and still have quite a way to climb.

But *Célie* was going to climb it. She was not going to get stuck here, no way. Her favorite dream of riding out of this place on the back of a motorcycle behind Joss washed through her, and she tried to stamp that pesky dream back down in with the rest of the wiggles in her stomach.

But ... it would be so perfect. They could go find some little town in the south of France that needed a baker and a mechanic, far away from drug trades and gangs and hopelessness, and, God, would she be happy.

"Coming, slowpoke?" she challenged over her shoulder, sticking her tongue out at him. Any time her crush tried to take over, she had to make sure it was obvious that she was just his friend's impudent kid sister and *not* stupidly in love with him.

His gaze flickered up from—her butt? Could it possibly be? Had he actually *noticed* she had a butt? But his expression was calm, neutral. "I'll try to keep up," he said, amused, reaching her with one long stride. "Célie, I still think pink is more your color." He tugged her braid again.

She frowned at him. "I'm far too tough for pink. Burgundy, now, burgundy makes a statement." A *tough* statement. Vibrant but not to be messed with.

They passed a *tabac* and a waft of cigarette smoke came through the door as someone left it, carrying a fresh packet of cigarettes. Célie craned her neck to take a breath of the smoke.

Joss closed his hand over her nape and kept her going. "Bad for you."

Célie rolled her eyes. "I *got* it, Joss. I'm not going to start again."

"Promise?"

"I already promised ten times!"

He didn't say anything at all, just kept walking, not letting go of her nape. Joss could out-stubborn her any day.

"I promise!"

"Even when I'm not around, Célie. Don't do it behind my back either." He held her eyes, something troubled in his.

God, did he blame himself in part because Ludo had gone so wrong? *Nobody* could have stopped Ludo. She could personally attest to that, as the little sister who had tried. Plus, plenty of guys his age did time for drugs or theft or assault around here, it wasn't like he was the worst guy in the world or anything.

Joss was, in fact, the only really good guy she knew. But he made up for all of them. In fact, he seemed to take it as his personal responsibility to make up for all of them—always the guy who shielded her from her brother's most irresponsible actions and kept her brother's other friends in line as she was growing up, growing more female and therefore more vulnerable. When she tried to learn how to flirt, she mostly practiced on him. He was safe. As she grew older, the safety stayed reassuring but it grew more and more frustrating, too.

"I *promise*, Joss," she said, holding his eyes in return, putting everything of her in it.

He held her eyes one more moment. Then his hand squeezed the nape of her neck and dropped away. He shoved it into his pocket, hiding that warmth from her.

"Is everything okay?" she asked.

He moved his shoulders in a minimal shrug.

She crinkled her nose. "No ... uh ... no luck on the job search?" she tested, and winced internally. She knew Joss's pride. She knew how much he hated looking like a loser in front of his friend's kid sister. And she never could figure out how to convey to him that she thought the world of him, no matter what. Didn't it show at all, when she brought out some special dessert for him every day and her whole self lit up just to see him? She couldn't *tell* him. If she exposed her crush too openly, he might distance her. For her own good, of course. Every time Joss did something that hurt her heart, it was for her own good.

His lips pressed tight, and for a moment she thought he wouldn't answer. But then he said, "I'll probably have to leave here, to have any chance."

Instantly, that vision flooded back: her clinging to him on the back of a motorcycle, *blowing* this place as that deep, powerful motor roared them out of here to a new life.

Her nails flexed into her palm, trying to drive that dream back.

It was kind of hell having such a crush on her brother's friend, when she knew it wasn't reciprocated.

But she still hadn't managed to get up the courage to just *leave him* and go find her own way in the world, either. *Come on, Célie, you're eighteen now. You've got to just do it.*

They reached the worn-out green space in front of their building that once upon a time had been some architect's idea of bringing nature to fifteen-story towers. All three of the limp, exhausted trees had their trunks covered with initials, bottles broken at their bases, here and there a syringe. Giant concrete towers rose above them, as if they'd been set there to turn humans into cockroaches and then crush the life out of them. Célie's apartment was up there, floor fourteen, its windows unbroken. Joss's was on floor seven.

A lot of stairs, when the elevator broke down.

"Where would you go?" she asked. *Maybe I can tag along.*

"Away from here," he said flatly.

Yeah. That was pretty much where she wanted to go, too.

She touched his wrist gently. Once in a while she tried something like that. *I'm sixteen now, all grown up. I'm seventeen now, all grown up. I'm eighteen now, all grown up. Are you ever going to notice?*

He turned and faced her, in front of the doors to their tower, under a lonely tree scarred with so many initials that there was even one that said *J + C* that didn't mean them at all. Over it, someone had carved an obscene symbol.

"Joss." Her heart broke a little for him. Sure, he tried to keep his expression neutral, but she'd known Joss a long time now. Behind that stoic expression, he held so much tense determination not to be beaten down by this place. And yet it was trying to break him. He was a *good* mechanic, she knew he was. He was a *good* guy. A *really good* guy. And yet just by association with her drug-dealing brother, he'd lost his job. He couldn't even find another one. It hurt her, every day that he couldn't.

"Joss. You know you're amazing, don't you?" She felt so shy to say it but *somebody* had to tell him.

"Célie." His eyes closed a second, and he shook his head.

She stuck her chin up. "Well, you are."

"Célie." He lifted his hand to cup her cheek, and she stilled. Even her heart tried to stop. Her lips parted, and she stared up at him.

Had he—was he—had Joss finally noticed her? As something other than his friend's pain-in-the-neck kid sister? Had Ludo's removal from their relationship somehow allowed him to *see* her?

"I'm *never* going to let you down," Joss said, low and fierce. "I swear it, Célie."

"No," she agreed firmly, making a fist of encouragement, cheering him on. "You won't. I know you won't." *You're such a good guy. My only good guy. And* behave, *you stupid wiggles.* "You can do anything."

"Right," he agreed, that monosyllabic intensity of Joss's that turned one short word into a vow. He shifted his hand to her chin, still holding her eyes.

She held very still. She kept her lips faintly parted. Just in case that was all the encouragement he needed to bend his head and ...

Kiss her on the cheek.

Damn it!

The other cheek.

Her heart sank in disappointment.

But he didn't let go of her chin, after the good-bye *bises* were finished. "Célie. I've got to go." That deep voice of his made her want to curl up with it so badly. Most nights, she pretended Joss and his deep voice were in her bedroom with her, just to comfort her enough so that she could fall asleep.

Something about the intensity in his eyes made her want to step forward and curl up in him now—press herself against his chest, get him to fold his arms around her, as if he was going to be wrenched from her if she didn't. But other than the time when she'd started crying after her brother was arrested, he never did hold her. She was the kid sister.

"I know," she said wistfully. Of course he had to go. He probably had a date or something. She was such an idiot.

His other hand shifted in his pocket. As if he was clenching it and unclenching it.

"You'll be all right?" he said.

Up went her chin. "Of course I will!" This place could *not* get to her.

He bent again. And—

Damn it.

A third kiss on her cheek. A fourth.

The full four *bises*, as if they came from some extra-affectionate part of France, the kind of regions where arriving at a party and greeting all the guests exhausted your cheeks. Not so common here, unless for a greeting after a long absence or a long good-bye. Or maybe, to give each other courage.

Or *maybe* because ... he was noticing her? Maybe *liking* her? Not quite ready to move straight to a kiss on the mouth, but getting interested? Wanting an excuse to touch her more?

She tried to hold very still, so as not to shake any possibility of a birth of interest away.

"Célie." He closed his eyes a moment. "The way you look at me."

What was wrong with the way she looked at him? Heat climbed into her cheeks. Damn it, if he knew about those wiggles ...

He opened his eyes, holding hers with that beautiful, beautiful hazel green. "Célie. You know I'm just a man, right?"

"No!" she said indignantly. She did not know that at all.

"Made of clay," Joss said, his mouth turning down. "I'm not good enough for the way you look at me."

Okay, now he was talking crazy. She put both hands on his chest. "You're *Joss*. You can do anything!" She shouldn't have to keep repeating that last part. It was so inherently true to who he was that she wanted to *kick* the world, kick her own brother, for vandalizing Joss's belief in himself. People around here got their graffiti on everything else, but they could damn well keep their grimy, destructive hands off Joss Castel.

He stared down at her a long moment. Then strength seemed to infuse him, even more strength than he always held, as if he grew three centimeters in every direction just from her belief in him.

Well, *good*. She willed more of it into him, trying to pour it through her eyes into his heart. *You are the biggest, best, most wonderful guy in the world. Don't let this get you down. You can do anything!*

"Right," Joss said. He took a deep breath that seemed to expand his chest to superhero size. He squeezed her chin one last time. "I *can* be good enough," he said like a vow. "Way the hell better than this."

Exactly. You can do it! Don't let this place get you down! She pushed the thoughts into him until her forehead hurt from the effort.

His hand left her chin—but then it was as if he couldn't stop touching her, because he stroked a wisp of hair back off her face, tucking it behind her ear. His fingers lingered over the curve of her ear and then, far too soon, fell away.

Célie flushed all through her, this rosy, starstruck hope.

"*Bonne nuit*, Célie." He started to turn away, then stopped, and looked back, gazing down at her as if he had to memorize her for a test. "You really are the best part of my day."

So Célie was *radiant* when she curled up in her bed that night. She glowed so much she could have been her own night-light. Tomorrow—tomorrow she was going to wear her sexiest shirt, the one with the deep V-neck, and the jeans that really hugged her butt, and, and ... she lost herself in dreams of what he would do, of how she might just *trip* a little when he kissed her cheeks, see if she might get their lips to meet for real tomorrow, because maybe he would *like it.* She dreamed it until those dreams blurred into sleep.

So it was a complete shock to her when his mother showed up at the bakery the next day in a hysterical rage, blaming Célie because the evening before, her son had caught a train south and joined the Foreign Legion.

Chapter 3

When Célie finally came out of the ganache room so people could work, keeping her head down, trying to get to the bathroom first to wash her face before she had to make eye contact, Jaime was sitting on a stool beside Dom, leaning back on one elbow on the counter, talking to him, passion fruit caramel hair angling against her cheek. Her blue eyes locked on Célie immediately. "Hey, Célie."

Oh, crap. Dom had called for female intervention. His über-freckled fiancée was exactly the perfect person to doggedly pursue the issue until she got to the bottom of some suspected abuse of the sisterhood. Célie scowled at her boss, for being so damn *bossy*, as if he had the right to interfere in his employees' personal lives or something, and went on to the bathroom.

Cold water on her face did not really do a whole hell of a lot of good. She turned her back on the mirror and sank against the sink behind her, holding on to it with both hands, and just—holding, there, for a moment. Holding everything. She drew yet another deep breath and sighed it out and finally went out to deal with things.

"So." Jaime scooped her arm up, elbow to elbow, as if they were best sisters about to go out for a walk.

Célie liked Jaime, so astonishingly different from all the women with whom she had been convinced Dom would screw himself over. In a good mood, she liked teasing Jaime, and even hanging out over a cup of tea or hot chocolate during a pause in the day. She'd been teaching the other woman how to inline skate, even. But still. They weren't actual sisters. Jaime had one of those already.

"Why don't we go for a walk?" Jaime said.

"He's still out there." Dom gave a greedy show of sharp teeth. "Why don't I go send him on his way first?"

"I believe we'll call the police if we need that," Jaime said very firmly. "Dominique. Let's keep you out of jail."

Dom brooded like a cigarette addict trying to make do with patches while somebody smoked right beside him. Célie thought it was so cute the way his fiancée called him by his full name all the time, *Dominique*, with that little careful accent of hers around all the French vowels. It was probably no wonder Dom was always kissing her. Célie practically wanted to kiss her herself, and she was *not* the type to go for small women who looked like they needed protection. She'd always kind of wanted to be the small woman who got protected herself.

It just hadn't worked out for her.

Well, Dom, but he was kind of on loan, really. He was her boss. He wasn't supposed to have to act like her big brother, too. Or in any other capacity, although she couldn't say that a few fantasies hadn't managed to slip past her guard on bad days, especially after she'd finally forced herself to quit fantasizing about Joss.

Well. Mostly quit.

"He's still out there?" Célie said, and repeating the words out loud made them true, made her heart beat harder, as if she was going to be sick. *He didn't just leave? Again.* "Dom, don't go get in a fight."

Joss had left her to go join the Foreign Fucking Legion, so by now, he was probably one of those people who knew how to kill others with his left pinky finger.

She didn't want either one of them to get hurt.

"I'll go talk to him," she said sullenly. She'd been so happy. And here, *bam*, let's just shatter that like crystal.

"Why don't you tell me a little bit more about what's going on with this guy, first?" Jaime asked, pulling her outside the glass doors to the top of the steps so they could tuck themselves into some illusion of auditory privacy, if they kept their voices low, even if they were pretty visible. "Was it a bad relationship?"

"No! It's not—it wasn't even a relationship. I just, I don't know—I just trailed around after him, I guess."

Jaime narrowed her eyes. "He had other girlfriends, too?"

"I wasn't his girlfriend, Jaime. That's what I'm saying. We just—we lived in the same HLM, and he was friends with my brother. Then he decided to make a better life for himself, and I haven't seen him in five years."

"Oh." Jaime sat still on the steps, trying to digest this. Since in normal times people ran up and down those steps between the *laboratoire* and the *salon* below constantly, they were really getting in the way, but no one pushed by them.

That was Dom for you. He'd be more willing to piss off any number of customers than shortchange one of "his" people.

"So," Jaime said slowly. "He never hurt you, and he didn't betray you?"

Célie's eyes filled again. "No," she said. No, it had all been her wanting, her hurting, her needing. He'd never deliberately fed it. And he'd left her with all of it, having better things to do with his life.

"Oh." Jaime eyed Célie doubtfully. Célie scrubbed at her tears again. Jaime sat waiting. The glass door nudged gently against their backs, and they scooted over to the far side of the top step, so that Thierry could squeeze out with a tray with a *mille-feuille* and a cup and pot for hot chocolate on it.

Sorry, Thierry mouthed, face scrunching with the force of his apology, as he snuck past them and hurried down the stairs. They must be getting desperately backed up, behind that glass door. Célie wouldn't turn around to see if anyone was watching them, or if they were all trying very hard to work—as long as that work kept them in full view of the glass doors.

Right now, she almost didn't care.

"Maybe *I* should go talk to him," Jaime said. "Do you want me to ask him to leave?"

Célie's heart seized. Leave? Again? Just disappear into that dark void again, and this time maybe she would *never* see him again. Never know what became of him.

She sprang to her feet. "No. No. No. I'll talk to him."

Jaime stayed seated, arms wrapped around her knees, watching Célie a long moment. Then she nodded and stood. "I'll make sure Dom stays upstairs. You promise nothing is going to happen that will make him jump through the window and break an ankle in his rush to go smash that guy's face in?"

Célie shook her head. "Joss would never hurt me." She hesitated, one step lower. "*Enfin* ... not like that."

Chapter 4

Joss waited.

He'd gotten good at it in the Foreign Legion, waiting. That grim, stubborn, determined waiting for someone to move, for a chance to kill or be killed to open up. For backup to arrive, for their unit to move on, for mail.

(That throat-tightening effort not to wait for mail, not to hope for anything.)

He could wait with purpose, as long as he needed to, for his opportunity to live to fight another day to open up.

This waiting didn't feel like any of those waits. It hurt his throat, this waiting. Struck in his chest over and over, this hard battering in time to his heart. Made him want to bow his head.

He tried to press his shoulders back against the wall, tried to make himself look slouching, because he was much less obtrusive that way, but he couldn't. His hands felt funny tucked in his pockets, chained, the hands of an idiot, and they kept slipping out again, where they could be ready for trouble.

He'd stuff them back in. Then a few minutes later, he'd realized they had pulled themselves right back out.

He missed the weight of a FAMAS across his chest while he waited—it would give his hands something useful to do at least—but an assault rifle would do no good here.

He only had a few skills transferrable to this situation. He couldn't fight that guy up there, her boss presumably, and mess up her life and her work situation. And get himself arrested, just as if he was still another loser from the *banlieue*.

But he could wait. He could persist. He could take hurt and keep going.

Sometime she would have to leave her hidey-hole. Have to go home.

Sometime ... maybe she would want to see him.

Célie used to like him, or she seemed to, anyway. She used to make him feel he could be the greatest man in the world. That he *had* to become a better man, to be worth the opinion she had of him.

He couldn't let that trust and pride she showed in him be misplaced, wither and die as he dwindled into yet another aging loser, still stuck in an HLM where he couldn't even make sure his own wife and kids were safe taking the elevator.

He'd had to do better by himself for her sake. Better by her.

But those postcards she sent him, there at the beginning, with the heart over the *I* in her name the way she always wrote it, revealing how young she was, how much of a teenager he shouldn't be hitting on ... those postcards had trickled and died from lack of response. From all the times he stroked them and twisted a pen in his hands and didn't find the words to write back.

They'd died quickly, within the first six months. And he never did find the words that paper could hold.

So now he waited.

Outside this fancy chocolate place Célie had found for herself, in *Paris* of all places. Not in its rejected fringe, where the idea of the romantic, glamorous city only a subway ride away left people bitter and desperate, but *here*. In its glittering heart. Instead of fleeing Paris as he had, for a better chance, she had marched right into the city's heart and made it accept her. His mouth softened. Wasn't that, when he thought about it, just exactly like Célie?

The beautiful glass doors—the kind of doors you could have in a country where bombs and guns didn't go off regularly—slid open. A small, curvy woman in a short-sleeved black chef's jacket stepped out, Célie, her eyes holding his even before the doors slid aside.

She flexed her fists uneasily by her thighs and then crossed the street to him. It was all Joss could do not to jump forward to cover her body with his, her crossing the street so recklessly, but he caught himself before he could act like an idiot. No snipers ever on rooftops here.

As she came up to him, she got smaller and smaller, until she was just the size she used to be back when she trailed around after her brother—small enough to fit under his arm if he ever forgot himself and draped it around her shoulders. Small enough to tuck up against his chest while his hand slipped down to cup her butt, if he ever let himself do that. Small enough he'd have to pick her up to get their bodies to fit right together. He still sometimes, at odd moments, remembered how easy it had been to pick her up to boost her over a wall in some of their escapades back then. At very odd moments, lying plastered on his belly in low cover, for example, that memory would ghost back across the muscles in his arms, as if they craved that lightness.

That spunky, stubborn cheer.

Her eyes and nose were red, this raw, swollen red, and his throat closed all the words out of him again. Deprived of words, his hand—which had known it needed to be free and ready for action, after all—lifted of its own accord toward her face.

She knocked his arm away before his hand could touch. Her mouth set hard, as she looked up at him, and her eyes shimmered again. "*Fuck you,*" she said bitterly.

The scent of chocolate came off her, strange and enticing, making him feel like one of his grandparents after four years of war and occupation, when the American soldiers started sharing their chocolate ration bars. She'd cut off all her hair and dyed it a vibrant red. His palm tickled with the urge to test what that winged, impudent hair of hers felt like now, compared to the long braid she'd self-streaked burgundy that last year in high school.

Of course, he hadn't touched it when she was in high school either.

His fingers closed slowly back into his palm, and his hand lowered to his side. He had no words, and no actions, and no idea what to say or do. He swallowed, trying to get her name out at least. "Célie."

His voice sounded rough, as if it'd been scraped too much in desert sands.

"You bastard," she said, and started crying again.

His hands closed into tight fists by his thighs. Utter paralysis of word and action. He wasn't even sure if he could have uttered his name, rank, and serial number.

She dashed her tears away again, and then again, until the water on her face was a damp smear rather than a flow, and glared sullenly at him. "What do you want?"

He tried to reach for her, to give her one of those dangerous hugs he'd twice or thrice given her at bad moments when she was eighteen and he was twenty-one.

She shoved both hands flat against his chest, pushing herself away since he himself wasn't very pushable. Anyway, his back was already up against a wall.

"What do you want?" she repeated, furiously.

That fist around his throat tightened and widened its grip, until it was squeezing all the way down his esophagus into his stomach. He had too much room in his chest, with so many things squeezed so tight. It hurt. And yet, like so many of the words he couldn't say now that he was back in polite society—even Paris was less riddled with swearing than a Foreign Legion unit—he also couldn't let himself say the one word, that one syllable that was the only one that could communicate the answer. *You.*

I'm bigger now. I'm stronger. I'm genuinely tough enough to handle any asshole you might ever encounter. So—I'm ready. Can't you see that?

Didn't it show in his arms, the width of his chest? Should he have worn a tighter T-shirt? *You told me I could do anything, Célie. Well …* I did *it. See?*

She was so full of so many temptations to touch, like something multifaceted and shiny being twitched in front of a cat. That perky nose, those flashing earrings. The second set of earrings were studs, but the first were more dramatic, and he reached again before he realized, this time aiming for the dangly part of the earring, to twist it just enough to see what it was.

She tossed her head, hard enough to knock his hand fiercely with her jaw, and took another step back, glaring at him.

He dropped his hands back to his sides. “Célie,” he tried again. He could say that. It made sense. It was even an answer.

“I’m working,” she said, furiously.

That shocked him. Her old home address had no longer been good, but people from around there knew where she worked. Of course he had come straight here, not waiting for working hours to be over. Five years, *merde*. She couldn’t take fifteen minutes to see him? She would rather he have *waited even more*?

“It’s a beautiful place to work.” Oh, look—words he could say. “You’ve done really well, Célie.”

For some reason that made her start crying again. “No thanks to you.”

The knife went right into his gut. He could only stare at her, while his whole body flinched around it, already starting to go into shock.

And ... of course no thanks to him, he realized slowly and dimly. Célie had still been in her pastry apprenticeship when he left. *He hadn’t been there.*

It was such a different perspective from his own. Because he was pretty sure that what he had accomplished—well, it was thanks to her. To that sassy, teasing teenager who had looked up at him as if he could be her hero.

But she didn’t owe him any of her at all.

He looked down, that skimming view of his own big body. Maybe if she could see that body in *action*, how much stronger and smoother he moved these days. "Can we walk a little?" He glanced up at her big, black-haired boss and the woman with reddish tawny hair watching them from a second-floor casement window, the two other people in chef's gear pressed to another casement window there. "Will it be okay? You won't get fired?"

She blinked, and just for a second past the swollen eyes and tears, he saw spunky Célie. "I'm Dominique Richard's chef chocolatier!" she said indignantly. "I won't get *fired*. I make those things!" She gestured back to the gorgeous glass doors and presumably the shop inside, that beautiful, luxurious space of exposed stone, velvet curtains, and white rosebud walls, with its steel and glass cases elegantly displaying beautiful chocolates.

That space that was like stepping onto another planet, as if none of his life matched any of hers at all. They weren't even the same sentient species, nor members of the same galaxy. And that was strange, because they'd grown up in the same building.

"The best chocolates in Paris!" she said.

His mouth softened, surprising him. He couldn't remember the last time his mouth had softened. But that was so like Célie, to stick her chin up and insist she was the best. Maybe it was part of the reason he'd wanted to *become* the best, so that they'd match. "Are they?"

"Yes." She put her hands on her hips. "They really are."

"I haven't tried them." Or any of the other chocolates in Paris. Back before he joined the Legion, he'd had to make do with supermarket chocolate bars, the gorgeous, elusive luxury of Paris well out of his reach, and not just in terms of chocolate. He'd given some special chocolates to Célie once, for her birthday, and they'd cost him far more than he could afford back then for something so ephemeral. But they'd made her really happy. She'd hugged him, and he'd had to use all his strength of will not to turn that hug into something else.

She stared at him a moment. And then she spun on her heel and stomped right back across the street. Again his heart jerked in his chest when she did that without checking the rooftops, and he had to force his reflexes to calm down and remember where they were.

The glass doors slid open, and she disappeared back to her safety inside that beautiful shop.

Damn.

He braced his feet apart and settled his weight into a soldier's waiting stance again, then reminded himself to press his shoulders back against the wall so he wouldn't look so obviously military in a city far from enamored of the military.

But only a few minutes later, Célie came back out, carrying a small, flat, shiny aluminum box aggressively, like she was going to attack him with it.

He almost managed not to jump out of his skin this time when she crossed the street without looking up.

"Here." She thrust the box at him.

He took it cautiously. Obviously she wasn't going to hand a bomb to him—not Célie, no matter how mad she was—so this might be a ... present?

He was going to go with the idea anyway. Pretend it was a present. Pretend she had given one single thought to his twenty-sixth birthday two weeks ago.

He eased off the tight-fitted aluminum lid stamped with an adamant *DR* and gazed at the contents. Nine exquisite, tiny chocolates, perfectly square, flat, each with a different elegant motif—a hint of green leaves, or a tendril of white, or a pattern subtly etched into the chocolate.

"You make these?" he murmured, fascinated. Célie did?

Wow, she must *love* that. Love it with everything in her.

Oh, thank God. Célie had grown up *happy*. Free. Big. He'd come back to get her out of there, now that he was big enough to carry them both to the top of the world's glass mountain, but she'd already done it for herself.

All by herself.

He lifted his gaze from the chocolates to her.

She'd forgotten to be angry or cry. She had a little curve to her mouth, utterly smug and trying not to show it.

He smiled at her in pure pride at what she'd managed.

She blinked, and her arms flinched around herself in a protective hug.

So he looked back at the chocolates, his smile fading. He was clearly supposed to taste one. He almost didn't want to, and he didn't even know why. This was going so badly, and—parting his lips left his insides vulnerable.

But he swallowed and carefully eased the edge of one thankfully clean thumbnail under the edge of a chocolate and worked it free from the others. *Merde*, the thing was no bigger than the pad of his thumb.

He looked at Célie again. Her gaze flicked eagerly between the chocolate and his face.

So he slipped it between his lips.

Sensation burst through him, this exquisite, hungry sensation of chocolate melting on his tongue, soft and rich and with some flavor to it he couldn't begin to identify.

"Wow," he said, and reached for another.

She smiled, for the very first time since he'd seen her. A real Célie smile, full of triumphant pleasure, her eyes sparkling.

The second one tasted different. Coffee? It melted, too, on his tongue, and the third was mint.

"Wow," he said again, and tried to take his time on the fourth one, to really look at it, how perfect it was, this tiny exquisiteness. How did she do that?

One of her eyebrows went up, a little scar in it from where she must have tried a piercing while he was gone. Smiling, she watched him eat the fourth, and then the fifth. By the time he finished the box, both her eyebrows were up in this blend of amusement and bemusement. "People, ah, usually savor these over a few days."

"Oh." He looked back down at the empty box. The square of metal was barely bigger than his hand. "Chocolate usually melts. In the desert." Which he wasn't in anymore. "I didn't want to waste them."

She shook her head. He couldn't decipher her expression.

"Why do they put off eating them, exactly?"

"Money, mostly. That's about forty euros worth of chocolate, so unless someone is rich, it's a luxury."

Forty euros. It was probably a good thing he stuck mostly with supermarket chocolate bars. He'd be spending hundreds a day otherwise.

"Plus, they *are* works of art," she told him, with her chin up in the air again.

Damn, she was cute. This sudden, fresh wave of her cuteness washed through him again, after five years of fading memories.

"Yes," he said. "I can see that." *Can I kiss you? Just right now?* He'd fought five years to be the man who deserved to kiss that mouth, and maybe he'd been assuming she'd recognize his right immediately.

Again, his gaze downward let him skim his own body. As far as he could tell, strength and competence and confidence pretty much radiated off his every cell these days. His personal radius felt about ten times bigger than anyone else he crossed paths with in the street. He tried to be polite and not pushy, but people shifted out of his way on the sidewalk before he could even start to shift out of theirs. "Walk?" he asked again, low.

She hesitated and then shrugged defiantly and turned to head up the sidewalk toward République. She had a brisk Paris stride, and he kept his much longer one slow, not in a rush to get to a café to meet with friends but in steady determination to get through terrain or his day.

It didn't take them long to reach the great Place de la République, empty of protestors today, people hurrying across it and a few families lingering at the fountains. Célie headed toward the canal, a nice, quiet place to walk. He only knew where they were because he'd had to look up her work address on a map of Paris and always liked to scout out the terrain before he stepped into new territory. Paris had not been his stomping grounds, in the old days.

The canal was pretty, though. Even prettier than in films, because now it felt like a real place. Shaded by plane trees, arched with bridges, filled with this quiet, dark water that rippled only when someone tossed a stone into it.

He glanced down at Célie and caught her in the act of sneaking a glance up at him. She quickly looked away.

"How's your brother?" he asked, for something to say.

"Oh, is that why you're here?" she demanded truculently. "You're looking for him?"

He cut her an astonished glance. Their whole *cité* and every gang in it had known that the only reason he kept putting up with her brother was that she came with him. If he had beaten the crap out of Ludo the way he'd wanted to when her brother started getting into drug trafficking and trying to drag Joss and Célie after him, he'd never have gotten a chance to see Ludo's sister again.

And he'd needed Ludo's sister. Seeing Célie nearly every day had made him feel like he had a—a teddy bear or something he could take to bed with him at night. Something that made him feel warm and secure and happy against darkness. He'd even tried as hard as he could not to fantasize about her too explicitly, because it had seemed wrong. Tender fantasies, more, where he tried not to let his mind go below her shoulders, and then tried not to let his mind go below her waist, and then the clothes above the waist had slowly faded away, and now, now … well, in the past five years, he'd long since lost all barriers to the fantasies. They'd gotten hotter and deeper, and she'd given more and more of herself, more and more willingly, every time. They'd kept their sweetness, though.

"I was looking for you," he said, and her brown gaze lifted and caught with his. He reached for her arm and pulled her out of the way of an elderly lady with a grocery trolley bag.

She jerked away and then had to apologize to the older woman for bumping into the groceries.

"Ludo got out two years ago," Célie said tightly, once the woman had moved on. "But he went to America. He said it was better than staying here. He didn't have a visa, but he didn't come back, so I guess …" She shrugged, in an aggressive display of indifference.

"So you've been on your own?"

She looked a little confused. "Well, my mom." She shrugged again. "Cousins."

Célie's mother and extended family were not exactly the rock on which a woman built a castle. "You've been on your own."

She shook her head firmly. "I've had work. Dom."

Dom. Joss frowned.

"Me." She lifted her chin.

Her. Yes. He realized that his hand had reached for hers only when his palm grazed over the knuckles of a fist tightened to ward off his touch.

He shoved his hand into his pocket to get it to behave. "You." He held her eyes. "That's a lot to have."

She blinked and her lips parted. She stared at him a second and then turned hastily to climb the steps of one of the footbridges arching over the canal, stopping in the middle of it to gaze at the water. As she stared down at it, not looking at him, a slow flush started to climb her cheekbones. She dashed at her eyes again.

He closed his much bigger hands around the railing, next to hers, but he made sure to leave enough space between them that she wouldn't jerk away again.

It hurt like hell when she jerked away. Like electric shocks or something, maybe it would train him to quit reaching for her.

The dark water gave him something to focus on. Its quiet, its stillness, its ability to adapt and survive, its depth. He could gaze into it like a mirror, catch blurred glimpses of her face in it, as if he was still looking at her in his memories from the distance of another life.

"You're mad at me," he said finally.

She shook her head, and then shrugged, and didn't look at him.

"Or upset."

She shook her head, and then gave that exact same shrug. And still didn't look at him.

He squinted over the canal, the banks to either side, the windows of the buildings, the rooftops—automatically checking everything in sight for possible trouble. But the only possible trouble he saw was the one he was already in. The one he hadn't predicted and didn't understand.

"I'm not very good at talking anymore," he said at last. Most of his vocabulary these days consisted of swearwords. Not that either he or Célie had exactly had clean mouths back in their *banlieue* days, but still. Maybe he needed to take up reading Racine or something, now that he was back. Give himself a vocabulary beyond *putain de bordel de merde* and worse. "You were always the one who was good at talking."

Laughing at him, teasing him, pushing for his attention. Saucy and amused and full of so much life that it had been all he could do not to grab her and pull her into his lap time and again as she laughed down at him while he was sitting on some graffiti-stained wall and she was bouncing around, too full of energy to sit. The number of times his palm had itched for that sassy butt as she glanced back over her shoulder, alight with mirth at some wicked, twitting comment she'd sent his way. But he'd known how a pretend swat of her butt would end. With his palm settling over that curve, taking possession of it, pulling her in.

His semi-friend's little sister. Who deserved to have an older guy in the vicinity who looked after her, who didn't harass her like every other damn bastard in their *cité*.

So he hadn't harassed her. He'd looked after her. He'd looked after her so well that he'd left, so he could turn into the man who could look after her properly.

And now Célie didn't say anything.

His hands tightened on the rail. "Are you not happy to see me?" The hurt of his own words sank deeper than any physical wound he'd ever had. No anesthesia for it, no way to get the bullet out, to stitch it up and help it heal.

Célie whipped around and launched herself so hard and fast at him that he barely caught her. He rocked back a step and seized her, and she seized *him*, this clawing embrace where her nails sank hard into his lower back, like she was going to rip his skin off. "You *bastard*," she said into his chest. *"Ton putain de Légion étrangère, va."*

"Célie." He tightened his arms around her. God, she felt good against him. Even angry or … or whatever she was, she felt good.

"How could you do that? Join the Foreign Fucking Legion? Just go and … be gone. Be *gone*. Nothing of you left here at all."

He blinked. Because he had been so solidly present wherever he was, it had never occurred to him that where he *wasn't* would leave much of a void.

She yanked away from him. His arms didn't relax fast enough, and she started squirming before he managed to release her, just as she shoved at him, bouncing herself back. She thrust a hand through her pixie hair. "I hate you. So, yes, I'm happy to see you."

"Ah." He closed his hand around his wrist behind his back, bracing himself in the position with which an *engagé volontaire* stood while being yelled at by some random corporal during basic training, and gazed at her.

Those happy, kissable, supple lips twisted unhappily and she looked away over the water. Over her head, he checked all their surroundings again. Still no trouble except the one he was in.

"Sorry," she said, low and rough. "I don't have the right to be so mad. I just, you know ... never mind."

He waited.

She shrugged, bitterly. "I know I was just Ludo's stupid kid sister who insisted on trailing around after you guys. I just, you know—I hero-worshiped you, I guess." She kicked the bottom of the bridge barrier.

Hero-worshiped him? His heart crinkled funnily, this embarrassed, puzzled, awkwardly crushed pleasure, like a butterfly squeezing out of a cocoon. How could she have hero-worshiped him back then? He'd gone away to learn how to be her hero.

To come back and rescue her, build a new life for her.

Around her stretched the beautiful Canal St. Martin, the buildings and old streetlamps and shady trees of this part of Paris. A vision flashed through him of her gorgeous *salon de chocolat*, of the luminous kitchens to which she had fled when she ran away from him. She seemed to have a pretty nice life already.

One she had built herself.

Without him.

"I don't remember treating you as a stupid kid," he said.

She looked up at him, brown eyes solemn and searching.

"As Ludo's sister, yes, granted. Since you were his sister. Still are, I guess." He'd kind of been done with Ludo well before Ludo finally got arrested. Maybe his desire to not be Ludo had helped fuel his enlistment in the Foreign Legion, too.

"Last I checked," she said dryly.

He sought words, filtering out swearing, trying to find a way he could say what he wanted to say. It was hard to tell someone something when you weren't sure you wanted her to know. "I'm not really Ludo's friend anymore." *You're nobody's little sister now.*

Fuck, that sounded alone and friendless, put like that. Unprotected. What he really wanted to say was: *I came back for you. Nothing to do with Ludo at all.*

"Yeah, well, you're not really my friend anymore either, are you?" Célie said.

Shock. This white-noise, buzzing, strange *thing* mind and body did when the hurt was too much to bear.

"If you ever were." She shrugged, flippant and dark.

Fuck.

His heart surely couldn't take much more pain?

"You just put up with me, I guess." Another shrug. He wanted to lay his arm over her shoulders and forcibly block them from shrugging.

"Célie, please stop now." *I changed my mind about you talking.*

Célie glanced up at him, her lips parting to say something else, to strike again, and then her gaze caught on his face and slid over it, then slid over it again. Her expression shifted. "I just meant—"

He shook his head and held up a hand to stop her, focusing on the water. His body felt suddenly utterly heavy and tired, a tired that went deep down into the soul, that wasn't a physical tired—it was hard to physically tire a man who had survived the paratroopers' Corsica march—but heart-worn weariness. He wanted to slump down onto the bridge with his back against the barrier, slump like at the end of that march and close his eyes and sleep for days.

If he was ever her friend?

Meaning, he'd never been a good enough friend to her for her to know it. And he'd tried so fucking hard.

He turned suddenly and sat down on the top step of the bridge. He shouldn't do that. His big body now blocked most of the passage across the bridge. But he did it anyway. Bracing his arms on his thighs, he let his face drop into his hands. He had killed two people in a nighttime combat mission in the Uzbin Valley, no deaths on his conscience ever and then all of a sudden two, and he felt now as he had then—not during the kill-or-die adrenaline of the moment, but afterward, the night afterward, when the adrenaline was all gone and all that was left were thoughts. Images.

God, he wanted to sleep. For years.

And then a small body shifted down on the step below his. Célie slipped her head between the bend of his arm and his torso, resting it against his leg. She wrapped one arm around his thigh, holding on to him as tightly as she could. And she started to cry again, these tremblings of her body, this slow soaking of his jeans. "I'm so glad you're okay," she whispered. "Damn you."

Slowly, very slowly, he unfolded one of his arms and settled it gently around her back instead. Slowly, very slowly, his other arm abandoned support of his face and dropped to her hair. It prickled faintly, from the gel or whatever she must use to give it that tufted-fairy look. His fingers sank a little deeper, down to the back of her skull, where her hair softened, gentle against her head.

His hand looked so big there. His thumb cheated and snuck out to trace over the curve of her ear, down to the two piercings, that dramatic one and that more discreet little jewel. If he kept going, his thumb would trace the line of her jaw, down over her throat.

But he didn't. He kept his hand on that quirky, attention-grabbing hair, on those earrings, all the ways

Célie tried to assert more space in her world. Cheerful, sparkling, happy ways.

"Me, too," he whispered. "I'm glad you're okay, too."

Chapter 5

La Ferme, Castelnaudary, four years and eleven months before

Failure.

It slammed at him from every direction, boots in the ribs, driving Joss down into the mud. The *adjudant* grabbed him by the back of the head and shoved his face into that mud. *"Abandonne!"*

No. I won't give up, you fucking bastard.

He'd joined the Legion so he *wouldn't* be a failure.

But if he failed, he could *leave*. Take back this stupid decision he had made, go back to a life in which failure now seemed by far the most comfortable option. He could go wait for Célie outside her bakery, and see her run across the street to him, with her face alight and something delicious held up in her hands. See that look on her face as she pressed her hands to his chest and said …

"*Tu es nul!*" the *adjudant-chef* shouted in his ear. Joss's muscles had long since turned to limp spaghetti, his will crushed like an earthworm under weeks of abuse and no sleep and tasks no man could do. Somewhere in his head he knew they were just trying to break him, and he had to fight through it, but he still felt broken. "Worthless! Weak! *De la merde!* No good!"

God, the man sounded like his *mother*, whenever she exploded at his father after the job loss and the alcohol took him. The way she even, as the bitterness grew and Joss kept bringing home crappy grades, exploded at Joss. *Not good enough! What's wrong with you? You're just like your father! You won't even try!* If Joss turned his head, he'd probably find that same lobster-red rage on the *adjudant*'s face.

"Give up!" the man screamed in his ear, spittle adding to mud. *"Abandonne!"*

Give up. After only one month. Give in. Go back to that girl who put her hands on his chest and said ...

You can do anything.

Brown eyes, rich and true in a way this mud could never be. Thank God he hadn't told her what he was going to do. Thank God she couldn't see him like this, ground down to nothing, already failing.

Goal. Focus on the goal. Brown eyes, bright smile.

"Give up!" the *adjudant-chef* yelled, shoving him down again.

He could hit the instructor and then crawl home. Home to *her*. And he could *eat*, for God's sake. Sleep ten years.

Be a failure.

Célie wouldn't mind.

She'd settle. After all, she'd been so desperate for a man to look up to that she'd even looked up to *him*.

She wouldn't know how he'd failed, because he'd made sure she couldn't see it. Only he would know.

She'd take what he could manage, as he folded in on himself. She'd take less and less, as they grew older and he never made her dreams come true, as that light faded out of her eyes, as she stopped believing and turned into every other middle-aged woman in that HLM.

You can do anything.

She'd stop saying that.

Maybe she'd even stop saying it to herself in the mirror. Dull-eyed when she looked at herself, all the light gone out.

"Non." He gasped it, in the first breath he could take free of mud.

"*What* did you say?" The hard grip on his neck shoved him down into the mud again.

He forced himself back up on arms that thought they had no strength left, struggling for breath. After five days with three hours sleep and one ration pack for food, he'd just finished a ten-mile race in combat gear, followed by an impossible obstacle course, and was now on his three hundredth push-up in the mud as punishment for having slid back down a mud-coated rope on a mud-slick incline before he made it to the top. He had an infection crawling up his right arm from a scratch that made even slight movements flame like fire and something wrenching his stomach inside out because he'd cracked and drunk water from a creek on yesterday's twenty-mile march. He hated this bastard with everything in him—but he didn't have much left. *Why the hell am I doing this? I could quit. I could give up. I could go back.*

You can do anything. Chin in the air, heart in her eyes.

"No." Joss spat mud out of his mouth.

"Non?"

You can do anything. He braced himself out of the mud. Fire lanced through his arms. His stomach heaved again. Mud coated his face. *"Non, mon chef."*

"Tu es sûr?"

Oh, fuck, here came more. It always did, when they asked if a recruit was sure. But ... *I can do anything. I am* not *a failure. I will do this. "Oui, mon chef."*

"You think you can take it?" the man asked contemptuously.

Joss gritted his teeth. "I can take it." Here it came. A blow, a kick, a shove into the mud. The order to climb to the top of a mountain barefoot. Anything.

The hard hand released his nape. The fifty-year-old career bastard who was their instructor stepped back, with a small moue on that merciless face. A *maybe you'll pass muster* moue. "Then you'd better get up and get back in line."

***

Well, she'd certainly made a fool of herself today, hadn't she? Célie thought, her face pressed into Joss's leg. Probably so traumatized him he'd abandon any plans of looking up any other old friends.

His thigh felt so good under her cheek, though. His arm over her back, his hand curving over her head. Warmth and strength and so much himness that it was all she could do not to turn her head toward his crotch, not to open her mouth there and shock-destroy all his defenses so that she could crawl into him, bury herself in his arms, get held close and hard.

She wrapped her arm even more tightly around his thigh to keep herself there and not twisting to kneel between his thighs and force her hands up under his shirt to just feel his damn skin, *warm* and *alive*, not grabbing his head in two tight, angry hands that held him still by the roots of his hair while she kissed him because she was so angry with him she wanted to kiss him to death, kiss him until he begged for mercy and said he was sorry, so sorry, and he would never, ever, ever—

Joss winced, under her cheek, and she realized she had dug her nails into the underside of his thigh, near the knee. She loosed them slowly, reluctantly, because the next and far more tempting target would be to dig that same hand into a fistful of everything she could manage to grab through the crotch of his jeans.

Yeah, I bet you wouldn't run away then, *would you, you bastard? Not if I've got hold of your privates. Men never leave that part of them behind.*

Priorities, after all.

She finally had to push herself away rather than do any of that. Scrubbing her hands over her face, she tried to figure out any way to redeem her behavior.

Yeah, there wasn't one.

"Sorry," she muttered. "I guess I just—I—you know—"

"PMS?" Joss suggested.

PMS? "Joss, you were already an idiot about women *before* you joined a military service that doesn't allow females in the ranks. Don't aggravate your situation."

Joss rested both his forearms flat on his thighs again and closed his hands over his knees. His body moved in one big sigh.

She studied his face. "Wait. Was that supposed to be a *joke*?" As in, that old thing friends did for each other, to try to ease a badly behaving friend back into the embrace of friendship, to show that it was okay, that was what friends were for?

Joss opened his mouth as if to speak, but then just took another of those deep breaths that shifted his whole body. Maybe he really had been joking, or trying to. He seemed so—tired suddenly. Flattened out. It was strange on such a big guy.

He'd already been a big, strong guy before he left. Working out, boxing, playing rugby, keeping himself big enough and tough enough to scare off most people who would mess with him. She'd loved it when she could walk through their *cité* by his side. Nobody ever messed with her when he was there. She felt entirely safe.

But now he was even bigger, stronger. He looked so tough, people probably crossed the street when they saw him coming.

The only person who would mess with him now was a man like Dom, someone who saw another big, strong male and went straight at him to confront him and get him the hell out of his territory. The kind of man who would rather kill or be killed than trust another strong man near anything his.

"Wait," Joss said suddenly, sitting up a little straighter. "How was I already an idiot about women? I did just fine with women, I'll have you know."

Célie stood up as fast as if he'd just touched a live wire to her and started striding away. But she didn't head back toward work. She strode farther north up the canal.

He swore under his breath and caught up.

Her phone burped. She pulled it out. Dom: *OK?*

Oui, she typed. *Laisse-moi tranquille.* Leave me alone.

Bossy idiot. Her heart warmed, though. It was good, really good, to have someone strong and with a good heart looking after her.

She glanced up at Joss, who had been that person when she was a teenager. He had angled his head enough to read the screen of her phone, and his mouth tightened.

She hit send and shoved the phone back in her pocket. "Sorry. I should get back to work."

But she kept walking the wrong way.

"This isn't going at all like I expected," Joss said.

Her eyebrows scrunched together. She looked up at his profile, that stubborn jaw, those straight lashes, and a glimpse of those hazel eyes. "So what did you expect?"

"I don't know." He shrugged, an odd movement on those big, square, military-straight shoulders, and shoved his hands in his pockets. "I guess I thought you'd still be in Tarterets, in your apartment with your mom, and that you'd look up at me, and your face would just *light,* and you'd throw yourself into my arms and not be able to stop kissing me from how happy you were."

She stared at him so hard she tripped over a cobblestone. His hands came out of his pockets, but she had already righted herself.

"I mean, kiss on my cheeks, of course." He touched one cheek and then the other, where *bises* would fall. Was that a tinge of color on his face? Impossible to tell, given how much the sun had darkened his already Mediterranean skin.

"I was just supposed to be sitting in my mom's apartment in the projects in Tarterets? Waiting for you? For five years? Not growing up, or accomplishing anything, or making anything of myself? Thanks a lot."

A faint frown. His hands went back into his pockets. "You could have kept writing," he said suddenly, low and rough. "Let me know what you were doing, what you were becoming. Sent a few pictures whenever you changed hair color, that kind of thing. I hear selfies are hot these days."

She glared at him. "Yeah. You could have written, too."

The strangest wistfulness crossed his face. "I thought about it," he said, the same way a man might say he used to dream of flying to the moon. "Once those first four months were up, and we had the right to send letters. I read once in a book about World War II how often soldiers would just make something up."

Kind of weird to think of Joss reading. But all at once she could imagine him, slow and painstaking, focusing on a book to pass all the dead downtime in some place like Afghanistan. Maybe books, which had always been his enemies in school where they were things he always failed at, had become friends when his real enemies fired bullets. She flinched away from the thought of those bullets.

"You would have letters dated from days of brutal bombardment and confrontation, written from the front lines, and the men would say, 'Everything's going well. Spending all my days playing poker with the guys. Miss you. Tell me more about you and the girls.' I thought about just making things up, pretending I was just a traveler enjoying the sights." His eyes closed for the briefest instant and opened again, immediately scanning the area for anything he might have missed during that second of weakness. "But my imagination has always been terrible. Even—" His mouth twisted with a wry wistfulness, and he broke off a second. Then resumed: "Even my best fantasies have always been ... well, at the time I thought they were ... realistic. Possible." A bleakness slid across his face and was stoically pushed back. He squared his shoulders.

Which was kind of a funny movement on him, given that his shoulders had never once lost that straight line. It spoke of a pretty rigid self-control, that he had to double-check that squaring of his shoulders no matter how automatically they were already squared. Maybe five years in the military did that to a man.

"What were your best fantasies?" Célie asked curiously. She'd always wanted to know what Joss dreamed. When he'd gone off and joined the Foreign Legion it had been a total shock to her. Never once had he mentioned military service as a possible ambition. In school, he'd trained as a mechanic, a career *she'd* certainly admired—all those things he could make work, all those motors he could soup up and get running, machines to take a girl out of there, take her anywhere she wanted. He'd been such an essential part of her life that she'd just assumed he would always be there keeping an eye out for her, providing her that strong body to walk beside through a tough neighborhood. That maybe they'd even speed out of their *banlieue* one day on the back of his motorcycle, with her holding on tight to that hard body.

Instead, she'd had to crush on a boss who drove a motorcycle and buy herself a moped.

Joss's lashes lowered, and now definite color burnished those stubborn, proud cheekbones of his. He pressed his lips together and shook his head.

Fine. Don't tell her. Célie stomped extra hard on the next cobblestone. That was just like him—bottle up everything that was fragile and beautiful and fanciful and then take it off to the Foreign Fucking Legion, never share it with *her*. Her and those stupid hearts she used to sneak in over the *I* in her name whenever she put her name on anything she was going to give to him.

Like he'd gotten *that* message. Or cared about it, if he had gotten it.

She cringed inside at the memory of her sappy, puppy-crush teenage self and gave herself a shake. "So how long have you been back?" she forced herself to ask briskly, as if they were just old semi-friends chatting now, catching up.

"My train got in to Paris this morning," Joss said.

Célie stumbled and looked back up at him. What? "Who—who else are you looking up?" Her voice sounded funny, not as casual as she kept trying to make it. "Your old girlfriend?"

His eyebrows drew slowly together as he searched her face. "What the hell are you talking about?"

"Sophie."

"Who the hell is Sophie?"

"*Sophie,*" Célie said incredulously. "Your *girlfriend.*"

"The only girl named Sophie that I remember is the girl your brother was sleeping with before he got arrested. Not that he ever gave her the respect of calling her his girlfriend. Your brother was kind of a bastard."

Célie blinked over that a moment. "She told everybody she was with you. Her boyfriend in the Foreign Legion."

Joss was silent for the distance between two bridges. "I guess that must have been better status for her than to be the ex-bootie call of someone in prison for dealing drugs," he said finally, with a quiet pity. "It's—not a good area to be a woman on your own with no protection, I guess."

"I managed," Célie said dryly.

Joss's face went blank.

"When she had the abortion, she said it was because you thought it would be better if the two of you waited until you were out to start a family," Célie said. It had made her throw up, when that happened—everything about it. That another woman should be pregnant with Joss's baby, and that Joss, the man she looked up to more than anyone else in the world, should say he didn't want his child. It made a woman never want to trust herself, her body, her chance at a happy life, to any man again.

Joss winced. "*Merde*," he said under his breath. "*Bordel de* ... Célie. That must have been your brother's kid. Or someone else's. But—but I can see why she would have wanted to tell that story instead of one where she was pregnant and alone and the dad was either worthless or didn't give a damn."

Yeah. Célie wondered if she would have told that kind of story about Joss, too, if she'd ended up pregnant in an area where a young woman was considered to be asking for it if she even wore a shirt with no sleeves, let alone a knee-length skirt. But there'd been no chance of her getting pregnant in those days. Joss had never picked up on any of her embarrassing attempts to sometimes get him to slide their friendship sideways into something a lot cuddlier.

She would have loved so much to cuddle with Joss back then.

Actually—she snuck a sideways glance at that big, hard, confident body—she would probably still love to ... she cut her thoughts off.

"What did you do?" Joss asked. "When she said that?"

"I cried. And I ripped up the postcard I was writing to you. And I ripped up your photos." And boy had she regretted that one. "And I took a train into Paris, and I knocked on Dominique Richard's door and told him I would work my butt off, if he would only hire me. That I'd work for almost nothing, if it was enough to be able to afford the rent on a nine-meter apartment in Paris itself and not the *banlieue*, that I'd live off chocolate and water if I had to."

Joss's hands curled into big fists. He glanced down at them and thrust them in his pockets. "And what did he do?"

"He said he'd better pay me enough that I wasn't forced to sneak all his chocolate for meals. That it would turn out cheaper for him in the long run."

Joss's hands shoved against his pockets. "So he was your hero. He saved you."

Célie considered that a moment. "Well, I mean ... *I* kind of thought I saved myself."

The expressions on Joss's face were so complicated and impossible to read. Not helped by the fact that he tried to keep all of them contained.

"I mean, that took some guts, the little nobody from the *banlieue,* to insist that one of the rising star chocolatiers hire me. And then to work my butt off making sure I deserved it, that I helped make us the best."

After a moment, he nodded, and his face softened. "You always did dream really big, Célie."

Well ... she supposed so. Dreaming of running off with Joss in some vague life of bliss and security had probably been dreaming really big.

Her chin lifted. A smaller dream, nevertheless, than the ones she had turned out to be capable of accomplishing, once she put her heart into them instead of into him. "So who else are you looking up?"

Joss had the blankest expression. Finally he shoved both hands across his face. "I hadn't really thought about looking up anyone else." And, while she was still trying to digest that, "You cried?"

She tried for a flippant shrug. "A girl can change a lot in five years."

Too late, she remembered that she'd pretty much spent the last half hour crying, ever since she'd first seen him.

Joss lifted an eyebrow but courteously refrained from pointing her tears out to her. He was silent until they reached the base of the next footbridge over the canal. "Célie." Abruptly he grabbed her by the hips, lifted her off the ground, and pivoted to set her three steps up on the bridge, so that her eyes were on level with his. The easy strength of the act rushed through her entire body. "I came back for you."

Her breath stopped, and it hurt that way, all stopped up in her chest. It hurt so much she wanted to cough it out, straight into his face, to hack him back from her happy life and all the hurt he could do to it. “I haven’t been waiting for you, Joss.” She made her voice mean. She made it as mean as she could. *“I’ve moved on.”*

He shook his head. “I can understand now why you didn’t wait for me, Célie. But I’ve been waiting for you.”

Chapter 6

"Work things out?" Jaime asked with quiet sympathy that afternoon.

Célie grimaced and shrugged, whisking her chocolate into cream. Across the steel counters of the hot room in the *laboratoire*, where all the burners were, she felt more than saw Amand, their sandy-haired caramellier, exchange glances with Jaime.

It was weird how subdued her own subsidence had left the *laboratoire*. As if she was its electric current and the power had gone out. Only Dom and Jaime resisted that power outage, and Dom had a particularly bad-tempered edge to him today. Every once in a while, he would look at her and then walk to the window to glare out of it and make sure Joss didn't stand below.

After each glare, Célie would find some excuse to sneak a look through a window and check for herself.

So far, no Joss.

Guillemette, from downstairs, slipped discreetly up to her. "Your, ah, friend just sat down at one of the tables. Should we serve him?" She tried to keep her voice low, but she underestimated Dom and Jaime's current state of alertness.

"Is that bastard stalking you?" Dom pivoted, chisel in hand. "I'll go take care of him."

"Or we could call the cops for that," Jaime intervened firmly.

A sharp, feral show of teeth in what was Dom's idea of a grin. "No, I want to do it."

"Dominique." Jaime laid a freckled hand over his muscled forearm.

Seriously, the way she said his name was adorable.

Dom glanced down at her hand on his arm, one black eyebrow lifting. "Is that supposed to be your magic trick to get me to behave?"

Jaime smiled. "Is it working?"

Dom held up thumb and forefinger, about a centimeter apart. "Only a little bit." But the energy of his body was shifting, as he turned more toward Jaime, as he focused on her. The aggressive gleam in his eyes was transforming to tenderness and a smile.

"Dominique."

There she went again. Of course the man was going to go all mushy over someone who said his name like that.

"I told you I was a bad bet," Dom said.

Célie slammed her big metal bowl of ganache against the steel counter. Chocolate fountained out of it, splattering up over her face and black chef's jacket. "Damn it, Dom. Look what you made me do!"

She swiped a hand across her face. Since her work in chocolate wasn't "hot" work, involving few things likely to burn her severely, unlike Amand, she was able to wear a short-sleeved chef's jacket, and a lightweight one at that. But that left her nothing to wipe with. She hunted around for a towel, growling under her breath. "Stupid bad bet thing. Men who ruin women's lives ... because they're stupid idiots ..." She sent Dom a venomous glance as she dragged a white kitchen towel across her face and chocolate-sloshed arms.

He gave her a bemused look back, both eyebrows lifting a little. Jaime nodded at her in firm approval of all that grumbling.

Célie threw her towel down on the counter. "I'll go talk to him."

Dom's eyebrows slashed together. "I don't think so. If he's stalking you, I'll take care of it."

"It's *Joss*, Dom! Don't be an *idiot*!" Célie stomped across the *laboratoire*. "As if he would ever—damn it, I hate you stupid men!"

The glass doors didn't slam worth a damn, probably just as well right then or she would have left glass shards all around her. She stomped down the spiral stairs with clangs of metal and glared at Joss.

He sat against the backdrop of the white rosebud-embossed wall. His little table looked oddly bereft in that salon. No one had served him yet, and he was such a big guy who had spent five years in war zones with the damn Foreign Legion and, and ... someone should be spoiling him. With all the delicious melts-in-a-desert food the stomach of a big guy like that could hold.

She stalked over to him. His gaze flicked over her face, and his eyes dilated visibly. "Hell, Célie, you know how much I like chocolate."

What?

"You've got it all—over—" His hand lifted toward her face as he drew his lip just a little under his teeth as if tasting something.

She jerked back a step, thrown completely off balance. Something started to fizz disturbingly in her stomach as she stared back at him. His hand dropped, and he swallowed.

Oh, hell. She tried to pull herself together. "Joss. What are you doing here?"

He just looked up at her with those gorgeous eyes and that stillness he had, emphasized by five years of military discipline. "Would you rather I wait outside?"

It was all she could do not to just shove the table aside and climb into his lap, bury her head in his chest and hold on tight. *Why did you leave me, you bastard? Oh, thank God you're home.*

Yeah, and that would be insane.

Plus she'd already done it once.

"Joss, you know I love you—"

A little jerk ran through his body. And hers, as the echo of her own words ran through her.

"Like a brother," she hastened to add.

"Fuck, Célie." He turned his head away, his jaw setting. "Like *Ludo*?"

Okay, well, maybe not like her actual brother. Or like any other male she'd ever known. But, but ... "But I'm not your person to come home to here." Oh, hell, had she just said that? *Yes, I am. Yes, I am.* "I've moved on."

"Moved on from what?" Joss asked.

She stared at him.

"We never dated, Célie. I wasn't Sophie's boyfriend, but I was never your boyfriend either. I was saving you for later."

Her jaw dropped. Fury sizzled once deep in her stomach and then just flared all through her. "You son of a bitch."

"For when you were *older*." He tried to regroup. "And I deserved you."

"I'm going to fucking *kill you*!" Célie pressed her hands into his table and her weight into them as she leaned her body over his.

"Okay," Joss said, and just lifted the table to the side to expose his body to her, shifting the table as if neither it nor her pressure on it weighed anything. "You can do that."

Oh, that bastard. It was now so easy to climb into his lap and bury herself there while she started crying again that her eyes prickled from it.

She turned away in dramatic temper before she could let him see that and stomped back across the room and up the stairs.

Dom and Jaime met her at the top of them, shifting from that spot in the glass walls where they must have watched the whole thing. Jaime shook her head with some bemusement. "It's fascinating how little you guys care about what your customers think."

Oh, yeah, Célie had kind of forgotten about all the customers watching that scene.

Dom gave that sharp, tear-someone's-throat-out grin of his. "They'll come back." He pressed his hand to his chest and gave Célie a hopeful look. "My turn?"

"Dom, I told you to leave him alone!" Célie stomped past him and grabbed a plated éclair off the counter in front of Thierry, whose job it was to both plate and descend the pastries and hot chocolate to the half dozen tables below. "Give me that."

"Hey!" Thierry protested. "That was for the woman at table three."

"Dom can make her another one." Because it wasn't as if she would have been able to talk him into making one for Joss. Célie stuck her tongue out at her boss and stamped her way into the ganache room with the plate. This room, on the opposite side of the *laboratoire* from the room with all the stoves and the variations in temperature and humidity that using them caused, also held the wire shelves scattered with metal trays of finished chocolates ready to be taken downstairs as the display cases needed replenishing.

Stupid men. She pulled out some of those trays. Arabica again, yes. He'd liked the touch of coffee. And mint, because he used to have a weakness for chocolate mint patties, and boy would her mint chocolates knock his socks off in comparison. And honey-hibiscus, because she had come up with it all by herself, experimenting, and she liked to think it tasted like she would, if anyone ever knew how to properly taste her.

Stupid, idiot men with their stupid, idiot excuses for making a woman cry her heart out for years. She slammed the little chocolates down on the plate around the éclair, a little circle of them, and then, remembering how fast he had eaten that box like a starving man, added a second one of each. Fine, a third.

She stomped back out of the room. "Here." She thrust the plate at Thierry. "For that idiot."

"Now you're feeding him?" Dom demanded, outraged. "My chocolates?"

She put her hands on her hips. "*My* chocolates. And don't you dare charge him. It's on me."

Dom made a feral noise between his teeth and pivoted back to his lion sculpture. At the first tap, the entire ear came off.

"Ha!" Célie said. "That will teach you to always want to use excessive force."

Dom gave her a dirty look.

"You know, I think I'll just do the rest of my work today from your office," Jaime said. "It's mostly calls and computer stuff, and God knows what trouble the two of you'd get into without me."

Chapter 7

Joss played with the chocolates on his plate. He'd eaten that little box she gave him too fast, and now he was almost afraid to eat these. They'd be all gone, once they were eaten, and he wouldn't be able to see it anymore—this visible proof that she cared about him. Still.

No matter how mad she was, she couldn't let him sit here without food.

No, it was more than food. These were her special accomplishments. The things she was so proud of, what she had made of her life when he left to make something of his. She was feeding him, but she was giving him something much more precious and intimate and proud than a croque-monsieur.

He rubbed his thumb gently along the perfect smooth edge, circling the delicate design, a stylized red flower. He couldn't shake the feeling that if he bit into that, he would be biting into Célie.

Damn, but he wanted to bite into Célie. Bite into that supple, saucy lower lip of hers, and bite into all those curves, that happy, athletic roundness of hers, vibrant with energy. As if it was her task in life to produce enough voltage to light a whole grim, bleak *cité*, all by herself.

Clean that chocolate off her, that had smeared her forehead and one cheek and spattered in her hair. That winged, asymmetric hair. Wasn't that just like Célie. Trying for the tough look and ending up resembling an elf longing for fairy wings.

I think I'm tough enough for both of us and all the world now, Célie. You can relax about the toughness and just let all that natural happiness play.

He bit into the red-flowered chocolate slowly. A hint of … something. It reminded him of the scent of Célie's hair. He couldn't put his finger on why.

The waiter wouldn't let him pay, when he asked for the bill. That made Joss smile a little and glance up at the section of glass wall visible at the top of those spiraling metal stairs. But he didn't spot Célie, peeking down at him.

Damn.

"When does Célie get off?" he asked the waiter.

"I don't think I should tell you that," the waiter said.

Joss sighed. These people acted as if he wasn't perfectly used to waiting all day in stillness if he needed to. Hell, he'd once had to wait three days, watching the entrance to a cave, with only a canteen of water and some rations to pass the time. "Fine. We'll do it the boring way."

He studied the line of people behind a velvet rope, all wishing they could get at his table so they could eat one of these éclairs themselves. He supposed he'd have to give up his position of comfort, too. "Can I have a piece of paper?"

"We've got this." The waiter handed him a postcard-size bit of heavy white card stock. It was stamped with an aggressive silver *DR* and then, in a corner, the formal details of Dominique Richard, store address, website, telephone number, info@dominiquerichard … Joss scowled. Then he drew a line through that *DR* and wrote "Célie" instead and flipped it over.

The blankness on the other side froze his brain, as it always had. He just didn't know what to write to her. He never had. He always, always had needed to *be* that thing he needed to write, to be that thing there, next to her, touching her. What the hell was there to *say*?

But maybe if he'd written back, after the first four months of training when he had the right to contact people again, she would have kept writing. She would have written, *What the hell is this story Sophie is telling?*

and he would have managed to answer that one at least, so she'd know the truth, and then he would have had new little cards and maybe eventually even letters that kept coming all through his stint in the Legion, instead just those first dozen cards he kept on the shelf of his locker so he could take them out whenever he needed to touch them.

He took a deep breath and scrubbed his face. God, it was a good thing he'd chosen the mechanic track back in school, because he would totally have failed his bac. He'd known it, too. Known he didn't have a chance in hell of sitting in front of a blank piece of paper with his whole future in jeopardy and filling it with anything that had any worth or made any sense.

What could he say? What could he possibly write that meant something and was true?

"Célie" he finally wrote. Okay, there, that was true. That meant something. He stared at it a long time and then finally put a comma after it. Then sat there twisting and twisting the pen between his big fingers. *Clearly* not fingers meant to wield a damn pen.

The waiter came back and hovered.

Joss lifted his head and gave him a long, narrow look, and the waiter found another table to take care of. The waiter also sent a quick look up to the top of those stairs, like a soldier going into battle and making sure someone was ready to lay down covering fire.

Joss followed the glance. Yes, Célie's personal hero, that big, black-haired guy *Dominique Richard*, was back in that corner where he could glare down at him.

Joss held the other man's eyes a second, all his muscles firing for battle. Then he bent his head to the card again and wrote, in his slow, deliberate letters that always meant in school that the teachers were yanking his exams away from him before he finished: *I would wait more than five years for you.*

He stared at it a moment more. And then he added a little heart over the *I* in her name.

He shoved it at the waiter before he could crumple it in his fist. “If this doesn’t get to her, I’m coming back and killing you.” Best sometimes to leave things clear.

The waiter blinked and backed up a step. “Dom won’t let you do that,” he said hastily.

“Yeah, right,” Joss said. “Him and whose army?”

He walked out of that beautiful, elegant, rough-and-romantic shop and went to find a much less comfortable wall to wait against.

Chapter 8

"If she wanted him to actually leave her alone, I think she would be handling this a little differently," Jaime said.

Ha! She knew it! Knew those two were talking about her. Célie pressed herself against the rolling wire shelves full of giant plastic containers of pistachios and almonds and raisins and every other possible chocolate ingredient that could be stored at room temperature in plastic containers, containers that currently shielded her eavesdropping on Jaime and Dom in Dom's office.

Dom rumbled something. Damn. She'd missed it.

"Well, yes, probably she is confused, but what's that have to do with anything? Caring about people is confusing."

"If he hurts her, I'm going to beat his damn brains out." Well, that one boomed clear enough.

A soft sound from Jaime. "You are such a sweetheart."

Célie rolled her eyes to heaven. Really, there was *no* reasoning with Jaime's insane idealization of Dom.

"I'm glad you're trying to take care of your people, but if you get in a fight with him, I'm going to be seriously pissed," Jaime said. "So just bear that in mind."

Dom grumbled something much lower and more wary.

"No, not pissed enough to dump you, you idiot. Dominique."

A brief silence. Célie stood on tiptoe to peek over the top of a container. Through the window in his office wall, she could see that Dom had pulled Jaime into his arms.

Oh, for crying out loud. If those two were going to get all mushy-faced again ... Célie started to turn away and get some actual work done this afternoon.

"You know she's always had a crush on you," Jaime said, and Célie froze.

Hey! Was that nice? To just *tell Célie's boss* about a perfectly private crush like that and embarrass the hell out of her for the rest of her career? What had happened to female solidarity and all that?

"*What?*" Dom said. "I've never—I swear—"

"Not a crush like that," Jaime said. "More like a safe-keeping crush, you know? A safe place to put her feelings while she's waiting for the proper place. Kind of like I used to crush on actors and rock stars before I met you. You know?"

Célie peeked again. Dom was shaking his head.

"You never did that?" Jaime said blankly. "*Everybody* does that."

"I think the only safe place I ever found for my feelings was you," Dom said, so quietly and with so little extra rumble to it that Célie could hear it very clearly.

It pierced her heart with this sweet tenderness for the two of them, this deep, precious gladness that the man who had been the big brother and refuge she had always needed and who had never believed he had the right to love himself had finally found that love. Finally found that place he felt safe.

Now if he didn't hurry up and set the date for a wedding, Célie would personally start hitting him over the head with something. Maybe buy one of those foam sledgehammers so she could bonk him with it every day he walked in still a coward.

She went back to her work while Jaime and Dom did the mushy-face stuff, and maybe she might have peeked out the window to see if any clouds had rolled in.

Joss looked up at her movement in it, but he didn't lift a hand and wave or anything. He just waited.

She looked at the card she'd propped in the corner of the marble counter, tucked under the wall of frames in all different sizes. She had it propped face forward, so no one could see what was written on the back, and because she liked the way Dom's eyebrow rose and the ironic, challenging glance he slanted at her when he saw his own name crossed out and replaced with hers. Ha! Take that. Because she didn't want the responsibility of running a business like this in Paris, and she didn't want the financial pressure, but she poured her life into these beautiful chocolates just like he did, and she *did* like getting some of the credit.

She touched the card. And then she knew she really shouldn't, but ... she peeked at the back again. That stubborn, determined handwriting, and the little heart over the *I* in her name just like she always did for him, as if he'd *noticed* that, and, and ... *I would wait more than five years for you.*

Her eyes filled again.

Blast it! She scrubbed at them, but not before two people spotted her and shook their heads. She knew she shouldn't have risked looking at those words again.

She glanced at the clock. It was nearly five. On normal days—not, obviously, the two weeks leading up to Valentine's or the week before Easter or the whole month of December—she left at five, having started at eight. Of course, her afternoon had been about as unproductive as it was conceivable to be, and she wouldn't normally leave without a heck of a lot more done, or else she'd have to come in at five in the morning tomorrow. And Dom got kind of grouchy when people came in too early unnecessarily—he liked having the kitchens to himself for a couple of hours. These days, he was torn, because he apparently also liked lingering in bed later than he ever had before he shared that bed with Jaime.

It must be nice, Célie thought wistfully, to like sharing a bed with someone so much you didn't want to leave it.

"I need to go," she told Dom abruptly, washing her hands. Dom came to fill the doorway of the ganache room and gave the quantity of work she had done that day an ironic look. "I'll come in early tomorrow," Célie said. That was a little meek. She stuck her chin up. "To make up for all those all-nighters I pull at Christmas."

Dom pretended to look grumpy, but his dark water eyes gleamed *touché*. "He still out there?" Dom checked the window. His hands closed automatically into fists. "Célie—"

"It's fine. Dom—I'm not worried. It's Joss, okay?" He often used to show up just a few minutes before she was due to get off, to lounge against the wall of the building opposite her bakery. It had made her heart sing, every time, when she saw him out there waiting for her. "You guys just don't understand because I overreacted."

"If you're trying to protect Dom—an effort I deeply appreciate—can I just mention that I could put a Corey security detail on you if you need it," Jaime said, coming into the room.

Dom stared at his fiancée. "I think you must have me mistaken for someone else."

Jaime smiled at him and shook her head, laying her hand on his arm. Dom sighed, looking down at it, and then covered her smaller hand with his.

"I need to go," Célie said again. She went into the bathroom to change into her street clothes—jeans and a short-sleeved knit shirt, because it wasn't as if she had been expecting to have to look hot on her way home from work—and grabbed her leather jacket and hibiscus-printed helmet. She hesitated, and then swooped back into the ganache room to fill a little metal box with chocolates. "Shut up," she told Dom.

He hadn't said anything, of course, busy rapping his knuckles against the nearest marble counter and looking from her to Jaime to the casement window.

"It will be *fine*," Célie said. "Damn it, men are such idiots." She stomped down the stairs.

Outside, she hesitated, glancing between her moped up the street on her left and Joss, leaning against a wall in the opposite direction. But she couldn't resist the pull of that muscled body, those hazel-green eyes.

She turned toward him, and he straightened from the wall as soon as she did, coming toward her. He moved differently than he had five years ago. He'd always been strong, fit, someone who made her feel safe, but now he had this hardness to him, as if he could cut a path through stone and steel just by walking toward it.

Or through bullets. Her stomach knotted even to think about it. She'd read about the Foreign Legion when he first disappeared into it—about the training he would be going through, about the brutal dog-eat-dog world of it, about the situations they were sent to handle in the world—and she would crawl between her own bed and the wall to hide, like she had when she was a little girl and her mom brought home a doubtful boyfriend. She'd clutch her arms around herself there, fighting in desperate anguish the knowledge of all he must be going through.

He stopped in front of her, taking her helmet for her but keeping his other hand at his side, his eyes sweeping over her face as if he was touching every part of it. Her skin burned from the look, and she flexed her hand around the box of chocolates so she wouldn't drop it on the ground and just fling her arms around him. *You're home, you're home, you're home.*

"You've still got chocolate on you." That sand-rasped quality to his deep voice now made her want to go up on tiptoe and kiss his throat, to slide silk over it so he remembered what softness felt like.

"I'm a chocolatier," she growled. "It's a hazard of the trade. Like mud and blood for a Legionnaire, only ... much nicer."

His face closed, and she wondered abruptly if she had just said something terrible. Like ... maybe that was a really stupid, flip thing to say to someone who might actually have seen a lot of blood in the past five years.

She thrust out her chin, somewhere between defiance and apology. "What I mean is, you might be tougher, but I taste better."

Wait. Did that sound—

Joss clasped his wrist behind his back, going into parade rest, his face almost completely blank. Except for the gleam of gold in those hazel eyes. "You don't know what I taste like."

A slow fire kindled somewhere down in the curl of Célie's toes and just started to burn, burn up through her. Joss didn't *hit* on her. He'd never, ever said anything sexual to her before.

And she'd never even imagined what he might taste like, until now. She'd imagined how warm he would be, in bed beside her. She'd imagined the texture of his strength. She'd imagined kissing him, even. But his *taste*—

If she opened her mouth against his skin, the taste of it would be—

No taste, maybe just a little salt, and ... and she realized she was actually sucking on the knuckle of her thumb to establish this for herself, right there in front of him. Whipping her hand away from her mouth, she shoved it into the pocket of her leather jacket.

"Here." She thrust her box of chocolates at him, pressing it flat against his chest, a metal shield between her hand and his heat. "Now you know what I taste like."

Wait. What the hell had she just said?

Joss brought one big, callused hand to cover hers, holding it against the metal she pressed against his chest. It must be her imagination that she could feel his heart thumping even through that aluminum box. It must be her own heart, beating in her brain.

Calluses and strength and warmth, sliding over the back of her hand. He held it and the box together, sliding it down, down his chest, to tuck the box in the waistband of his jeans. Célie's brain fused. She just stared at that flat silvery box angled there where it was absolutely too hot for chocolates ... they were going to melt ... it ...

He linked his fingers with hers, these big, firm fingers that felt *way* better than she had ever managed to imagine, making their space in between her smaller ones, and brought her hand to his mouth ... to suck on the knuckle of her thumb. "Hmm," he said. "I expected something a little more exciting."

Hey! More *exciting*? She was going to dissolve in a puddle. Her heart felt like one of those cartoon hearts, thumping in great zigzag elastic bounds outside her body as if it wanted to break free.

"Maybe you'll taste different in other places," he said.

Her brain had turned into chocolate too long in the sun. Nothing left of it but something a greedy person could lick off his fingers.

What was he *doing* to her? Joss had always been her brother's friend. She'd had a crush on him, sure, but no matter how many ways she'd tried to hint them into something more than friendship, he'd never taken her up on it. He'd been safe.

Until he left her and broke her heart into a million tiny shards that cut in her throat and her eyes all the nights she cried over him, hiding between her bed and the wall and hoping no psychopathic sergeant was making him do a thousand push-ups without food or water at noon, or carry rocks in his mouth for three hours in the hot sun while he did them, or beating him to broken bones for some infraction, or all the other things she read about the Foreign Legion training. That was in the first six months. Then, when she knew the Foreign Legion was being called into action in Mali and Afghanistan, she'd had to worry about whether he might right that second be in a firefight, whether—

She jerked her hand away. It didn't jerk very easily. First his grip tightened and restrained her, until he made himself loosen it and let her fingers free. "You are five years too late for this, Joss. Too bad you *saved me for later* when I actually had a crush on you. And ditched me. What, did you think our HLM was your own personal little walk-in freezer for me and you could just thaw me out when you got home?"

His face closed again immediately, hiding his weaknesses from anyone who might see a chance to exploit them, and it made her want to *cry*. Their *cité* had taught him that skill, but the Legion had perfected it. "I screwed up with you," he said. "I'm sorry about that, Célie."

She frowned, discomfited. He *had* screwed up, and it was much too big a screw-up to be solved by a simple apology. What was she supposed to do? Shrug and say, *No problem, it's all okay*?

"That doesn't mean I'm going to give up, though, Célie. I don't actually know how to quit."

It was true. He never had. That's why she'd known, once he'd signed up for the Legion, that he wouldn't be back. No matter what kind of hell training was, he would see it through those whole five years.

She thrust out her jaw. "You quit on *me*." *You left me there. You just ... left me. As if I was nothing.*

I guess I was nothing. A drug-dealing pseudo-friend's little sister.

Hell, if the thought of her on the back of a motorcycle flying out of there with him had ever even ghosted across his mind, the thought of them going *together*, he must have instantly dropped her out of that picture as dead weight.

"Célie." He struggled visibly for words. She hesitated, caught by that as she always had been—by the desire to know what he was thinking that was so very hard to say. "I did it for you."

Her fists clenched. A scream rose up in her, strangled by all the city around them, this primal scream that needed an entire empty desert or mountain range to let it out. "*Fuck you,*" she said again and pivoted, striding for her moped.

"Célie." He came after her. Not even hurrying to keep up with her, just this easy, ground-eating walk. Her chocolates still rode against his waist.

She swung back, putting the moped between them. "Don't you *tell me* that you did it for me, you *bastard.*" She yanked her helmet away from him and thrust it onto her head. "And quit stalking me! It's creepy! They're about ready to have you arrested!"

An eyebrow went up a little, and he rubbed the back of his military cut. "That would be weird. And I'd have to go quietly to be polite? Or were they planning on sending a SWAT team?"

"Aaaarghh." She strangled the scream as best she could, but the sound vibrated in her throat. She zipped her leather jacket.

"I didn't realize I was stalking you. I was just waiting. Do you—" Straight brown eyebrows drew slowly together. "Do you want me to go away?" His words came out hard, jumbled, as if he was back in school, having to make sense of a text while the letters danced and twisted in front of him.

And her eyes filled again *of course*. Of course she had to keep crying in front of him. Wasn't that perfect? "Don't you—don't you—" She had to gasp through the threat of sobs. *"Don't you dare go away again."* She yanked the metal box out of his waistband and shoved it into his hand. "And this is to be eaten! Not melted against your skin like you're some ... *porn star*!"

She swung onto the moped, starting it, wishing she had a big, growling motor like Dom on his real motorcycle instead of her silent little electric thing.

Joss reached out and grabbed hold of the handlebars. "Célie. I don't know where you live. I don't have your number. You don't have mine. And I can't give it to you, because I still need to buy a phone and find a place to stay. I don't even know when you usually get off. If you don't like me waiting outside where you work all day, can we come up with some plan for how I'm supposed to *not go away*?"

She stared at him, wishing for once she had a face shield on her helmet to provide a barrier against the world. “Fine,” she snapped. “Get on.”

And instead of roaring out of their *banlieue* with her arms wrapped around him on a powerful motorbike he’d souped up so he could rescue her on it as she used to daydream, she wobbled carefully with all his weight behind her and his thighs pressed against hers on her little moped into the mass of traffic circling République.

She’d always known she would regret not getting the pink bike.

Chapter 9

“You need a helmet,” Célie grumbled, sitting on the edge of the quay of the Île de la Cité. She folded her legs under her, so she wouldn’t be tempted to lean back against the wall instead and ... tuck herself up against a shoulder.

She’d always wanted to do that. Tuck herself up against his shoulder. She’d been looking for another guy against whose shoulder she would love to tuck herself for five years, but ... yeah, no. No, the last thing she wanted to do was lower her guard to someone else, depend on someone else, and have him disappear in pursuit of all those big dreams that had no room for her.

“I need a car,” Joss said. “And a phone.” He leaned back against the wall behind him, stretching out his legs and folding his hands behind his head, contemplating the Seine. “*Merde*, but it’s good to be out of the Legion.”

I didn’t tell you to join it, Célie thought bitterly. She pulled her jacket off and draped it over her helmet, using it as an armrest. “Was it terrible?”

“It was challenging,” Joss said, of what was supposed to be one of the most brutally demanding military services on the planet. “Especially Corsica. It changed everything I understood about my own limits, about what I could do. But in the end, you’re under the orders of officers you don’t always agree with, and politicians, and, God forbid, sometimes even the UN. Also, while there are some of the best men in the world there, men you can look up to, there are definitely also some psychopath officers and NCOs. I hated having to do things I didn’t agree with, so I couldn’t see myself doing it another ten years.”

“What are you going to do now?” she asked warily. Wait, Corsica?

“I don’t know.” He shrugged. The river stretched behind her, the sun setting beyond the bridges and the Louvre and the Eiffel Tower, and she couldn’t tell if he was looking at her or looking at the view of Paris with that hint of wonder that even seemed to ease the hardness his eyes had gained in the past five years. “I imagined taking you to the south of France or even one of the islands, like Tahiti or Réunion, and living there. But you seem to be happy here in Paris, so I’ll have to readjust. Unless Tahiti appeals.” A questioning lift of his eyebrows.

“Every time you talk about all the plans you made for me, like I was a snack in the refrigerator you were looking forward to eating when you got off work, it makes my head want to explode,” Célie growled.

His expression blanked again. He did that even better than he used to—hid his thoughts and feelings. Yeah, she could imagine that skill standing him in good stead as he went through training under those psychopaths he mentioned, and she could imagine that skill getting honed relentlessly. Coming as she did from an emotive and unstable family, something about that control of his reassured her. But it could also drive her completely nuts.

“You never thought about me, Célie?” he asked carefully.

Oh. She wrapped her arms around herself and the pain in her middle. Oh, yes, she had thought about him. Sometimes, when she had a bad day, particularly if that bad day included yet another dating disaster, she would curl up with the thought of him in her bed, as if he was still her old dream of happily ever after.

He had been thinking about her, too? Imagining all his own happily ever afters with her? She hugged her knees harder, a sweetness and a wistfulness calming her frustration, turning it into something more painful and more longing. “You were in Corsica?” she asked warily. “Isn’t that where the paratrooper regiment trains?”

He nodded, his hands still clasped behind his head.

Holy crap. She'd read about them, of course. She'd read obsessively about the Foreign Legion, the first six months he was gone. The Legion itself was already considered elite, albeit insane, but the 2e REP was the elite of that elite, one of the most elite combat regiments in the world, with the training to match.

And it hit her that he could not possibly be her same Joss anymore. That everything she knew about him was like knowing what cocoa beans were like before they got turned into chocolate. No. Nothing as soft and sweet as chocolate. Like knowing what fresh-mined iron ore was like before it got turned into a steel blade. She stared at him, wondering if his heart had changed, too.

He gazed back at her, his face hard to read but his eyes still that same steady hazel green. He did look hardened, everywhere hardened, even his eyes and the set of his chin. And yet ...

There was this quiet to him, still. That same quiet strength that had made her crush on him so hard back when she was a teenager.

That made her shiver with hunger now, so that she had to rub her arms to disguise herself, as if the evening was bringing a chill.

"A porn star, hmm?" Joss's voice was so neutrally musing, but a little curl snuck into the corners of his lips. He lounged there against the rock, with his hands behind his head, and his whole body in this lazy display of ... of ... something a woman could really easily jump on.

Heat chased the chill away from her skin. "That was not a compliment!"

"Oh, trust me. None taken." But the curve of his mouth deepened.

"Only a man would think it was a compliment to be compared to a porn star!"

"No." He shook his head. "But it's a compliment to know you were thinking about sex."

Oh. She gasped, both her fists clenching against it. If the Seine wasn't such a disgustingly dirty river, she would dive right into it this second and maybe swim around to the opposite end of the island before she came back up for air. Then just sneak away and go hide between her bed and the wall, the way she did so many nights worrying about him.

God, he looked so freaking gorgeous, stretched out almost to the point of *relaxation*, there so close to her. He looked real. He looked as if her Joss had come back, only ... not hers and completely different.

And her mouth watered to know what he tasted like.

He picked up her box of chocolates from the stones beside him. "If I eat these up again now, are you going to be mad at me?" He pried the metal lid off.

"Maybe you need dinner." She watched the strong fingers ease free a small, perfect piece. He sure could consume a lot of chocolates.

The thought made her happy. She could *make* a lot of chocolates. She might be the only woman in Paris who could keep this guy filled up.

He shook his head and slipped the entire chocolate into his mouth in one bite. She stared at his mouth, as her whole day of work, everything she had accomplished in the past five years, just melted in a rush of flavors inside it. "It gives me something else to focus on," he said. "I'm thinking about sex, too."

Her lips parted. She squeezed herself so tightly her feet came off the stone, and she wobbled on the edge of the quay.

He lunged forward and grabbed her arm, pulling her back into steadiness before she'd even properly lost balance.

The sudden surge of power, just to capture her, made everything inside her go still. Waiting to be captured. His lashes lowered, as his gaze fixed on his hand, firm on her arm. Slowly, his grip softened, and his fingers spread, his hand rubbing gently back and forth once against her forearm. "You're cold," he said softly.

Yes. It was midsummer, and yet the hair rose all over her body at the need to bury herself in the closest source of warmth.

"Célie." His voice dropped deep and low and sand-rasped. "I could warm you up."

"I *know,*" she said between her teeth. It was her deepest, most persistent fantasy about him, the one she still, even just two nights before, had used to ease herself to sleep—that his big body was there, warming her up. The fantasy she found more soothing to cuddle into at night than any actual male body of any man she had ever dated.

She patted blindly for her leather jacket and pulled it back over her legs. *I can take care of warming myself up. Since I had five years of knowing I, and only I, was ever going to take care of me.*

"I want to go home," she lied fiercely. The thought of leaving him on this quay, of separating herself from him by more than a meter, made her feel as if she was prying her own skin off.

His mouth twisted. "I can't do that. Until my home decides to let me back in."

That made her feel like an apartment broken into and wide open, a flimsy sheet over the door, no possible way to shut him out and keep herself safe. "Joss—"

"Here." He pulled her very carefully into his arms, lifting her easily and settling her between his legs, as he leaned back against the wall of the quay. "Does this help?"

She bent her head, defeated, into this, her very favorite fantasy. His warm body. His hold. "You left me with nothing," she whispered. "For five years. Nothing but me."

His arms tightened gently on her. "That wasn't leaving you with nothing. That was leaving you with everything."

Yes, clearly. She'd made herself from that point. Everything she'd become had come from inside her, and her *everything* was a good *everything*. It was a proud, happy everything.

"I thought leaving you with only me was leaving you with nothing." That deep steady voice, coming from inside his chest under her ear, rasping over her head. "Back then."

He had been her everything. The only reason she didn't already have a concrete plan for getting out of that *cité* the day she turned eighteen. The person who made it bearable, on whom she could put all her focus. The dream she rode with out of there.

"I could *bite* you," she said. *Nothing. Him!*

"You can do anything you want to me. I'm sorry that I hurt you, and I can take pretty much any punishment."

Her eyes filled again, and her head collapsed back against his chest in defeat, her hand rising to stroke right where she had been so tempted to bite. *I'm sorry. Why did you have to go join the goddamn Legion?*

Oh, God, the heat and scent of his body. In *real.* She hadn't even known he smelled like that—this rough, sweet, piquant scent of him, as if he'd absorbed all the odors of the pine and wild-herb-clad hills of Corsica and baked in them. Which, God, he probably had—crawling through brush, doing those two hundred-kilometer, four-day marches in full gear in the hot sun. And that was just the training. That was before he must have been sent to Afghanistan to march right into explosives or an ambush of bullets while he was doing them.

"You were never *nothing,*" she said flatly. "You made it worth getting out of bed every morning and braving the damn walk past those gangs of assholes, just knowing I'd get to see you. You were everything to me back then, Joss." She lifted her chin, sat away from the warmth of his body. "But these days—I've got all this." She gestured to the whole beautiful stretch of Paris in the setting sun and back to herself, finishing with a flick of her hand up and down her body. She had herself, too.

Joss gazed down at her. The sunset glimmered rose across his face. "Good," he said finally. "I'm sorry that I hurt you, Célie, but I'm glad you ended up with all this"—a copy of her gesture, to include the whole Seine and all its palaces and bridges and Eiffel Tower, and then a slower, gentler shift of his hand up and down, to include her—"instead of just me."

Oh.

Now what was she supposed to think or feel about that?

"I would have been happy with just you," she muttered. *Just.* How could he even say that about his strength and kindness and steadiness, all those things he had shown her back then, in a world where everyone else's strength always seemed to be primed to cause harm?

"In Tarterets?"

"It never crossed your mind that we could make something of ourselves *together*? Drive south, me hire on with a baker, you with a mechanic in some likely town, and we make just a ... I don't know ... a stupid, happy life together?"

He stared at her.

Yeah. It obviously hadn't occurred to him.

"I wanted to be bigger," he said stubbornly.

"Yeah, well ... forgive me for ever imagining you could become a bigger person with me there to help. I didn't realize I would have kept you small."

Fine. That choice would have kept him smaller than he was now, true. Some small-town mechanic, while she was a small-town baker.

She sure did love being the best chocolatier in Paris. Even if Dom did get all the credit.

Okay, fine, maybe Dom deserved a smidgen of the credit. But still ...

"You wouldn't have kept me small." Joss was gaining that obdurate tone he got, when he had to keep forcing the same words out because he couldn't find the perfect ones. "But I had to get bigger."

"Congratulations." Still in his hold, Célie brought both hands up so that she could bury her head in them instead of his shoulder. "You clearly succeeded in your goal."

"It was my first step." As always, Joss's words were simple, his gaze direct. "You're the goal."

Chapter 10

Célie's heart clenched when the door into her building swung shut with Joss on the other side of it. The darkness tightened her lungs as she set her foot on the first stair. Every breath grew more panicked, that she would never see him again, that closing that door on him had shut out his existence. She couldn't do this, walking away from him, climbing and climbing up a dark stairwell by herself while she left him behind.

She had to, though. Because he had done the same thing to her, left her behind while he disappeared up a dark climb where she could not follow. And she couldn't be the person left behind again.

She was as unable to let him back in as she was to send him away.

She smacked on the timed lights at every landing, but the one flight lit above her seemed like some wimpy candle against a grief or a fear, and the darkness pursued her from below, as the lights went out behind her with each flight she cleared.

In her apartment, at least, she could leave the lights on. Her home in expensive Paris was essentially a bed with a tiny amount of space on either side of it to move around. Joss couldn't come up here. If he came up there, she would ...

He would ...

They would ...

How did Joss make love? She had no idea. Urgent and hungry, pushing her down onto that bed as soon as they bumped into it for lack of other space to move?

Quietly, slow and easy, letting her lead?

Tantalizing, starting at that knuckle he had tasted and slowly drawing her finger into his mouth as he massaged her hand and let his palm rub down her wrist, calluses over her skin as he worked his way into greater and greater intimacies, not one of which she could deny?

Why did he have to have such a hot body? That wasn't fair. All muscled and perfect and stubborn and those beautiful eyes focused on her, as if he'd hike two hundred kilometers for her with a fifty-kilo pack on his back any day of the year. *You're the goal.*

She wanted to *smack* him when he said that. She wasn't any damn freaking goal, she was a *person*. She'd rather they have been walking hand in hand toward any goals.

She'd rather have come home, the first time she succeeded in making a perfect chocolate for Dom, and crawled onto their bed in their tiny apartment because it was the only space they had, to show it off to Joss excitedly and watch him eat it. Maybe even bring it to his lips with her own fingers, because he hadn't yet had time to wash the grease off his hands from working on some car.

That was what she would have rather.

They would have been *happy*.

He couldn't take back all those nights she'd had to curl up between her bed and the wall, in those black hours when she went into panic attacks over what he might be going through.

It had been bad enough when she thought he just didn't care about her that way.

But *to have done it for her?* To have *liked* her and still left her that way?

It made her want to rip him to shreds.

Only, she was afraid if she touched him, she might just rip his clothes off instead. That when her fingers tried to sink into his actual body, they would end up doing something else.

She washed her face in lieu of being able to clean up her mind and went to the window, hugging herself, looking out at all the other lights that used to console her a little during those black moments. She was alone, but she wasn't. Millions of other people were out there being alone, too.

Or finding someone.

But Joss had never been part of those millions. Always before, Joss had been somewhere off with the Foreign Legion, and even thinking about him had made her brain shy away from all the imagined nightmares of who might be shooting at him or what he might be doing.

She leaned on her little window railing, like a princess whose Prince Charming never did remember to stop by and serenade her, and blinked at what she saw below.

What in the world was Joss doing now?

***

Joss punched his jacket into a comfortable shape under his head and settled back on the bench, gazing up at the light in Célie's window. Six floors up. He'd picked it out by the timing of when the light went on, after she left him at the door, and confirmed it by the shape of her silhouette.

It would be easy to climb the face of that building. Really easy. Just his own body weight to carry, and there were balconies and ledges every floor and even some grimacing old stone faces for handholds. It would feel like strolling in the park, to climb the face of that building.

So climbing up the stairs inside with her would have felt like ... floating. Magically rising above the earth just by the wish of it.

Maybe she knew that. Maybe she didn't think he deserved anything that easy.

She'd worked hard, too, after all. He pulled out his little metal box and gazed at the three chocolates he had saved for later. His thumbnail traced carefully around the edge of the one with delicate green twining across it, the mint one. She must have worked her butt off, to get this good.

Célie. He smiled. She'd never been afraid of work, or at least not work per se. She'd been afraid of ending up in a mind-numbing job in a factory, but that was why she'd focused hard on her pastry apprenticeship, because it made her happy and proud. Some people would consider pastry work mind-numbing, too, but not Célie. His mind flashed to all those memories of her face when she ran out of her bakery with a box full of something she was so proud to offer him.

Célie. With her burgundy braid and her bright eyes, always so happy and vibrant and bouncy. Sometimes she'd twitch that saucy butt at him on purpose and stick her tongue out at some excuse she'd found to tease him, when she met him leaving his work or he met her leaving hers, and his fingers would itch and he'd shove his hands in his pockets, to save her butt from them.

To make sure that first he became the man she'd really dreamed he would be. Her hero.

He clasped his hands behind his head to get comfortable, gazing in some awe at the wide open sky, the lights sparkling in windows on the buildings rising around him—people changing, eating, arguing, gazing out the windows at the night. He supposed he should go to a hotel until he found an apartment, but he hated to waste money on something stupid like that. He had plans for that money.

Besides, it had been a year since his last leave. And right now, being outside like this, under the non-starry sky of bright Paris, with people of both sexes all around just *living their lives*, no real menace to him anywhere, instead of in barracks surrounded by the solidarity and snores and problematic temperaments of other fighting men or outside where he had to keep an eye out for snipers or someone smiling coming up to him with a basket of flowers that hid a bomb … It felt so free, it was almost like flying. He didn't even know if he'd be able to sleep. He might want to pace Paris, see it with all its lights and cynicism and the profound romantic innocence of its sleep.

He turned his head toward Célie's window again, wondering what she looked like when she slept. Romantic? Innocent? Cynical? Cute. He was pretty sure about the cute part.

He couldn't see her moving in her apartment anymore. A sigh of wistful arousal ran through him at the thought of her, either in the shower or already tucking herself into her pillow.

"Joss."

His head twisted at her voice coming from across the street. What was she doing back down here and not in bed? Oh, hey, had she missed him? Maybe even ... started thinking about inviting him up?

She crossed the street determinedly as he stood and stopped in front of him, her hands on her hips. "What are you doing?" she demanded.

He looked from her to his jacket in a pillow position on the bench, not quite grasping the question when the answer seemed pretty obvious. "Nothing much," he admitted. "Just going to take a break for a while." He'd been up a lot longer than twenty hours at a stretch before. Sleep deprivation to push a man past his breaking point was a key component of Legion training, a well-founded component it turned out later, given what they had to deal with in actual combat situations. But that sleep deprivation was also how a man learned to catch sleep when he could, too.

"Are you *sleeping* on that bench? Joss—don't you have anywhere to stay?"

"I hadn't gotten around to it. I just got into town this morning, and ... I've been busy." Besides, originally, he hadn't intended to stay. He'd thought he'd sweep Célie off to some place like Tahiti, and they'd spend the rest of their lives in some dreamy paradise. Now ... well, she seemed happy here.

"Do you want to help me find a place?" he asked hopefully. That way, even if she tried to be noncommittal, he'd know exactly how much or little she liked his options. He could read Célie like an open book.

Actually better. He could focus on her longer, without the sense of her swimming away from him. She ... rested his eyes. His brain. Made him feel as if everything was clear now, beautifully so, as if all that energy and tough-hearted optimism in her washed the world around her clean and made it sparkle.

Every time he thought of her insane little chocolates, that so-easily-melted, delicate perfection held out to the world with all her heart, it made him smile. Maybe the smile didn't show, because he'd spent the last five years in situations where you didn't want to give anyone a weapon against you, but it curled up there, deep in his middle. *God, I want to kiss you.*

"Joss." She put both hands to her head. He loved it when she did that, the way it showed off her whole body—energy and curves and gracefully determined muscle—in some dramatic chiding. He liked being the focus of her chiding. He got off on it a little bit, to tell the truth. "People already want to arrest you as a crazy stalker."

He stopped smiling. "Damn it, now I can't even sleep on a bench? *Merde*, Célie. It's a nice night." Nice night to be alive, nice night to be out of the Legion, nice night to gaze up at an apartment window and contemplate his goal and how he was going to get to it. He sure as hell had spent nights in far worse conditions contemplating his goal and how he was going to reach it and, ideally, survive.

Of course, in those cases, sometimes he had to *kill* his goal, which was another of the contrasts that was so nice here.

She jerked her hands down from her head and folded her arms across her chest, a look he didn't like on her at all. It closed her off. "And that's a load of bullshit," she said stiffly.

Oh, really? He clasped his left wrist behind his back in parade rest. "What is?" he asked coolly.

"That you *did it all for me.* First of all, if you did it all for me, I'll kill you. And second, you damn well did not. You must have just started some fantasy thing about me to get you through."

One thing a man learned fast in the first four months training in the Legion was when to keep his mouth shut, no matter what someone said or even yelled in his face. Just because somebody said something completely idiotic and insulting didn't mean you had to react to it. Plus, she'd put him in the typical drill sergeant lose-lose situation there—damned no matter what point he argued.

"Just like some—some calendar pin-up girl or something," Célie muttered.

Joss grinned before he could catch himself, a sneak escape out through his neutral expression, at the idea of Célie as a pin-up girl. "You'd make a rather unique Playboy bunny."

Her hands dropped to her hips. There you go. He liked that position, too. Much more open than the arms folded one, and, yes, yes, getting in trouble with her *did* give him a hot erotic charge. Made him want to just ... mess with her. Get her more riled up until they were wrestling on a big bed and he was proving to her exactly how much she liked the kind of trouble he could get into. He'd never done it in real life, but always in his fantasies, that was a familiar tussle, one they got into a lot.

But Célie was scowling. "What's that supposed to mean?"

He imagined that scowling position naked, perhaps with some skimpy erotic lace covering certain bits. His grin snuck back out. "You'd definitely be different than their norm."

Hurt flashed across her face before she covered it with a deepened scowl. "Well, now you've dashed all my hopes of building a career out of exposing myself so that perverts can jerk off fantasizing about me."

Pervert seemed a little harsh there. What else was he supposed to do, find a brothel?

"I always kind of liked the idea of you being unique to me," he said apologetically.

She stared at him.

He tapped his temple. "My, ah, pin-up girl in here. No one else gets to see."

Her lips parted. She licked them, and then pressed them abruptly together, stiffening her stance. "I'm going to hit you now."

He laughed. Damn, she was cute. All those fantasies had gotten so faded and worn-out over time, and her real-life presence recharged them *hard.* As if they'd been hit by lightning and most definitely needed some kind of surge protector to keep from shorting out his whole system. "Okay. Am I allowed to duck and block, grab my attacker and subdue her, or do you want me to just stand still?"

Grabbing his attacker and locking her in right up close to his chest while she wiggled ...

Her hands went back to her head again instead, and she gripped her skull as if to keep it on. "Joss, I *can't* put you up in my apartment. It's basically just a bed with walls."

Oh, wow, hell. Definitely needed a surge protector there.

"I mean, you can barely squeeze around in it, without falling on the bed."

Holy shit. His brain fried. His breaths started to come in long and deep, as his whole body went hot and hard.

"You have to go to a hotel."

He frowned, and his hand tightened around his wrist behind his back. Damn it, she just didn't get it, did she? How much easier it was for him to be a little uncomfortable than to get far away from her again. He'd already screwed up once by committing to five years away from her. "I think I'm more used to roughing it than you realize. I was enjoying being outside. It's a nice night. It's Paris. I suppose you're used to it being Paris."

She nodded uncertainly, her arms back across her chest. She just couldn't stop moving, could she? He'd always loved that contrast with himself, with the way he knew how to be still. And wait for her. "Joss—can you not afford a hotel?" she asked cautiously. "You know I'd help you out, if you needed it, right?"

Right, because that was the whole point of joining the Foreign Legion—coming back to sponge off an old semi-friend's little sister, helpless to take care of himself. "I'm fine, Célie. I've actually got enough for—well, it depends where you want to live, but a nice house in some places or a down payment here." He nodded at the expensive Paris streets.

She gasped, one hand flying to her lips as she stared at him.

Now what should he not have said? Shit, the Legion lessons were right—a man was really better off, in all circumstances, just keeping his mouth shut.

"A—a house?" she whispered. "For you and me?"

"Not a house *here*. It's the Legion, not a millionaire's club. Here it would have to be an apartment."

Her head bent. She looked as if she might be on the verge of tears again. He wanted to touch her, but it was night in a romantic city just below her apartment that was *all bed*, and his body was already so freaking charged up. He tightened his hold on his wrist, struggling to ride out the urge.

"Joss...I know letters aren't your thing," she said low, desperate ... and angry, too. She lifted her head. "But five years saving up for a house together and you couldn't have *written*? Found a phone once in a while and called? Come see me on leave?"

"That wouldn't really have been fair to you. To ask you to wait for me." Plus, he hadn't proved he deserved her yet. Lots of men failed out of the Foreign Legion. And it made his stomach jittery to even think about how much it would have cost him to come see her on leave and then turn around and say good-bye again.

Her hands sank convulsively into her fairy-punk hair. “Oh, my God, I’m going to kill you.”

Well … if she ever did actually go through with that plan to kill him, he couldn’t say at this point that he hadn’t been forewarned.

“Joss.” Her eyes were anxious, confused, pleading. “Please go to a hotel.”

His hand tightened on his wrist behind his back until it hurt. Fine.

So he went to a damn hotel. Some cheap place that was the closest he could find to her apartment, where he looked out the window at the wall of the other building across the alley and some guy deliberately exposing himself to the hotel guests, instead of up at Célie’s window. He tilted his head back to catch a glimpse of Paris night sky, a tepid darkness compared to the black and starry sky in Mali or Afghanistan. Hell. Now *those* were real skies.

He’d like to take Célie to see a real sky sometime. Not in a war zone, but somewhere safe. She’d *love* it.

But meanwhile, she was in her apartment a couple of blocks over, and he was here, closed in, with this stupid, empty bed behind him and some guy mooning him from the fourth floor across the way.

What a boring letdown for his first night back.

Chapter 11

"Everything all right?" Jaime asked.

Célie straightened guiltily from Dom's in-progress sculpture of a lioness. No, she had *not* been thinking of biting that other ear off. "You're back again? Already? I thought Dom had started sleeping in later."

"You're here pretty early yourself," Jaime said.

Dom came up the stairs, his short delay after Jaime suggesting he'd taken care of a couple of things downstairs on the way in, and gave Célie a disgruntled look at having to share his space so early, but otherwise didn't say anything, moving to hang up his leather jacket.

"I promised to come in early," Célie said. Plus, she'd needed the reassurance. *Here I am. All these things I made of myself.*

Her card from Joss was still tucked in the corner of the counter in the ganache room. *I would wait more than five years for you.* With a heart over the *I* in her name.

"Did you ever feel like knocking Dom's head against a wall?" Célie asked.

"No," Jaime said.

Oh. Now Célie felt guilty.

"I wouldn't want to hurt him," Jaime admitted. Dom gave her a wry look as he moved to double-check his lioness. He seemed pretty darn big and hard to hurt, especially in contrast with Jaime's size.

Célie scowled. "Fine. I'm a bad person." Didn't that just figure?

Jaime smiled. "You're maybe just more physical in your mental imagery. That or Dom's less frustrating."

Dom's eyebrows rose a little at that, his lips curving ruefully, and he ran his hand over his lioness, exactly like someone petting an actual lion. Well, someone like Dom petting an actual lion. Célie liked the *idea*, but was worried she might cop out about actually touching a lion in real life.

"It's just—I mean, it was bad enough when he was just my brother's friend, whom I had a secret crush on, and he went off and joined the Foreign Legion. Then, you know—well, having a crush on a guy a few years older than you who doesn't reciprocate, you just have to tough it up and get over it, right? But when he tells me he did it *for me*, I—" Célie's teeth ground together, and she grabbed a big bag of chocolate blocks and slammed it against the counter to break them up, helping relieve the stress.

Dom frowned at the noise, sighed, and focused on his lion again. He really did hate sharing his space at this hour of the morning.

"Seriously?" Jaime said. "He abandoned you for five years for your sake? No wonder you want to hit him over the head."

"Yeah, Dom might be an idiot about wanting to wait until he's proven his worth, but at least he's being an idiot *at your side*," Célie said.

Dom gave her a look. She stuck her chin up at him.

"True," Jaime admitted. "You're doing much better than Célie's guy," she told Dom approvingly.

Hey. Both Célie and Dom gave Jaime indignant looks, for opposite reasons.

Dom focused on his lioness, picking up a small knife, working on detail. Célie had dumped her chocolate chunks into a bowl before Dom suddenly spoke, without looking up. "Of course, I'm older."

Célie blinked. Had Dom just defended Joss? Dom? Of all people?

"How old were you when you first started working for me, Célie? Eighteen?" Dom shaved a long, fine strip of chocolate off the lion. "So that made him, what? The same age? A couple years older?"

"Twenty-one," Célie said stiffly. Hey ... hadn't it been Joss's birthday a couple weeks ago? She'd gone out with another guy, to better ignore the date and embrace her happy life without him, but the guy hadn't inspired in her any desire to invite him up or curl against his side.

"And still stuck in the *banlieue* and in love with you?" Dom nodded, still focused on his sculpture. "Yeah, that would do it."

Both women stared at him.

"Do what?" Célie finally asked between her teeth.

"Motivate him. *Merde,* Célie, a man's either an idiot or very determined to change his life, to join the Foreign Legion."

"Or both," Célie said tightly.

Dom shrugged acknowledgment. Jaime picked up the sliver of chocolate that had come off the lion and nibbled at it. A little smile flashed across Dom's face as he glanced at his chocolate on her lips.

"I didn't ask him to change his life for me," Célie said. "Maybe if he was in—in—in—if he had a crush on me, he should have talked to me about it before he did something so asinine. Maybe we could have come up with some mountain we could have climbed *together.*"

"Yeah," Dom said, almost absently, focused on shaping the leg of the lion. "Men don't always think that way." He gave Jaime an apologetic look. "We're kind of raised to want to go out on quests to earn the princess's hand by becoming a hero. It's, ah, hard for us to wrap our minds around a princess who wants to do all that dirty work with us. Makes us feel—insufficient. Not man enough. Not good enough."

Jaime reached out suddenly and rested her hand on Dom's biceps, flexing as he worked.

Dom met her eyes just a second and then focused again on his lioness. But the line of his lips was softer, a little vulnerable. "And, you know, he was barely out of his teens."

Célie scowled. "I was *in* my teens."

"Exactly. Still time for him to get worthy of you while you were growing up."

Oh, for God's sake. Men were so annoying. Célie went into the "hot" room, where all the burners were, from which she could still see Dom working on his sculpture and Jaime leaning against the counter on which the sculpture was posed, out of his way but still close.

"Did anything else happen just before he joined?" Dom asked, eating a bite of his own chocolate and then offering the other half of his bite to Jaime as a peace offering or an apology. Or just to get her to kiss his fingertips, as she did. For crying out loud, those two were so mushy.

"My brother got arrested for drug dealing," Célie said bitterly. Yeah, it had been a *banner* year for her. First her stupid brother and then Joss, both gone. Her on her own.

"There you go," Dom said. "It makes sense to me."

Jaime's eyes narrowed fractionally. "Does it?"

Célie thumped her wooden spoon down in her melting bowl of chocolate, muttering about maybe just taking Joss's and Dom's heads and knocking them both together. Knock sense into two idiots in one go.

"Well ..." Dom eyed his fiancée with cautious apology. Jaime was the only person in the world who could make Dom look cautious. "Yes."

"Maybe I can see your point," Jaime told Célie. "Maybe I could be tempted to knock some sense into somebody, in your shoes."

"See?" Célie flung out her hands in self-justification and accidentally spattered chocolate off her spoon across the stove. She cursed and wiped it up. "Anybody could be driven to it, in these circumstances!"

"*I* could knock some sense into him," Dom said hopefully.

Jaime put her hands on her hips and frowned at him.

"Except that I believe in a nonviolent approach to life," Dom corrected hastily. "Definitely. I definitely believe in that."

Célie banged pans in lieu of people's heads.

***

Joss pulled out his little metal box of chocolates and studied the last one. Perfect and sweet and tucked up into the corner, just waiting for him.

Kind of the way he thought *Célie* would be, but okay. He should have known better than to underestimate her that way. Good for her.

It made him smile, to think of how happy she must be making these chocolates, and he resigned himself to it: Tahiti was out. Who ever heard of making top chocolates in the tropics? He'd have to get an apartment in Paris.

But just for a moment, before he got to work on the hunt, he stretched his arms out along the back of the bench, fascinated by this wide-openness of his body, this stretch of it that seemed to say to any possible sniper, *Here, let me just paint a target on my chest to go with it.* And yet there *were* no snipers. He could just lounge here, watching the passersby.

Time to start looking for work, too. It felt weird to have nothing to do today, no end to his leave in sight. The last time he'd been unemployed, he'd ended up joining the Legion.

Seemed like a better thing to do than turn into a loser.

But employment wasn't *urgent*. He did have most of his salary for the past five years saved up. He'd always sought out the opportunities for greater certifications and advancement, done the corporal training and the sergeant's training, so his base salary had increased commensurately, and he'd earned two and a half times that base whenever he was deployed. Which had been a lot. The Legion had a lot of hot spots to jump into, these days.

The Legion had covered lodging, uniform, and food, and didn't allow recruits cars or even phones for that first contract. So there wasn't a lot to spend money on. He'd never really seen the point of gambling it or drinking it all away.

He didn't want to waste it now, after five years of economizing toward his and Célie's future, but a day off wouldn't *kill* him. Interestingly, he was pretty sure that nothing in this city could really kill him. Or, better yet, would even try. Oddly relaxing, that.

And he was almost giddily tempted by the idea of taking a day off. Of just wandering around this city, with no orders as to how he should spend his time, no constraints, no hostiles. It was *Paris*. It was incredible to be sitting on this green bench, watching the people pass, and not thinking bitter thoughts about Parisian wealth and privilege and the contrast with the *banlieue* but to be thinking, *Hell, this is as much my city as anyone else's. If Célie could make it hers, I can make it mine, too.*

Paris. Right there, like his own personal world in an oyster.

He might not wander along the Seine in his explorations, though, because walking along that lovely and romantic stretch of the city might actually hurt in weird parts of his body, like the hand Célie wouldn't be holding, and the heart she wouldn't be eagerly welcoming, and his butt where her hand wouldn't be slipping possessively into the back pocket of his jeans, like girlfriends *did*. There was a woman doing it in a couple walking past right now.

Célie would be possessive, if she decided to possess him. She'd do it in a funny way, mostly, teasingly minatory if he happened to glance at a nice ass passing by, but she'd very definitely make sure everyone, including him, knew he was hers.

The fantasy of it returned so easily, and he grimaced wistfully, rubbing the bench.

"Hello," a female voice said, and he looked around in surprise.

A woman with reddish hair stood a couple of meters away from him, kind of a big distance for a greeting, but maybe he looked dangerous.

Which he was, but not to women or children. Not even to men unless they were dangerous to him.

Except possibly that damn boss of Célie's.

"Hi," he said briefly so as not to encourage her, sitting up straight and dropping his arms from the back of the bench. It was true what he'd quite stupidly told Célie before, that he'd never had much trouble attracting women, but after five years in a rough, wild world of men, he'd lost even the most basic skills and now felt awkward about how to politely show a strange woman that he was unavailable.

"I'm Jaime Corey." She held out her hand, coming toward him, kind of in an odd way, as if she knew that some men were best not approached suddenly and needed to see you weren't carrying any weapons. "A friend of Célie's."

Oh. Joss shook her hand, intrigued now. Wow, she looked *really* different from the friends Célie had had before. More—together. Nice clothes but casual, not skintight, and her nails weren't even polished, let alone two centimeters long and covered with patterns. It reminded him that the last time he'd really known Célie, all her friends had been teenagers whose main hope for the future had been catching some *banlieue* version of Prince Charming.

"It's nice to meet you," he said. "Did I see you yesterday?"

He'd been focused on that black-haired boss of Célie's, as the person he might have to fight, and on Célie herself, but there might have been hair that color in his peripheral vision.

"In passing. I believe you were choosing not to fight my fiancé at the time."

Her fiancé?

"Dominique Richard. You know, black hair? Scowling? Big?" She did a thing with her arms that was apparently supposed to indicate bulky muscles and was kind of cute on such a slim form. Joss found himself starting to smile, despite the man they were currently talking about.

"The two of you are engaged?" That completely changed Joss's perception of the man's relationship with Célie. He immediately wanted to ask if the man had ever cheated on Jaime with his employee, or maybe had a thing with that employee before he ended up with Jaime, but had the sense to bite both those questions back.

Jaime nodded. "Good choice, by the way. The choice not to fight."

Self-control was an absolute necessity for any man in the Legion. Men of action, yes—men who could control that action. Always. In every situation. "I didn't come here to ruin her life. She's made a good one for herself."

A smile broke out on Jaime's face as if he'd said something she deeply approved of. "Tell me a little bit more about being in the Foreign Legion." She actually sat down on the bench beside him.

Joss rubbed his thumb over his jeans, schooling himself not to let his eyebrows raise. "That fiancé of yours going to come out here looking for a fight if I do?"

Because *that* would be okay, right? If the man came looking for it out here, outside Célie's place of work? Or could Richard still conceivably take it out on Célie if Joss broke his nose?

Also, would the two of them even be able to fight and it stop with nothing more than a broken nose? The man looked kind of hardwired to keep fighting even if he was at the bottom of a heap of enemies, and Joss was kind of hardwired that way, too.

"I'll talk to him if he does," Jaime said, shrugging.

Yeah, right. That was going to work, all right. Maybe she could try throwing her slim body between two freight trains next, as an encore. And Célie would be super pissed.

"I'll tell you what, I'll stand," Joss said, and did so, leaving her the bench.

Jaime smiled. "Why don't I buy you a cup of coffee?" She waved a hand to indicate the multiple terraces with café tables within sight of the great *place*.

Joss's eyebrows drew slightly together. He searched her face. "You're a friend of Célie's," he repeated. "And you're engaged."

Jaime's blue eyes widened a fraction, and then she smiled and shook her head, standing. "I'm not hitting on you. I'm being nosy. And I, ah, work with a company with a very high interest in effectively managing security issues in countries in upheaval. It sounds as if you might have some experience with that." She gestured with her head toward the nearest café. "So come on. Let me buy you a cup of coffee."

Chapter 12

"I like him," Jaime said that afternoon around four thirty, having come back by the shop after her afternoon of meetings with undoubtedly more of the one percent of the world.

Dom, who'd only just gotten a chance to return to work on his sculpture for a bit, stared at his fiancée from his bent position over the lioness's claws. "How do you know that?"

"I had coffee with him this morning." Jaime shrugged.

Dom straightened slowly, his brow lowering. "You did … what?" His voice went deep into a growl.

"I wanted to get to know him better."

"You had coffee with a dangerous stranger who's acting like a damn stalker?" Dom's growl vibrated so down deep and low that the hairs on Célie's nape stood on end.

"He's just very intently goal-focused and used to having to pursue those goals through an incredible number of obstacles. I think I might try to hire him to consult with us on security issues."

Dom's lips pressed together in visible anger. He started to speak, stopped himself with an effort, and abruptly reached for the buttons on his chef's jacket. "Let's go for a walk."

Jaime's eyebrows went up a little as she took in his expression, but she went with him without question, not forcing any imminent issue in front of his employees.

"Although I do sympathize," she added on her way out to Célie, who was still standing stock-still, trying to figure out what she thought about Jaime inviting Joss for coffee. "I mean, I like your Joss, but I'd be pissed at him in your shoes, too."

Célie hurried to the casement window, watching, her stomach knotting anxiously. The last thing she wanted was for the world's mushiest couple to get in a fight over her—her—her—

Not boyfriend. *Not* friend.

Her ... Joss.

On the street below, when the couple came into her range of vision, Dom had his hands shoved in his pockets, every line of his body hard. She could tell that the two of them were arguing as they walked, that Dom was seriously pissed off and Jaime was standing her ground, fighting back, her gestures growing increasingly exasperated. Célie's gut knotted. They were, like, the magic couple. They made her believe happy endings were possible. She didn't want her problems to hurt the magic couple.

Dom's steps slowed as they reached the end of the block. He turned toward Jaime. Jaime lifted her hand to cup his cheek.

Dom's eyes closed a moment, and he angled his head to kiss Jaime's wrist.

Oh, for God's sake.

Célie grabbed some more chocolate to break up, brooding over how easy those two found it to make up when her own anger and betrayal and pain lodged deep in her where she couldn't let it go.

***

"This one's a really dark chocolate," Célie said. "Bitter."

In Joss's big hands, that bitterness looked fragile and insignificant, all too ready to melt at his heat. He treated it with respect, though, studying the nine chocolates in their little metal box, the adamant rippling pattern stamped on their surfaces instead of any color or stylized motif. "Can I eat them? Or am I supposed to take my time, let them last?"

He hadn't come inside the shop that day, nor spent his day waiting for her outside it, but when she left it, he was leaning against a nearby wall. Shades of when she was eighteen, when he often showed up a few minutes before she got off and waited for her. His shoulders were straighter now, almost no ability to slouch in his stance, his face sterner even in repose. But he still picked the same position—not directly across from the door but a little up the street to the right, where her gaze went to him automatically. He still straightened immediately, exactly as he once had, and came toward her without any pretense that he had been there for any reason other than her.

They stood now in the Parc de Belleville, Célie's favorite park in Paris. Close to her little apartment, it was built on a hill in the old immigrants' quarter of Paris where a little patch of a vineyard could still be found and children played in waterfalls built into the slope, and a view of Paris spread out below it, as if the city belonged to her. It was rare for tourists to find their way to it. No, this park was for Parisians, a spatial feast for children and parents and all the people from the quarter who sought this park for the same reasons she did. Peace. Play. Dreaming.

Trees lined the gravel path. A woman sat on a bench some way up it, reading. Shadows and sunlight dappled them.

"I don't know," Célie said uneasily, her gaze going from those dark chocolates in his callused palm up the muscled arm to the mouth that would close around them, in which they would melt. At twenty-six, he had lines already at the corners of his eyes from squinting into the sun and sand, and his lips had a firmness to them from being so long pressed into a stern line. Her lips and her eyes didn't have any of that. Full, wide lips, generally laughing eyes. Even despite the pain he'd left in her middle when he left her.

He'd counted on her resilience. And, well ... she'd had resilience. She had, in fact, bounced up, blossomed without him, lived a life she still wanted to hug to her for how vivid and delicious it was.

"I can try one now?" Joss eased it out of the box with a blunt-tipped finger.

"That's … that's kind of the point," Célie said. To let him eat that bitter darkness up.

Was that, in fact, her point?

She stared at his fingers bringing her helpless chocolate to his lips. Stern lips that softened for it, eyes that brightened at the rush of flavor in his mouth, the subtle shifting of his facial muscles that indicated how he savored it. Heat climbed up her back, making everything in its path shiver.

"In … in milk chocolate, you can get away with lesser quality," she said. "The sweetness will offset the cheap. That's why candy bars are mostly sugar. But the darker it gets, the more the chocolate has to be the *best*, the ganache the most melt-in-your-mouth smooth and perfect."

Joss's eyes focused on her mouth and stayed there. Her lips started to burn, this soft, buzzing burning that made her want to lick them, made her want to swallow. "Do you like it?" he asked. "This dark."

She nodded slowly. "I have to savor it. I … need to."

"I like it, too." His rough voice was like being grazed with quiet. As if quiet had rubbed its five o'clock shadow all over her skin. "It's as if you made it just for me."

Well … yeah.

"If I eat it all up, will you be mad?" He touched the edge of another square hungrily. Shadows and light played over his face from the shift of leaves above them and the angle of the afternoon sun across Paris.

"I—I don't know," Célie said, mesmerized by his mouth, by the thought of more bitter-dark chocolate melting so easily. "I—I didn't expect for you to make it all disappear this fast."

"Maybe just one more." Her skin prickled with the texture of that quiet voice. He loosened the chocolate from the box and brought it to his lips. "Or maybe two," he murmured as the chocolate disappeared. An expression of concentrated pleasure suffused his face, his eyes closing.

In that instant his eyelids protected her, Célie stole a lick of her lips. When his eyes opened, she was somehow closer to him. Able to see all the flecks of hazel and green in his eyes, locking with hers. The afternoon sun kissed one side of his face. She followed that kissing light with her eyes, helplessly, wanting to press her lips to the corner of his, there where the sun touched.

"I need to warn you about something," he said.

She waited, while children laughed out of sight in the distance. He didn't chatter much, Joss. He would answer her questions, but if he told her something gratuitously, it was always because he thought she needed to know.

"Before I left, I tried really hard to be your friend and your brother's friend and not to touch you. I tried not to go after you. I succeeded."

She scowled, reached for one of her chocolates, and ate it herself. The bitter darkness stung her tongue even as it melted.

"But you're all grown up, and I've become someone closer to the man I wanted to be for you."

"I'm going to hit you if you say that one more time," Célie said between her teeth. And licked chocolate off her lips. It tasted bitter. And sweet.

"So it's going to feel different to you. Because now I can try for you. And you don't actually know what that's like, when I try."

She struggled to stay stiffened against him. But she felt like her own stupid chocolate, vainly struggling not to melt at the temperature of touch. "What's it like?"

She'd better get him to tell her, because he might never get a chance to show her. The odds of him having to actually exert himself to get her seemed woefully low right then.

He searched for words like an alien trying to convey his world so that an Earthling could understand. "I don't give up. I don't let go when the going gets tough. I'm not very crushable by even the worst insults, and you could strip me naked and humiliate me and I'd still keep going even if I had to crawl through the mud to my goal. I can be patient, and I can be persistent, and I can endure, and if something hurts, it doesn't stop me." A slight, wry twist to his mouth. "I suppose you could get a SWAT team to bring me down, though. I'd eventually respond to enough bullets."

She put her hands on her hips. "And that's not the least bit creepy."

That straight, serious gaze. "Is it? I may not have very good judgment anymore, about what average people think is acceptable effort."

She rubbed her arms, which kept missing his warmth despite the summer and her leather jacket. "It would be nice to have a stop button on you, short of shooting you."

A tiny, perplexed wrinkling of those stubborn eyebrows, a search of her eyes. "You are the stop button, Célie. You can say no."

She frowned, in a sudden surge of panic at that ability.

Energy ran through all the hard lines of his body. His focus honed in on her. He took a step closer. "Do you want to say it?"

She bit her lip, unable to look away from his eyes. She felt like a kitten, begging him not to drown her. And utterly mute. If she tried to speak, she might only manage a whimper of a meow.

His hand lifted and touched her face. She gave a little gasp. The last time her cheek had felt the gentle, callused warmth of that hand had been in some teenage bout of furious tears over her brother, when Joss was trying to coax her out of it. “No, Célie?”

She swallowed.

He shifted in, this unhurried, gentle motion, easing her back against a tree, leaning over her, closing her in. “Not one little ‘stop’?” His hand slid to cup her head, his other hand bracing against the tree above her.

She licked her lips, her breath coming in hard and deep. She had to grab enough oxygen before she went under.

“Not one little ‘no’?” His head bent closer to hers, this hot, strange hunger flaring in his eyes, as if all that steady hazel had been hiding a wild creature.

She tried again to speak and could only swallow. His lips were so close ...

“Maybe a hand raised”—his leg shifted so that now a thigh framed her, too—“to push me back?”

Her fingers flexed into her palms, in this hot, still panic that any move she made might be the wrong one, might tell him *no.*

And she was supposed to be telling him no. She was supposed to be saying *stop. Stop, go away, leave me alone* ... her insides whirled in fear that he might hear the attempted thought, might do it.

He’d left her alone before, after all, without her even asking.

His palm ran down her arm, a strong rub of warmth, until he reached her hand. He lifted it and set it against his shoulder. “I’m right here.” His breath brushed her lips, every line in his body taut with barely restrained energy. “If you need to shove me away.”

And then he kissed her—this sweet, firm closing of his lips over hers, this rushing, thorough heat as he lost control almost instantly, his kiss deepening, his hands gripping the tree hard on either side of her head, his body pressing into hers. Arousal and heat, hard strength, this intense, starving *hunger.*

She'd dreamed of kissing Joss so many times, and it wasn't like *any* of them. It wasn't *dreamy*. It was so damn physical and hot and real. The bark pressed against her head, and his hard body surged into hers, so obviously wanting more, and she couldn't stop kissing him back. She just couldn't stop.

She kept climbing into him, trying to eat him up, trying to make him hers, take him inside her where he could never get away from her again. Kissing and kissing, seeking the texture and hunger of his mouth, his tongue, the strength of those shoulders as she dug her hands into them, as she dragged her fingers down to squeeze his arm muscles, too, as she slid her hands around to climb up the hard, broad muscles of his back.

"Hell." He shoved away from her and staggered to the next tree over, pressing a hand against it and hanging his weight against that arm. A flush ran over his cheekbones, his lips damp and full as if somebody had just tried to eat him up.

She held herself back against her own tree, trembling with the need to go after him, to *not let this stop*, and weak with the fear that she had already drowned in him. That she wouldn't find her way back to herself.

"Holy shit." Joss pressed his forehead against his tree so hard that the muscles in his neck stood out. "You're going to have to shove me *really hard*, if you kiss me that way. That's almost too much for me to handle. I shouldn't have—*hell*, I shouldn't have tried this in public."

Thank God it had been in public. If he'd kissed her like that in her apartment, they'd be ... right this second, they'd be ... She covered her face, pressing the heels of her palms into her forehead to drive in sense. "I told you I couldn't let you come up to my apartment."

He turned his head against the tree to look at her. One of his arms looped around the tree and tightened, holding himself there. "That was for *you*? *Merde*, Célie, I thought ... I thought it was for *me*. Because you could guess how hard it is for me to hold back and didn't want to torment me. Or maybe didn't trust me."

Torment him. Her thighs squeezed along with all those inner muscles right above them. "For both of us, I guess. Mostly, um ... me."

"Oh, hell, sweetheart. Célie." He turned back to her.

She backed away, holding up her hands, eating his body hungrily with her eyes over the barrier. She wanted him so badly that hunger made tears well out of her eyes, and she didn't realize until she was sobbing. Oh, God, not *again* with the crying. When was she going to get this all out? She covered her face, but the tears kept coming, until she had to sit down on the nearest bench. "I can't do this, Joss. I can't do it. It hurt so much when you left."

A big body dropped down in front of her. She dragged her hands far enough from her eyes to see him. That corded strength knelt beside her thigh, Joss taking her hands, his eyes intense. "I'm sorry, Célie."

How could somebody whose whole body communicated lethal power *apologize*? To her?

"I know you are," she whispered. "I just ... can't get over it this fast." She gestured to the box of chocolates. And suddenly, bitterly, it burst out of her: "You don't *deserve* me."

Not the *her* she had made without him, happy and energetic and most definitely independent, not needing any man. Because a woman couldn't let herself count on any man. Not her father, whom she'd never even met, not her marijuana-smoking, dog-fighting cousins, not her older brother, and most definitely not her older brother's sexy friend, who might run off and join the Foreign Legion without even warning her, as if she didn't matter at all.

Joss's body tightened, and his arm went out to press across the bench just beside her thigh, gripping the opposite edge. Anger flared through every line of his body, locking his lips into a tight line. The way he'd looked at Ludo when he first realized Ludo was dealing.

"I did all this to deserve you, Célie." His arm tightened on the bench, his voice dropping low and harsh. *"Do you have any idea how much I did?"*

Her eyes widened as she stared at him, and she wanted to pet those broad shoulders just in front of her, to pet down over those straining arms. That must have strained so much more than this, over and over and over. Up cliffs. In two hundred push-ups because some sergeant was pissed. Hauling himself on his belly through the mud in training. Training the whole purpose of which was to teach him to handle the next four years of his life, when any cliff he climbed or mud he dragged himself through would be for life or death.

"I'm sorry." Her hands did reach out of their own volition and pet down over his biceps, tentatively, a thief stealing the texture of those muscled arms to carry away with her in her palms. "I didn't mean that, exactly."

"Then what did you mean?" This deep vibration of anger.

"I just—" She pushed a hand across her stupid streaming eyes. Her voice dropped to a whisper. "I just—I really loved you, Joss. Just the way you were. You made me—happy. To know I might see you that day."

"Célie." His hand gripped the edge of the bench until she thought he'd break it on the metal. He pulled himself a taut five centimeters closer to her. *"Do you think I didn't know you had a crush on me?"*

She gave a little gasp.

"Of course I did. It's not like you had a lot of other options for halfway decent guys there. *But you deserved better.*"

She stared straight into his face, only a forearm's length from hers, his eyes blazing.

He thrust himself back and to his feet. "So I got that for you." He gestured to himself, a slashing, angry indication of his body. "Better."

Célie stuffed her arm into her mouth—still clad in the heavy-duty protective leather that she wore for riding on her moped—and buried her primal scream as deep in her throat as she could.

The woman reading a few benches down, who had ignored their sexed-up clinching as the normal backdrop to an evening in a Paris park, now looked around, frowning.

Célie pulled her self-imposed leather gag out of her mouth and made a little motion with her hand to indicate the woman didn't need to worry. Then she tried taking deep breaths. She even closed her thumb and forefinger together into those circles she saw eccentric tourists do sometimes when meditating in the more tourist-central Paris parks. The circles didn't help.

"I know I was just a stupid kid." She folded her arms, as if that could protect her wounded middle. "And ... weak. I know I was acting like a five-year-old who can't handle her nightmares. But I used to hide between my wall and the bed almost every night, because the panic attacks were so bad, after you left."

His eyes widened, and then his eyebrows drew together. "What were you afraid of?" His anger honed in on this new focus. *"Who was threatening you?"*

She shook her head. "I wasn't afraid for me. Although," she couldn't help adding, "if anyone had threatened me, you put yourself out of range to be able to help for five years."

His face blanked again. This hard blankness of a man who'd learned blank from a merciless military.

She pushed her hands across her face, trying to clear away the wetness. "I was afraid for you." And, in a whisper, "*God,* I was so afraid."

He stepped forward and just wrapped her up, pulling her up and in for a strong, firm hug against his body. She could still feel the hardness of anger in him, but he didn't let it leak into the pressure of his hug. Or maybe his body was just always that hard now, anger or not. "You don't have to be afraid anymore." His voice vibrated under her ear against his chest. "I'm here now. I've got you. I'm sorry, Célie."

She tilted her head back. "I taught *myself* how to be brave. I conquered those nightmares *myself.* I don't need you anymore."

Pain shocked across his face before the blankness caught up and hid it. He started to drop his arms.

She grabbed onto his shirt with both fists. "Please don't let go!"

He hesitated, staring down at her.

"Please don't," she whispered, holding on tight enough to rip the shirt if he tried.

His arms slowly settled back into that firm hold.

"Please don't," she whispered again, letting her head rest on his chest.

He didn't.

He didn't, and he didn't, and he still didn't.

No matter how much she had said to drive him away, he didn't abandon her, cold and alone, for such a long time, that the skyline of Paris stretching out below them slowly turned pink, and her body slowly started to relax into his. As if her body had latched on to this absurd, ridiculous optimism that someday, she might be able to trust him again with her.

Chapter 13

He was kind of a bastard, Joss thought.

No, he really was a hopeless bastard, no *kind of* about it.

Because all he could think about was how much he would like to turn this hug into something else.

It was driving him absolutely out of his mind.

Five fucking years he'd been fantasizing about Célie. No, who was he kidding, longer than that—back when she was a damn teenager and he was supposed to be her brother's friend, the guy who looked out for her, he'd been fantasizing about her. She was the only reason he'd put up with Ludo as long as he had.

One of the worst duties during Legionnaire training was guard duty. Everybody hated that one. It was nothing like actual, practical guard duty later. No, two solid hours you had to stand without moving a single damn muscle, which felt like two days. Two years, sometimes. You'd be ready to kill your relief by the time he showed up, because you were so convinced he was late, but he never was. (The relief *engagé* knew better, knew somebody might really beat the crap out of him if he was even five minutes late.)

He tried to call on it now, that guard duty training. *Don't move. Just hold. Don't get aroused, damn it!*

But he did get aroused. Her body felt so sweet and good and *real* after all those fantasies. His own body just pressed and pressed more insistently into her belly, against all his will, rising of its own volition. It was all he could do not to press even harder. Not to lift her so he could fit that pressure between her thighs, press her back against that damn kissing tree and have at it again.

Better yet, haul her back to her damn apartment that was *all bed*.

"I'm sorry, too," Célie said suddenly into his chest.

He latched on to the words, trying to focus on anything besides what her body felt like pressed against his, besides what she would look like caught between him and white sheets, besides what should be the very first item of clothing he removed. Should he unbutton her jeans? Work down that zip? Slide his hands under her knit shirt first and push it up? Get this damn leather jacket out of the way ...

"I know you had the right to live your own life and make everything you could out of it. I don't mean to be this way. I just—can't—every time you say you did it for me, it makes me want to *pound* on you."

He did do it for her, though. So was he supposed to lie to her? Or just not talk about it? Célie was the one person he talked best to.

He gazed down at the fists that still clutched his T-shirt, the fists that wanted to pound on him. He knew her hands must be incredibly capable, to produce those chocolates, even more capable than when they'd kneaded dough and made croissants as a pastry apprentice in an average bakery in their *banlieue*, but ... he covered one fist with his hand. Yeah. His hand completely engulfed hers.

It made him feel big as the universe, to be able to so completely embrace her within the size of his own body.

When she was sixteen, seventeen, eighteen, and he was nineteen, twenty, twenty-one, his much greater size had always made him feel a breath away from being like every other loser, user guy in their *cité* to her. Literally a breath—that if he ever bent his head and breathed in the scent of her when she was teasing him, he would just grab her ass and pull her against his body and take every advantage he could of that cursed, so-tantalizing, so-flattering crush she had on him.

But now he felt made for her. Made *by himself* for her, through the crucible of the Legion, so that his size and strength and control, everything about him, now was just right. He could protect her hand from all the world.

He slid a thumb under her fingers to loose the clutch of his shirt and then gently struck his chest with her fist, again, and then again, in a pretense that she was pounding on him.

She turned her head suddenly and kissed his hand covering hers. The touch of her lips lanced through him in ways he didn't have the words to describe. A heat and hunger and sweetness that went so far beyond sex.

He held both their hands very still, so as not to shake away that press of her lips.

"I wish I could touch you all over," she whispered, and his whole body jolted. "You have the most amazing *texture*."

Oh, yeah. Hers was amazing, too. "I can grant that wish," he said, rough and harsh. Heat was rising in him like an inferno, engulfing him. "Hell, Célie."

"But I'm still so *mad* at you," she said fiercely into his chest.

"You could have mad sex. And I could have just ... sex." If she poured all her anger and hurt into sex, maybe she'd almost match the fierceness and intensity coming from him. He wanted to beg. *Merde, Célie, please.* His fingers flexed into her butt.

"And I don't even know you anymore," she said.

Merde.

She drew far enough back from his chest to look up at him. "You're really a stranger. And I'm a stranger to you, too."

No, she wasn't. She was still exactly Célie, bigger, brighter, stronger, more accomplished, but as vibrant and gutsy and beautiful as she had always been.

Fuck.

He drew a deep breath and then another. And managed to ease his hips far enough away from hers that he wasn't grinding his damn erection into her in a vain, desperate pressure for more. He braced his arms on the tree by the bench to help him, framing her.

She looked smaller and more vulnerable than usual, vulnerable like when Ludo had been arrested, vulnerable like when she'd pressed her face into his thigh there on that bridge over the Canal St. Martin. In both cases, she'd trusted him with that vulnerability. He'd been the man she turned to with it.

The man who had never taken advantage of her vulnerability. Never used it to lure her into anything she thought she was ready for when he knew neither of them really were.

"Maybe we should date," he said. His hand left the tree to frame her face. She looked startled, as if her cheek had no idea what a man's hand felt like up until that very moment.

Or maybe just not what his hand felt like.

Her face crinkled up so funnily, happiness and wonder and fear and the threat of more tears. "*Date?* Like ... like we might have done if you hadn't *saved me for later*?" Her eyes flashed on that phrase, but the flash faded into a curious hunger. "As if ... as if you wanted me to be your girlfriend?"

He stroked his fingertips over the curve of her ear, gently rubbing those two piercings. "Exactly like that." Exactly what he had always wanted her to be. "Does that work for you?"

She nodded vigorously.

His face relaxed into a smile. "Then it works for me, too."

Chapter 14

"I'll take it," Joss said. Hell, he couldn't believe his luck. Sixty square meters and with a view right on Célie's favorite park, the park where he'd kissed her for the very first time. The place where he'd known: Yes. She was going to forgive him, and this was going to work out.

And it was an utter dump, so the owner, who had inherited it from an old aunt who passed away, wanted to get it off his hands as quickly as possible, meaning that Joss could buy it cheap, remodel it, and flip it for a great profit, if Célie decided she'd rather live in Tahiti after all.

Something *physical* for him to do. Something for him to build, accomplish. Clear out the trash, get rid of the rotting floorboards. The bathroom needed a total remodel, the kitchen was like some nightmare out of a haunted house from the fifties, and he'd bet that plaster covered up some gorgeous old brick, given the age of the building and the Belleville location. There was even a fireplace, which he could keep, if Célie wanted to stay in Paris, or break and remove to add an extra square meter to the surface area—and thus tens of thousands of euros to thc apartment's market value—if he resold.

He'd build a full wall of shelving into the walls here, to maximize storage space, remove the old bath entirely and replace it with a luxury shower, open up the kitchen and put down ... had those been granite or marble counters upstairs in Dom's shop? He'd figure out a way to get her to tell him what she preferred, without letting her know what he was doing.

And then, when he had it beautiful, perfect, the most perfect apartment she could ever imagine ... he'd show it to her.

And her face would light up, and she'd run her hand over those granite—or marble—counters, and she'd run to the big windows that gave her a view onto her park and the Eiffel Tower. She'd bounce the hell all over the apartment, she'd be so happy.

See? You were right about me, Célie. I can *do anything. Even give you this.*

And then, maybe, she'd cuddle up with him on a ... really comfy couch.

Yes. Definitely a big, deep couch.

"I'll take it," he repeated. "Let's get the paperwork started."

Célie was going to *love* this.

As soon as he got it into a shape that he could be proud to offer her. He was damn well not showing her the dump it was right now.

***

As soon as Célie spied Joss through the window the next day, happiness leapt inside her. He was in his spot, over there to the right. His leaning stance held a lot more hardness to it these days, though, hard not just in the presence of muscles, since he'd been in great shape before he left, but in the way those muscles seemed ready for anything.

She finished up, cleaning chocolate off her hands, changing out of her chef's jacket into a sexy, sleeveless, cream-colored silk top that draped with affectionate looseness against the curves of her body down to graze over some butt-clinging leather pants. She jumped up and down in the bathroom to try to get a glimpse of her butt in the small mirror over the sink, hoping this outfit looked as good on her as it was supposed to, but the glimpse was far too inadequate.

She poked her head out. "Have you ever thought about installing a full-length mirror in this bathroom?" she called to Dom.

He glowered at her. "No."

"Can I organize the workers and go on strike until we get one?"

Dom stared at her.

"And a makeup mirror," Célie said. "Or at least proper lighting. Honestly, I don't know how I've put up with these working conditions so long." Apparently she hadn't been that worried about what someone else thought of her post-work appearance before this.

Dom groaned and swung back to his work, muttering about how "this kind of thing never happens to Sylvain." Célie grinned, grabbed the box of chocolates she had made and slipped it in her messenger bag, then ran down the stairs and across the street.

Joss jerked away from the wall in what almost seemed the start of a hard lunge toward her, as she darted across, but he caught himself and stilled on the edge of the sidewalk, waiting for her.

She sank into happiness until it was slowing her down, until it was like too much caramel and she was an ant trying to make her way across it. It bogged up her feet, it pulled her under, until by the time she reached him, she'd remembered why an ant should never get close to caramel in the first place. The infinity of sweetness might seem like paradise, but that was before your six little feet got caught in it and you ended up smushed and limp, all the life sucked out of you. Like last time.

Joss let out a fast breath as she stopped in front of him, his gaze going quickly up and down the street to either side of her, checking high and low, and then back to her.

Célie went up on tiptoes to kiss him on each cheek, feeling solemn, as if she was re-opening a long-abandoned ritual: Joss waiting for her after work, as she danced across the street to him and kissed him on each cheek and they walked home together, and she was full of happiness just to be in his company and nobody messed with her.

Joss turned his head and caught her lips with his, his hands closing around her hips to pull her in closer to him.

Oh.

Oh.

Memories of what they had been blurred with all those unfulfilled dreams of what she'd wanted them to be. Firm hands pulled her against a hard body, lips opened on hers as hers opened against his, as she got lost in him, sinking deeper and deeper into the kiss, into the slide and shift of lips against each other, into the hunger to take it deeper still, to take it horizontal, to use tongues and teeth and ...

Joss lifted his head, his hands flexing into her hips. She stared up into those beautiful hazel-green eyes of his, her hands on his shoulders. She caught a breath and then another, and then found herself up on tiptoe, seeking his mouth again.

"*Ça va, les jeunes?*" an amused old man asked as he passed, and Joss lifted his head again, taking a deep breath.

Célie pressed her fingers to her lips to hold the feeling of his kiss there better, staring up at him. Vaguely, she started to remember that all her colleagues were probably peeking through the casement windows, commenting on her, right about now, but she stroked her hands over those hard shoulders and chest, through the fine knit T-shirt, and didn't care.

"Nice color," she said randomly of the soft sea green with its hint of gray. "It brings out your eyes."

"I went shopping." He, too, seemed to have difficulty focusing on his own words, thrown out randomly. And Joss was almost never random. Thus the even greater shock when he ran off to join the Foreign Legion. "It's the first time I've been able to choose my own clothes in five years, beyond choosing whether to wear camouflage shorts and a muscle shirt or camouflage pants and a T-shirt in my downtime."

Célie instantly planned a secret shopping spree in her head. Hey, if *she'd* spent five years stuck in uniforms and camouflage, she'd *love* it if someone came home with sacks of brand-new clothes for her to try on.

"And I opened a bank account, got a phone. All the paperwork things."

"You got your nationality back?" Yet another layer to why she'd been so pissed at him about the Foreign Legion. Couldn't he have just joined the *regular army* or something? Sure, it wasn't as dramatic and glorious, but ... to give up *everything about himself*, his nationality, his name. Her.

It was as if he didn't have any hint of the true value of who he was at all, to give it all up to the Foreign Damn Legion. Or of the value of who she was, to give her up. Which she'd kind of accepted as his right, to not value her, but it had hurt her terribly just the same.

And she'd been *livid* about him giving himself up. Who *he* was.

He nodded.

"What were you, while you were in?"

"Monaco." He shrugged. "Marc Lenoir. Castel is what we call one of the regimental training bases, at Castelnaudary, so it avoided confusion."

"Did you change it back after the first year, when you were allowed?"

He shook his head.

She frowned at him. He hadn't wanted to be Joss?

He spoke slowly. "It seemed easier to just stick with Marc than try to make everyone change what they called me. And it ... kind of protected Joss from them. Kept him safe ... for you."

She stared up at him, her eyebrows drawing together as she processed that. "So ... after getting out of the Foreign Legion, do you need therapy now?"

He smiled slightly and shook his head.

A sudden thought startled her: in five years, had she been the first person to call him by his real name? By who he used to be? "Is it weird? Changing back to Joss?"

"Not when you say it," he answered simply.

And while she was still hugging that to her and thinking it over, he reached into his pocket and pulled out a little paper bag and handed it to her without a word.

She opened it to find a necklace, nothing expensive, just a little red hibiscus, hung on a simple chain.

Her heart brightened. "Thank you."

He shrugged, disconcertingly awkward for a man who exuded so much power and confidence in every situation but dealing with her. "It's just a little—I just wanted to—" He stopped.

"You were just thinking of me," Célie supplied, stroking the delicate petals, ridiculously pleased, far more pleased than if it had been a calculated and expensive diamond. Diamonds were insistent and demanding, even burdensome, like an investment against some return. This ... this was pure sweet. That sweetness of a quiet thought. *I was going about my day, and I saw this, and it made me happy to bring it to you.*

Joss shrugged again.

"Thank you," she murmured, and went up on tiptoe to kiss him again. At the last second, she pressed the kiss against his chin, to avoid starting more public displays of affection in full view of her colleagues.

He rubbed the spot on his chin, watching her as she dropped back onto her heels. He was still so hard to read. Harder even, than back before he left. She reached behind her neck to fasten the necklace, and his big hands took over from hers, fastening it for her far more slowly than she would have managed. The graze of his hands against her nape sent shivers down her spine.

His callused fingers trailed down the chain to touch the little hibiscus with his thumb. "Perfect," he said, of that cheerful, sweet flower against her consciously sexy, leather-pants-and-silk outfit. "It looks just like you."

"Do you know, sometimes back then I would get my hopes up about you," she whispered to him. "We got along so well, and you were there so much for me, that I'd start to tell myself, *Hey, maybe ... just maybe ... he likes me.* And then I'd see you again and try to flirt with you and you'd keep me at a distance and I'd realize, *No, no, he must just be a nice guy. Or need a friend.*"

"I liked you. And I was trying to be a nice guy. And your friendship was the most valuable thing I had in that damn place."

Her smile softened in a trembling way. "Yours was my most valuable thing, too," she said, and just managed not to add the thought that immediately sprang to mind: *Which was why it hurt so much when you took it away from me and left me with nothing but myself.*

But then, of course, she had had to learn how to value herself much more than she might ever have done, had he stayed. Possibly the same way he had had to learn his own value, through and through, to handle the Foreign Legion.

A long, slow sigh moved through his body. "I should have written." He touched her face. "Found a pay phone and called. Gone to the cybercafé and sent an email."

She nodded.

"I'm sorry, Célie. I did do it all for you, but I may have done it in a very self-absorbed way."

"Well ..." Célie hesitated. "You *were* only twenty-one. And clearly clueless."

"I'm very, very proud of you." He ran his hand down her back to rest on her butt, in possessive approval. "Of who you became."

She beamed, her eyes stinging. "Me, too. I'm so proud of you, too." God, she was proud. Every passerby whose gaze lingered on him made more pride swell inside her. But that was a superficial pride, smugness because he was so hot. Deep down, this hot, powerful, passionate pride burned in her center, at the man he had always been and the man he had become.

"When I look at you, bouncing out of that shop, I think, 'That's my Célie.'"

Really? She hugged herself, even though it bumped her arms against his chest and even though she wasn't supposed to want to belong to anyone else. She was too independent. She whispered, "Can I think, 'That's my Joss'?"

His smile lit his face for just a moment, this brilliant flash of light. And then it was gone, disappearing under some serious, intense emotion. His hands closed over her shoulders, thumbs rubbing her collarbone, eyes fixed on hers. "Yes."

Too much emotion swelled up in her, too many things that were too complicated: so much joy it was terrifying. *You left me, and I don't even know you anymore. And I would still, if I saw you watching me with that steady gaze from the other side of a street full of hot coals, walk barefoot across them just for the chance that you would hold me.*

Hell, I'd do it just for the chance that you might smile *at me and say, "That's my Célie."*

"I brought you something." She reached into her messenger bag for the box of chocolates.

Because when he saw her bouncing out of the shop, when he thought, *That's my Célie*, she wanted his mouth to automatically start softening in anticipation, his lips to part, his tongue to ...

She swallowed.

He smiled, opening the box. "Just three bitter dark this time?" he asked softly, at the array of patterns in the rows to either side of that center dark row.

"The others are just different ones I thought you might like." She pointed. "This basil one, that was Dom's idea. I thought he was crazy. Especially when our first test batches came out tasting terrible. But he insisted, and we kept trying it, making the flavor more elusive, until we got ... well, try it."

Joss tried it, but his expression stayed disappointingly closed, unmelted. "I like your flavors better."

"He's Dominique Richard, Joss."

"I like your flavors better."

"I made that ganache that's melting in your mouth right this second! Just because it was his idea doesn't mean I didn't do any of the work involved!"

"Fine." His jaw set a little as he forced himself to concede. "Then I guess I like it very much."

She put her hands on her hips. "Men are idiots."

His lips quirked up. "I see your sexism hasn't improved."

And she laughed. It was funny how much she had always loved teasing and being teased by Joss. It just charged her up. Made her tickle everywhere inside. "This one, we came up with this little hint of spices the first year we opened, for Christmas, and the demand for it and our other flavors caught us all only halfway prepared for it. We'd work through the night—I remember us taking turns catching an hour's sleep on that divan in the salon—and Dom would go grab everyone breakfast and—"

Joss tried it as she talked, his face relaxing as he gazed down at her. And then he did something he had never done, when he picked her up from her work back in the old days. He *took her hand* as he turned them down the sidewalk, strolling together as she told all the chocolates' stories.

Célie stared at her hand in his. Her breath got too short, and she had to fight to calm it. His hand was so solid and large around hers. Calluses rubbed against her skin, which was kept soft by all that cocoa butter.

It was what a boyfriend and girlfriend did, hold hands. It was what a man did when he wanted to tell the woman with him, *Our hands belong together. I like to touch you. I like to make sure you're in reach. I like for everyone who sees us to know you're with me.*

It made her happy.

As if a dream had come true.

Which was disorienting because that dream was supposed to, long ago, have declared itself an impossible fantasy.

Chapter 15

"Who. Is. *That?*"

Propped on one elbow on the edge of a picnic blanket spread across stone, Joss kept his expression neutral, not glancing toward Célie's friend, a long-legged blonde who favored form-fitting leather and who apparently didn't realize how well her voice carried. She and Célie were standing a little apart from the group of friends on the blankets, Célie having just finished dancing salsa with one of the many friends Joss was meeting tonight. She had a *lot.* Far more than she had had as a teenager. What, was she trying to give herself spares?

In case one of them up and left her? he realized soberly.

"Where did you find *him*?"

"Umm ... an old friend," Célie said. "From high school."

Joss snuck a fast glance at her. She was blushing.

Hey. That blush spread through his belly and out through his body in a warm and tender pleasure. It was *amazing* how much he liked her blushing over him.

The blonde stared. "*That's* one of your old friends? Why don't my old friends ever grow up like that?"

Célie tried so hard not to look smug that Joss had to press his lips down against the upsurge of his own pride, swelling from deep inside him at her expression. Maybe he could handle this evening, after all.

It wouldn't have been his choice, to hang out in a crowd of careless people among whom he couldn't relax, but her evening out with friends had been planned before his return to her life, and she'd seemed eager to include him in it.

It was good to know Célie had friends, that they were friends with whom she had fun, that she'd been thriving without him. He'd told her the truth when he said he was glad to know that.

But it made him feel a little precarious. Like—if she could do so well for herself without him there, what exactly was his role in her happiness?

Did he get to have one?

He thought of the apartment and smiled at the image of her face lighting up as she looked at that view of her park. *That* would make her happier. She'd love it so much.

"So is there anything—?" The blonde let her question trail off into a wiggle of her finger between Célie and Joss. "Or—?" Another wiggle, this time toward herself, with a teasing lift of her eyebrows. The blonde woman looked as if she could have been a Bond girl, with those high cheekbones and that tough leather, looks that apparently made her pretty confident about flirting with men.

Célie stiffened, glaring at her friend. "He's *with me.*"

A grin escaped Joss, and he quickly suppressed it, rubbing his fist against the picnic blanket. *You tell her, Célie. Fight for me. I'm with you.*

With Célie. He took a deep breath, trying to get used to being with her. Her world was so alien to him now.

Happiness spilled across the quay around them in careless abandon. People laughed and talked and danced as if happiness was some basic human right and not some miracle conjunction of space and time. Lights from the opposite bank of the Seine stretched across the darkening water toward them, as if those lights desperately wanted to reach the dancers and shake some sense into them. On the tip of the Île Saint-Louis halfway across the trembling water, a smaller, saner group of people gathered, the kind of people who said: *That looks fun, but let's keep a safe distance. If trouble starts, I'd rather be on the other side of the water from it.*

Masses of people were tempting targets.

Happy people, on the Seine, Notre-Dame glowing just down the river. You'd think a terrorist attack had never occurred on French soil, the way these people acted. That their government didn't have men like him fighting extremist armies right this second, factions that had more than proven their willingness to strike wherever it hurt the most, as well as their belief that no one in Western Europe was innocent, not civilians, not women, not children, and certainly not smugly happy people dancing on the edge of the Seine just beside one of the great symbols of European culture and achievement and in the heart of one of the most powerfully emblematic cities in the world.

Nobody was even controlling the damn perimeter, checking the bags of those who joined the laughing, happy crowd of dancers and observers.

It was all Joss could do not to jump to his feet and start patrolling the area, and he missed the feel of a FAMAS under his hand like an itch of panic.

Anyone could be carrying a bomb, or a gun. That man in his young twenties approaching them right now, for example, with a backpack on his shoulder and a leather jacket still zipped despite the warm summer evening. Joss surged to his feet as the younger man reached toward his backpack—and caught himself as the greetings from Célie's friends rang out.

Ah. Yes. The young man was pulling out baguettes and wine, kneeling on the edge of the picnic blanket now, unzipping his leather jacket which he'd almost certainly been wearing because he'd gotten here on a motorcycle or moped like Célie.

Joss took a deep breath.

"Who is he?" he heard someone else ask Célie. A girl with loose black curls and a bronze tone to her skin. "He looks like he's CRS or something."

Ouch, really? The national police force was less than popular among those of them who had grown up *en banlieue*. Also, these days, he liked the Gendarmes much better, after being in a couple of training courses at their facilities, and they and the Legion cooperated well together, but ... well, no offense, but one Legionnaire could eat five CRS for breakfast and still be hungry.

"Umm ..." Célie's blush deepened. "Foreign Legion."

Her two friends turned as one to stare at her. The blonde's jaw had dropped. "*Foreign Legion?* Are you kidding me?"

The black-haired friend's eyes narrowed. If her golden skin came from any of France's former colonies, then her parents and grandparents might have adamant opinions about the Foreign Legion.

"He just got out," Célie said.

"Are you sure it was the Foreign Legion he just got out of?" the black-haired young woman asked dryly. "It would be easy for a man to claim that instead of prison, say. Or just running off for five years."

Joss sighed.

"He wouldn't lie to me," Célie said firmly, and some tension in his chest relaxed. He wouldn't, actually. He was glad she still knew that. Glad she still believed in him.

Her friends both gave her pitying looks.

"He got my cards there! The Legion couldn't have passed them on to him if he wasn't a Legionnaire."

Her friends looked disappointed at having their cynicism dashed. Then the black-haired one brightened. "Aren't they psychopaths in the Foreign Legion?"

"Lina!"

Psychopaths now. Great. He went over to Célie before this conversation could get any worse, and also just because he couldn't stand lounging on the blanket anymore and needed to move.

Her gossiping friends grew quiet, their eyes widening as he approached, checking him out. "Damn, Célie," he heard the blonde mutter, with a nudge into Célie's ribs, just before he reached them, and he worked valiantly not to let himself smile, as he took Célie's hand.

Certain looks from women just did a man good.

Célie was bursting at the seams with smugness, too, and that did his heart even better. He smiled down at her, tugging her into him, enjoying immeasurably that he could do that now, flirt with her with these little invitations of his body to come in closer, rather than always, always, be the good guy maintaining barriers between them.

"Joss, this is Vi. Violette." She indicated the blonde. "And Lina." The black-haired woman. "We met when we were the junior team for France, in the International Chocolate and Pastry Competition."

"Nice to mee—hell, Célie." Joss stared at her. "You represented France?"

She nodded, her pride radiating out through all the cracks in the shell of her effort to contain it.

Damn, and he'd *missed* it. He hadn't even known. "Sweetheart." He grabbed her before he even thought about it, squeezing her so hard he lifted her off her feet. "*Good* for you."

"We won," Célie said, that shell of attempted modesty bursting wide open, her pride in herself like a sunburst. She reached past his shoulder to give a fist-bump to Vi and Lina. "We *won*, Joss. First place. First all-female team ever. For France."

His arms tightened on her, and he lifted her up, spinning her around once to try to express all his frustration at missing it and all his pride. "Damn, I wish I'd been there."

"Yeah." A shadow across Célie's bragging.

"Good for you." Joss lowered her down his body. "*Good* for you." He nodded to the other two women, who were trying not to look smug but who had angled their chins at a proud, of-course-we-take-this-level-of-success-for-granted angle. "And good for you. Congratulations."

"It was three years ago," Vi said.

Ah.

Three years.

And he hadn't even known.

She hadn't sent him a little card to tell him, for example. But then, why would she?

"Vi's about to take over her first starred kitchen now," Célie said. "We'll never see her again."

"Yeah, after I'm jailed for murder over all the male chauvinist crap I'm going to have to squash, it's going to really cut down on my social life," Vi said darkly.

She and Lina both gave him dark looks, too. Possibly having spent the last five years as part of a military service that was so notoriously macho it didn't even allow women to join might put him on bad ground here. "Do you need help?" he asked Vi.

"No," Vi said calmly. "I need to do it myself."

Yeah, and she probably did at that. Women had it crappy. They had to handle men his size, and they had to do it with half his physical strength. "Still," he said, "if you need backup ..."

Vi gave a sweet smile. "I'm really good with knives."

Nice to know he wasn't the only pseudo-psychopath on Célie's side. "I like your friends," he told Célie.

"You relieve our minds," said Vi dryly.

"Infinitely," Lina ageed, in a tone that clearly communicated: *You can kiss up all you want, but we're still reserving judgment about you.*

He smiled. Yes, Célie definitely picked out better friends for herself these days. He looked down at her, his fingers flexing into the curve of her hip, enjoying that possession. Enjoying his arm around her, and the fact that she hadn't pulled away.

"Want to dance?" He bent to whisper in her ear. "I'll try not to act too psychopathic."

Célie put her free hand on her hip, turning to face him and raising her eyebrows in laughing challenge. "You can dance the merengue now? Boy, they really do teach you guys everything in the Foreign Legion."

She might be surprised by all the talents Legionnaires could produce in their down moments—art, dancing, guitar, piano. Hell, Captain Fontaine actually knew how to waltz, and Adjudant Valdez—Delesvaux—one Christmas had cooked them a dinner that would make a tough man cry.

But Célie, of course, thought he didn't like to dance, because he'd refused all her sassy attempts to get him to as a teenager. He'd known better than to let his body get pressed up close to hers while she teased him. His attempts to stay her big brother substitute would have shattered like car windows when riots broke out in their old *banlieue.*

So he just smiled, which eased his tension. He could handle this crowd for her sake. It wasn't a restful evening, but he'd had plenty of non-restful evenings, and she'd brought him here to share in her fun. "No, but I figure if I can do some of the things we did, I can manage to figure out how to wiggle my hips."

She laughed, a rainbow shimmering of all that old saucy happiness of hers, and grabbed his hips, pulling him toward the dance space. "I'll teach you."

He smiled down at her, letting her position their hips close together. *Sure, sweetheart. You want my hips to do something with yours? Feel free to grab them and pull them as hard as you want.* "You teaching me how to wiggle my hips the way you like it sounds like a fun evening to me."

She stilled just a second, gazing up at him. "I can't get used to you *flirting* with me."

"Well, that's why we're dating, isn't it? So you can get used to it?" So *he* could get used to it? *She's not eighteen anymore. I'm not her substitute big brother. No holding back. Unless she says stop, I can go all out for her.*

She flushed a little with vulnerable pleasure, and then caught herself and tried to cover it with that sauciness of hers. "All the times I tried to flirt with you and you acted as if flirting wasn't even something that ever crossed your mind." Her eyes narrowed.

"I was trying to be good," he said apologetically. He hated to bring it up again, given how badly she had reacted so far to the fact that he had protected her from him until he grew big enough to deserve her.

She sighed despairingly. "Joss. What am I going to do with you?"

It sounded like a sincere question. As if she genuinely believed she needed to figure out how to pick up his twice bigger body and fit it onto the proper shelf or make him behave the right way.

He bit the inside of his lip to prevent a doubtless infuriating male grin and bent to whisper in her ear. "Maybe you should be wondering what I'm going to do with you." Sliding a firm hand against the small of her back, he pulled her hips in snug against his, so that he could let his glad-to-be-alive dick just glory in that sensation.

She flushed crimson.

He laughed as the heat of her blush ran through him and twirled them around in complete inconsistency with the music, enjoying the power his size and fitness gave him over her body, enjoying the press of her hips to his and the way she allowed it and seemed to enjoy it, too.

Even if she was pretending to narrow her eyes at him.

They didn't stay narrowed, though. As he set her on her feet and made an exaggerated attempt to rock his hips side to side like the nearest other couple, she started to laugh, too. She gave him a part of her happiness, with that laugh. He still wanted to take her happiness away from all this crowd of people where he could keep it safe, but at least it felt like something his.

"Like this." She resisted the pressure of his hand in order to wiggle her own hips in a different rhythm than his, which slid their hips in opposite ways across each other deliciously.

So deliciously that he let himself be utterly incompetent at mastering this physical task for a little while, his hips shifting again and again just off rhythm of hers. The sliding grind was probably going to kill him, but it would be such a better way to go than all the other possibilities he was used to having to consider.

She couldn't quite figure out whether he was doing it on purpose or not, checking his face. He tried to look helpless and clueless, not an expression he got to try out very often around anyone but her.

Her eyes narrowed. It made him laugh out loud, a reckless happiness bubbling up inside him. In the moment of laughter, his hips fell into the rhythm of the music, and he realized how much he'd been missing. Moving in sync was *far* better than moving out of it.

Oh, yeah. Just let him replace that side-to-side sync of their hips with a backward and forward motion and he would die happy.

"So you're having a good time?" Célie's eyes searched his. He turned their bodies yet again, so he could keep checking their surroundings.

"Mostly." He let his hand slide down from the small of her back to the curve of her butt. Oh, *yeah,* that butt. Round and perky in his hand and begging to be squeezed. "It's nice to meet your friends. And it's a beautiful evening."

"And ... ?"

He grinned down at her. "And I'm really enjoying this merengue."

"But ... ?" Célie pushed. "You said 'mostly.' What are you not enjoying?"

Careless slip of the tongue, that "mostly." He should have known better, after watching his tongue so long in the Legion. "Nothing." He made his voice surprised. "What's not to enjoy?"

"You tell me," Célie said, exasperated.

He looked down at her. She was getting frustrated with him again, and he probably should never tell her how much he enjoyed that. At least half of him, whenever she started simmering, got all excited that she might actually put her hands on him and try to work her frustrations out.

But another part of him worried about it quite a bit. She'd asked him what was wrong. He'd said nothing. Why was she frustrated about that?

She never used to get so annoyed with him. She'd … hero-worshiped him too much, maybe.

Which was all backward, because *now* she was supposed to be able to properly hero-worship him. He should be able to *relax* into it. Feel as if he finally deserved it.

And instead he didn't seem to be getting much of that hero-worship at all.

"I'm enjoying everything," he repeated. "Except maybe that you're frustrated with me, but, to tell the truth, I'm even half enjoying that."

There. He'd been honest with her.

She gave him a look that was apparently supposed to make him quiver in fear. He'd probably better not tell her the parts it really made quiver. She might be able to feel them herself, with this damn merengue. "Joss Castel."

He smiled, on a kick of pleasure at his name in that minatory tone.

"Joss." She sighed in exasperation. "I can *tell* something's wrong."

Seriously? How the hell had he let it slip?

"Will you just tell me!" she snapped.

He sighed, looking down at her as their hips rocked together.

He'd gone through the Foreign Legion so he'd never have to disappoint that hero-worship in her eyes. But he missed talking to her. Missed the way she bounced her laughing and teasing off him, but also missed just those quiet, easy conversations about anything and everything except, of course, the most dangerous anything and everything back then—that he didn't have a platonic bone in his body, when it came to her.

"I can't relax," he admitted.

Her hand pressed over his chest, where his heart beat too rapidly, keeping him primed for anything. She searched his face.

"It doesn't matter how many times I tell myself that I don't need to keep an eye on everyone in the crowd, I can't turn off the instinct, and I keep doing it. Checking every movement, every person carrying a backpack or wearing loose enough clothes to conceal a gun or explosives. This is about ten times worse than any market I ever had to patrol. It's okay, it's not a big deal. It's good practice for me to get used to being back in civilian life, and it's a beautiful evening. It's just ... tense."

She was silent for a moment, and he braced, feeling bad. See, this was what he hadn't wanted to do—ruin her evening. Her forehead stayed crinkled, but the exasperation faded. He missed the exasperation. And he definitely didn't want that crinkle to be in concern or pity instead.

"I have an idea," Célie said. "Why don't we say good night to my friends and take a walk on the Seine? Just you and me."

He gazed down the dark river toward Notre-Dame. Somewhere past the crowds in that direction, quiet and peace lay. A beautiful evening where he could walk hand in hand with her and maybe find a spot to kiss her again.

But he was copping out if he did that, wasn't he? Giving in to a weakness and robbing her of her fun evening with her friends? It was something else she could later blame him for, right?

"I've always wanted to do that," Célie said wistfully. "Walk on the Seine at night with someone I wanted to hold hands with."

And she never had? A hot, painful joy surged through him to know that. She'd been lonely ... but *she'd stayed all his.*

"Then let's do that." And for good measure, since she seemed to have a taste for romance, he lifted her hand off his chest and kissed the palm.

Wow, the look in her eyes at that. You'd have thought he had slain a dragon for her.

Interesting, since he *had* slain metaphorical dragons for her, over and over, and the thing that had made her eyes go starry was one easy kiss of her hand.

Women made no sense sometimes, especially not Célie, but he kissed the tips of her fingers next since she liked it so much, and held her hand snug and warm as they took leave of her friends and headed off for a walk.

***

The farther they got from her friends and that bright center of happiness and dancing on the quay, the tenser Célie got.

The security and confidence drawn from the friend-filled evening drained away from her as they kept walking, leaving her support network behind. All the bright, vivid life she had made sure to build for herself, in defiance of anyone who might have left her with nothing. Each step took her further outside her comfort zone, to this isolated place where her happiness depended on one person.

On the way he held her hand.

On that neutral, quiet expression of his as he gazed at the luminous bridges and old palaces and glanced regularly down at her. On the size of his body, an impenetrable barrier against the world. Not a single group of guys called out for her attention as they walked past. She would have shot them a bird and kept on walking if they did, and it felt weird and weak not to do that, not to be depending on herself or the strength of a group of friends.

She couldn't relax. Her stomach tightened, and her heart started to beat too hard. It was too romantic. It was too dependent on him. Bad enough taking him to the Île de la Cité just toward sunset, bad enough taking him to her favorite park, but the Seine at night ...

It just slapped its romance down and *slayed* you with it.

Utter obliteration of a woman's heart and strength and sense.

As they passed the islands and continued toward the Louvre, the groups hanging out drumming or drinking beers or playing some card game thinned out and quieted. Joss didn't really lose his alertness, but some of the tension in him seemed to quiet. His breathing slowed and deepened.

Her hand tightened on his. "Joss. Why didn't you tell me?"

His eyebrows knit, and he gazed down the length of the Seine as if trying to interpret a particularly cryptic crystal ball. "I ... couldn't. I had to do it first, before I could brag about it. If I told you I was going to do it, and then *failed* and didn't ... what would that make me? To you?"

She was silent a second, adjusting to his subject of conversation. "A ... young man who had lots of dreams and realized some of them were crazy? After talking them over with the girl he claims he liked?"

He frowned. "I need to teach you to have higher standards for men."

That annoyed her so much. She scowled, and her hand flexed for freedom, but he firmed his hold, not wanting to let go. "I *meant* why didn't you tell me just now? That it was hard on you, being in a crowd like that?"

"I did," Joss said, confused.

"I had to drag it out of you! After we'd already been there an hour! Why didn't you just *tell* me, when you saw what it was like?"

His jaw hardened in that obdurate way. "First of all, I didn't realize immediately. And then I thought I'd manage to get over it. There was no sense ruining your evening from my..." He paused, his lips curling as he tried to force a word out: "Failure." From his expression, he was trying to swallow something disgusting and shameful, even to say it.

Célie was silent a moment. "You know what I do with my failures?"

He looked at her, his expression gone very neutral again.

"The chocolates that don't come out perfect enough, because we get a batch a tad wrong? I send them home with any of the team who wants to share them with their family. Sometimes, we make little packets of two each that we keep under the counter, and whenever any kid looks wistful because his mom tells him the chocolates are too expensive, we slip one to him. Or if there's a big batch, we give them to schools in some of the poorer areas. We share them with the soup kitchens or with homeless people on the street. And they make everyone happy. Everyone appreciates it very much. Because we still gave them something that was a hundred times better than anything else they could have had."

Joss's lips tightened. God, his jaw was stubborn. "*Merci.* If I ever want to treat you like a homeless person who should be grateful for whatever you can get, I'll let you know."

"Sometimes," Célie muttered, "I would like to beat my head against your chest as if it was a damn brick wall."

He shrugged, not letting go of her hand. "Okay."

Which just made the urge more intense somehow. "You don't *listen* to me, Joss."

He gave her a puzzled glance. "I'm listening to you right now, Célie."

"You don't let me *affect* you. You just dismiss what I say and do your own thing."

Damn it all.

They passed a couple sitting on a bench together, the young man's arm around the young woman, his hand on her chin, coaxing her face up to his, and Célie wanted to yell at the other woman: *Are you out of your mind to be out here on a night like this? Run! Run the other way! A man could do anything to your heart, if you hand it to him on the Seine at night.*

Women were so reckless. They didn't stand up for their own hearts *at all*. It made Célie want to grab them and thump her head against theirs to try to knock some sense from her brain to theirs. *Just woman up, darn it. Quit expecting everyone else to take care of you instead of doing it yourself.*

But here Célie's own hand was, held by the very man who had hurt her heart the most in her life. Danger was everywhere—in the glow of the bridges against the dark water, in the sparkle of the Eiffel Tower there in the distance, in the locks of lovers weighing down the Pont des Arts and in their keys lurking below the gold-gilded black surface of the water, clogging the river. Stubborn, self-entitled lovers, convinced it was more important to declare their love to the world through a lock on a bridge than to protect a world heritage.

Also oblivious lovers—blind to the fact that regularly, the city removed the grids on the bridge and replaced them with new ones, tossing all those old locks for scrap.

Every brain cell Célie had kept noting the danger to her, the irony of reality.

And yet she couldn't quite get herself to flex her hand free.

Because his strong, callused hand felt as if hers had found the safe place it had always longed for.

As if she could lower her guard and let him take that guard duty up.

She set her jaw, turning her head away a little. So much bullshit, her heart could come up with. It had done it before, where he was concerned.

"You don't *affect* me?" Joss said incredulously.

"I'm not talking about sex!" Célie shouted, and the romantic couple looked up, startled. Then both of them grinned.

Célie flushed hot.

"Neither was I," Joss said, and her flush got even hotter. "Célie ... I joined the Foreign Legion for you. That's an effect."

Célie gritted her teeth. "I swear to God, I will push you into the Seine."

Joss was silent for a moment, and then he lifted her hand so that he could gaze at it in his hold. His thumb rubbed over her knuckles, and he sighed. "You can't really do that, you know. I'm not that pushable."

"Yeah," Célie said darkly. "I noticed."

"So we have to figure out some other way to communicate."

"*I'm* talking to *you*!"

He nodded, his expression as unreadable as ever. Except for maybe the very slight frown between his eyebrows as he gazed ahead, the length of the Seine.

And a wave of forgiveness came back at her, rocked toward her by the Seine and the stupid *Bâteau-Mouche* that passed playing "La Vie en Rose." The forgiveness washed over the bitterness, which struggled to hold on. He'd barely been out of his teens. She'd still been in her teens. It was fair for him to make something larger of his life before being saddled with her.

Saddled. See how her bitterness tried to trick its way up through her brain again? A resilient thing, hurt. Hard to kill. It didn't melt away like a sandcastle under a wave of forgiveness, just maybe got a little less sharp at the edges.

"You gave me this," she said suddenly.

He glanced down at her and followed her gesture to indicate the whole glorious Seine, all its glow and darkness. "No, I didn't. You got it for yourself."

Well ... that was true. It warmed her that he honored that and understood it. But ... "I guess what I mean is ... you were right. If I'd still been hanging all my hopes and dreams on you, I never would have come here and taken Paris."

He smiled a little. "You shouldn't underestimate yourself, Célie. You always shone as bright as a star."

Oh. What an incredible sweetness came from that. But didn't he understand that the truth of him, the strength of him had helped her shine that bright? That he ... he kept the grime off her, back then. Just by existing.

It was as if, underneath the pride that drove him away from her, into thc Legion, he hadn't valued himself at all.

"I don't know," she said slowly. "I don't think I could even imagine being better than you, back then. But when *you* didn't think that was good enough, when you left to become the best that you could be ... I guess I decided I'd darn well be the best I could be, too."

She certainly had been determined not to stay there, without him, and fade and fail under the weight of that place. Become "not good enough" hcrself.

And now Paris was hers. She was part of this city, part of its vitality and strength, absorbing its heart and energy and pouring her share of it into making the best chocolates in the world. She was part of what people flew here from all around the world to enjoy, part of what made people glad they lived here—*her*, her contributions to this city.

So the Seine was hers. The luminous bridges were hers, arching over the water one after the other, as far as they could see. The Louvre was hers, that long, glorious palace, lit with its soft, warm light. The Eiffel Tower was hers, sparkling at her as they crossed the

Pont des Arts. She tightened her hand on Joss's and pointed at it.

My world. Look! I'll share it with you. You can have it, too.

He stood still to watch it. The nearest lamp cast those cheekbones into stubborn relief and shadowed his eyes with his own lashes. She could not read his expression, as he watched the sparkling Eiffel Tower.

Then he looked down at her. "I think you underestimate yourself, Célie. You were only eighteen, and you had so much energy and hope in you. *I* had to do something so that I could keep up with *you*."

"Meaning we could have talked about it," Célie said before she could stop herself. "If we both wanted to make something more out of ourselves. Maybe we could have encouraged each other. Become better together."

The sparkles of the Eiffel Tower died back to its regular nighttime glow. He gazed at the quieter tower a moment and then turned that seriousness down on her. "What do you want me to do, Célie?"

"Not treat me like some princess in a tower. Not go off to become perfect for me when I'd far rather you were imperfect and *here*."

His jaw set. "*You* are going to talk to *me* about trying to be perfect?" He reached into the messenger bag he'd taken for her and pulled out the box of chocolates. "The woman who makes *these*?"

"I already told you! If it's not perfect, we still get good out of it. We don't ship it to Pluto!"

"Corsica is not Pluto."

"It might as well have been to *me*!"

He fell silent.

She sighed, wishing that bitterness hadn't caught her again. And muttered, "I know damn well you guys get leave, Joss. Forty-five days a year. It's on the Legion's damn website. You could have kept in touch. You didn't because I wasn't real to you then. It's ... like the Playboy bunny. I was just an image you could focus on to help you reach your own goals."

If she didn't know better, she'd say Joss was flushing a little. It must be a trick of the glowing lamp under which they stood. Or ... oh, Good God, he *had* used her as a Playboy bunny, hadn't he? He'd even said something about it. That was ... he must have ... Her eyes grew wider and wider as she tried to imagine all the ways *he* might have imagined *her*, in his head.

They might have been *way* more explicit than her dreamy cuddles.

And she couldn't figure out whether her body was flushing with annoyance at that or ... curiosity.

"Célie. I'm trying to listen to you, but I don't even know what you *mean*. In my entire life, you're the most real." He lifted his hands and framed her face. "Everything about you is true."

Oh.

His hands rubbed over the shape of her skull, tracing the curve of her ears, shaping her cheekbones. "And deserves the best I can be."

The texture of his palms against her cheeks caught her, lured her in past argument. That texture made it seem as if he wasn't some great granite rock rising out of a sea—glorious and obdurate. The sea dashed against a rock like that, but the waves didn't penetrate, and it didn't change. Not in a human lifetime.

And the touch of his hands, the look in his eyes ... none of that was like a rock at all. Strength and warmth and tenderness.

All given to her.

"You deserve the best I can be, too," she whispered, before she'd even thought it through. But the whisper ran through her: he really did. So did *she* deserve the best she could be. That was why she had tried to become it.

Actually, why she was still always trying to become it—every single day in that *laboratoire*, pouring her all into being ever better.

Exactly like him.

"Joss," she sighed, soft as wistfulness.

Soft as wanting.

You're not a rock. All those muscles, as hard and strong as they are, have a little human yield in them. They'd take the pressure of my fingers. That pressure would change you, you'd respond to it, your body would be mine.

And I wouldn't feel anything at all like a sea trying to get a rock to change.

His thumbs ran over her cheekbones, and he bent and kissed her, as if he couldn't resist a taste.

Velvet heat spread through her body, this fuzzy heat that softened all the sharp edges of hurt, that turned off her brain. She found her hands climbing up his arms, and she was right—those hard muscles were warm and alive and human. They responded to her hands, not as if he was a rock against which she beat herself but as if her slightest touch could change his entire existence.

I don't want to be up on a glass mountain or in a tower waiting for you, Joss. I've always wanted to be human and real to you.

So she kissed him like somebody real.

Eager.

Melting.

His lips shaped to hers, his hands pulling her hard up into his body, harder and harder, more and more eager. His palm ran up her back, his fingers cupping her butt. The press and shift of his lips, the graze of his teeth, the touch of his tongue ...

The jazz band busking on the bridge started playing them a love song, and Joss lifted his head. "God, this hurts. Kissing you and ... only kissing you. I love it, though. I'll do it as long as you want."

She didn't know quite what he meant. She didn't think any man she had ever dated had ever *hurt* for her. The couple of sexual relationships she'd tried in the past five years had been, well ... *friendly*. That was, she and the guy had started out getting along, hitting it off, and he'd nudged for sex, and she'd thought, *Well, I should try it, he's a nice enough guy,* and ... it all felt really, really limp and tepid compared to this, like the hot chocolate some cafés in this part of Paris tried to pass off on tourists.

Like somebody shouldn't have forced her to try to make do with that shit instead of him.

She scowled at that somebody.

"What?" he asked. "I mean it. You set the pace."

"Sometimes it's so hard not to hit you."

His lips curved so wryly it was all she could do not to kiss them again. "What did I do this time? Too greedy?"

"No. Not greedy enough."

He drew a hard breath that she felt through his entire body still brushing hers, and then pulled her in close and kissed her again, ignoring the jazz band and their public exposure, ignoring everything but her.

Joss lifted his head and swept a hard look over hers. She blinked at the four men hovering near them, each with a lock held up for sale, each trying to be the first to catch their attention. At Joss's look, they all took a step back, hesitated, then moved away.

Célie squinted her eyes and tried to pack her own gaze with power that way, practicing on Joss's chest this sweeping *back off before you die* look. He didn't even have any meanness in it. No squint, no effort, just this relaxed swing of a blade. The sweep of a sharp sword wasn't mean, it was just a fact that you'd better be out of that blade's way when it swung in your direction.

"What did I do this time?" Joss sighed, and she hastily tried to smooth her expression.

"Oh, just, you know ... practicing."

His eyebrows went up. "Practicing?"

She sighed. "It's never going to work the same when I do it." She tried her approximation of his look on him, her face scrunching into it.

He smiled. He tried to press the smile out, but this rumbling started passing through the chest on which her hands still rested, and then it escaped out of him, as he started to laugh. He laughed so hard he had to sit back against the bumpy locks along the railing. "You're so damn cute. *God*, I've missed you."

She put her hands on her hips. But she could only pretend to be minatory. Because the sight of Joss laughing, his big, lethal body framed by the Seine, the Eiffel Tower glowing in the distance beyond him ... just that *laughter*, it ... "*You're* so damn cute," she said helplessly. "Damn you. I've really missed you, too."

He caught her fist and thumped it twice against his chest in pretend punches, then reeled her in with it, tucking her between his thighs. "I want to take you somewhere private," he breathed, this rough, sand-grained sound. "But if I did, I'd kiss you all the fuck over, Célie. And squeeze you and..." His hands flexed into her hips, too hard. "*Hell*, but I want to do things to you. You have no idea."

She stared at him, her jaw dropped, heat flaring through her. "No, I don't!" she said, indignant. "How would I have any idea, when you would *never even flirt with me* before?"

"Now the trick is to get you to want to do all kinds of things to me." Again his fingers flexed into her, a little gentler this time, but still harder than he must realize. "Besides punch me, although honestly, at this point ... any excuse to get your hands on me works for me. Besides"—he smiled a little and lifted her fist to kiss it—"punches from this thing would probably feel like a massage."

Okay, that was just flat-out ... annoying, that was what that was. She glowered at her fist, which did indeed look extremely little and incapable, in his big one. She'd put a hell of a lot of effort into making her hands capable of everything amazing. She transferred her frown to his face.

He smiled. "Kiss me or kill me, sweetheart? Which one do you want?"

So she kissed him because ... well, he really was that infuriating. A woman had to do *something*. Killing him out here in public like this would get her arrested.

His arms wrapped around her, pulling her in tight, hand sliding to her butt to press her hips against his, now level because of his half-seated position against the rail. Fire ran through her everywhere, this hunger for more and more and more—rubbing, contact, heat, texture, skin—more of *everything*.

She twisted her mouth away with a gasp. "I think that ... even for the Pont des Arts on a Friday night, we might be getting a little out of hand."

"Are you telling me to stop?" Joss asked roughly. "Or are you telling me to take you somewhere more private? The only thing is, if I get much more out of hand than this and no one can see us, I'm going to start ripping your damn clothes off."

Every deep, fast breath Célie took felt as if she was inhaling a drug, this intense rush. *I want to be real. I don't want to be your damn goal anymore. I want to be with you.* "Do you ... do you want to go back to my apartment?"

Joss's hands yanked from her body to catch fistfuls of locks and railing, holding on to them as if they were all that kept him from falling into the river. "The apartment that's *all bed*?"

Célie's cheeks heated deeply. "It's the only one I've got."

Joss jerked upright. "Hell. Fuck. *Yeah.*"

Célie took a step back, licking her lips, her body on fire. Awkwardness and embarrassment and want, all aflame.

Joss shoved a hand over his face and over that buzz cut of his. "Oh, *merde*, am I supposed to try to survive riding on that little moped pressed up behind you to get there? Do you mind instead if I just run?"

Chapter 16

But he did ride, squashed behind her, that easy, firm balance of his body against all her movements of the moped, his thighs pressed hot the length of hers, his hands trying to rest lightly on her hips and entirely failing—kneading and kneading until her driving fell all to pieces, until all she could think about was how much she wanted one of those hands to slide across her pelvis and settle its hard heat between her thighs.

Right in the middle of Paris traffic, she scolded herself.

But she almost didn't care.

She wanted him to do more—slide both those hands up under her jacket, cup her breasts through her silky top …

"Watch out!" Joss yelled, and she dodged away from a car changing lanes.

By the time she parked in front of her building, she was already going out of her mind.

"Are you crazy?" She jerked her helmet off. "Are you trying to get us killed? I have to concentrate when I'm driving!"

"What did I do this time?" A flush rode on Joss's cheeks, his eyes dilated. All the muscles in his body strained, visibly fighting against his will to hold them in check.

"You—you—you—" Nothing. Just ridden behind her.

And she was a hot mess of hunger and nerves. He was her *friend*. He was the guy who had strolled off as if she was nothing more than some dumb girl trailing after him. He was—he was—

She wanted those callused hands to do things to her body. She'd always wanted him for hers, always dreamed about him. But how had her wants gotten so explicit, so fast? Not vague dreams of warmth and kisses, but hungers to be squeezed, rubbed, explored.

She pivoted and tapped in her code, her breaths short and shallow, embarrassed, as if she'd stepped across some important line in the sand.

Joss caught the door when it clicked and pushed it halfway open but stopped there, his own breathing hard and deep. "Maybe I should meet you at the top," he muttered.

Meet her … ? "There's only one staircase."

"I could just climb up the outside." A hard rise and fall of his chest, his hand fisting on the door he still held open. "It might be easier than trying to get up all those stairs behind you. It would give me something to do with my hands until we get to the actual bed."

She stared at him, then up at her apartment window six floors up. "Are you like one of those guys who climbs the Eiffel Tower and all that?"

"No, I'm more like a paratrooper in the Foreign Legion. The Eiffel Tower has so many holds anybody could climb it."

Célie was pretty sure that by *anybody*, he meant *anybody but the vast majority of the population including her*, but … but … she lost her train of thought before the intensity of his look.

Burning, she took a step back from it, her brain short-circuiting.

He licked his lips and gave his head a tiny shake as if to clear it. "God. I can't believe this is actually happening."

Her whole body itched. Standing so close to him but not quite touching made her feel like one giant frantic case of chicken pox. "Please just come with me up the stairs." Her fingers flexed into her palms to keep from grabbing him and trying to haul him forcibly. "If you fell off the building, I'd kill you."

"Climbing those stairs behind you without touching you might kill me," he said roughly.

He got her mind and body so tangled up and confused with hot wanting. The Joss she thought she knew had been an honorary older brother, tolerant and quietly patient with her and subtly protective. He'd been the focal point of all her teenage fantasies, a safe place to put them, the only decent guy she knew. It hadn't been reciprocal. He'd been the guy who had been able to leave her for his own dreams without a second thought.

To discover ... *this*—this burning, flushed, taut hunger of his that pursued her up the dim staircase like a lion after its prey—was as if her whole world had been picked up and shaken until she fell out of it naked and wanting in front of a man who was half a stranger.

It felt real, though. It felt as if she was down out of her tower and aflame with realness. Or at least he'd finally invited himself into that tower instead of standing on the ground below.

She stopped just short of the top of the first flight. "Joss." Her whole back burned, and her buttock muscles would not stop clenching and releasing even when she paused in her climbing. "You're ... looking at me or something. I can feel it."

"Fuck, yes, I'm looking at you," he said, low and strangled. "I can't believe I'm finally going to be able to touch that ass. *Merde*, all the times you've twitched that thing at me and I haven't grabbed a handful of it."

She twisted her upper body cautiously, just enough to see his face. They hadn't turned the lights on, so he was almost all shadow.

In the dark stairwell, his focus was intense, absolute, as if every flex of her body was being burned into him. All that rugged power was primed, ready. He had one hand closed around the railing, the muscles on his forearm standing out as he gripped it.

"You go first," he said roughly. "I'll try to give you a head start."

She climbed three more steps and looked back down. He was so big and powerful and predatory just below her, held in check only by a clear effort of his own will. Half a stranger, half a friend.

What are you doing? she thought. *Don't let him in. Not in where he can break everything you've built of yourself down into nothing.*

Her steps sped up. *Not* because she was running from a predator. Not at all. She was *naturally* this fast, that was all—a thousand times a day, she raced up and down the stairs at work, in a hurry to get everything done. She glanced back down. He still gripped that railing, staring up at her.

Her steps managed to speed up a little more. Adrenaline raced through her. When she glanced down from two flights up, he still hadn't moved, straining against his own hold on the railing. Their eyes met. His locked with hers from two flights below. She licked her lips.

And he let go of that railing and surged up the stairs, in an explosion of lethal power. He barely made a sound, taking the stairs two at a time, in this smooth, clean burst of a predator in pursuit.

Her heart kicked into overdrive, a terrified prey but with this surge of laughter through it, too. It was a challenge now. And she'd always loved challenging Joss, teasing him.

Now she had to beat him. She raced up the next flight. A sixth-floor apartment and running up and down the stairs at work a thousand times a day left her in excellent stair-climbing shape. And gazelles were faster than leopards. She could do this. She could—

She tripped in her rush and started to fall, just as that dark pursuit surged up and caught her. A hard grip pulled her in.

"Joss," she whispered.

He pressed her back against the door. "*Merde,* Célie."

The jacket she'd been holding in her hand had fallen when she tripped. Without it, she could feel the nakedness of her arms, the bareness of her shoulders, how thin and fragile her silky top was against that strength and that gaze. He braced both hands on the door on either side of her.

"I'm going to screw this up," he said hoarsely, big hands flexing against the door. "I want it too damn bad."

She squeezed her eyes tight against her own wanting. "Me, too," she whispered. It confused her, because she hadn't known that her body could want sex this intensely. Sex had always made her feel anxious, naked, wishing the guy would quit touching her because his touch felt so totally wrong against her bare skin. She hadn't done that much of it, in fact, and she'd always felt guilty about how rare her efforts were, as if she wasn't properly trying.

"Merde." A rough expulsion of breath. Joss's hand left the door, lowering to just above her breast and hovering there a second, open. She tried to breathe deeply enough to lift her breasts to his palm. "God, Célie."

His hand shifted enough to finally cup her breast.

Both of them stilled at that claiming. The first time Joss had ever touched her there. The first time Joss had ever touched her anywhere a man could only touch in private and with permission.

His hand felt so hot and big against that fragile, intimate part of her. Within seconds, he had lost his paralysis, and his hand was shifting, massaging, his body pressing in closer to hers.

"Hell," he said. And then a string of curse words in this mix of languages that must be the way he had learned to curse in the Legion. But he said all those profane curses in this wondering, incredulous tone, his hands squeezing her breasts, sliding down her ribs, rubbing back up to her breasts to squeeze again.

She shivered and flexed against that door and dragged her hands over his torso. How could anyone be so *muscled*? This lethal, intense strength of a body that could meet any demand anyone made of it.

Except, perhaps, hers.

Because that body flinched and tightened under her touch. His breathing grew labored. His hands slid down her body and grabbed her ass, gripping too hard. He lifted her until he could press his hips against hers, driving her back against the door. "Tell me to slow down," he said roughly. "I'll do it if you tell me. You have to keep telling me and not let me forget."

"God, your shoulders are hot," Célie whispered, dragging her hands over them and down. She found the hem of his T-shirt and shoved it up so that her hands could slide bare against those muscled ribs. "*Merde*, Joss, your body."

Ripped, hungry strength. As if every ounce of fat had been sacrificed to maximize its power.

"Give me your keys," he muttered against her mouth.

"It's"—she gasped and pulled her mouth away—"It's not my door."

He turned toward the other door on the landing.

She pointed upward, desperate. "One more flight."

A far more violent stream of mixed-language curse words erupted. He dipped down and caught her jacket in one hand.

And then he just scooped one big hand under her butt and lifted her up to him, starting up the stairs. She wrapped her thighs around his hips instinctively, for security. "Joss"—the shifting pressure of his erection against the crotch of her jeans rocketed through her—"you can't carry me up the stairs."

"You really have no idea what I can do, do you?"

His strength and agility didn't seem challenged by carrying her up those stairs one-handed, but his control did. Hunger built with every step. She felt halfway to being devoured already.

"Keys." He set her down in front of her door. His hand pressed against it, and he put all his weight against that arm above her as she twisted to try to unlock it. "Honest to God, I could tear this door down right now, Célie, if you fumble too long."

She got it open and stumbled in.

He closed it with too much of a slam behind them, and she looked back as her fourth step away from it brought her to her bed. He pressed himself back against the door as if he was afraid to leave it. "I'm going to screw this up," he said again, his eyes eating her alive. "I'm not going to get this right. You're too—I'm too—"

She felt as if she was burning up, frantic with the itch to be touched, handled, squeezed. "It's all right." *It won't be the first time a guy has screwed up sex with me.* But she realized just in time that the wry comment would not go over well *at all* and kept it back. "It's not really about the sex."

"Hell. It's *not*? That's all I can think about. My brain is going to explode. Or something else."

She hesitated a nervous second. And then she just caught the hem of her silky top and pulled it over her head.

Joss made a sound as if she'd punched him in the stomach. "Célie." His hands flexed against the door behind him. He took a harsh breath. "We should slow down. It took me much, much longer to ease your shirt off in my fantasies. A month, I think."

"That's because in your fantasies I must not have been helping," Célie said dryly. "Real, live women, we do all kinds of things on our own."

One corner of his mouth twisted. "Right." He left the door and came toward her, carefully, as if he suspected land mines.

"We might be different," she said defiantly, "in real life than in fantasies. We might have minds of our own."

"I got it, Célie," he said, very evenly. He stopped only a few inches from her, his fists at his sides, clenching and unclenching as he stared down at her breasts, pushed up by her bra. “Trust me, I know the fantasy was a poor man’s substitute for the real you.”

Her mouth trembled all of a sudden. “Do you?” she whispered. Because it was hard to live up to a fantasy a man had been building for five years without any contact with the real woman.

“Yeah. Nothing compares to this.”

“This?”

His eyes burned down over her body, his fists flexing by his thighs as he held himself in. “This moment. Right here. This.”

The room felt too hot, too tight. She twisted away from him suddenly, around the bed, to open the casement window. Street noise invaded immediately, echoing up between stone buildings from the cars and voices six floors below.

She turned back.

Joss still stood where she had left him, still holding himself in. Energy came off his body like a force of nature barely contained. He tilted his head just a little ... and then held out a hand, fingers curling to coax her back.

She came because she couldn’t say no. She wanted to touch him so much. Be pulled in against that hard chest. Be held.

Know he was alive.

Somewhere inside her flared the panicked sense of rolling down a mountainside, of going too fast, flailing for holds and unable to stop herself. They weren’t ready for this. They hadn’t made that transition from her brother’s patient friend to *this*, this fire and storm of hunger.

But as soon as her hand touched his chest, he pulled her in with a groan, hands pressing into her back and butt hard as he lifted her into him, kissing her.

He kissed her so hungrily, so intensely, his hands running so hard all over her body, fingers digging into her, gripping her. He kissed her until he’d toppled them on the bed behind her with the force of the kiss. And still he didn't stop, pushing his hand up her ribs, squeezing her breasts.

She'd imagined making love to Joss, too, and it hadn't been anything like this. It had been quiet and protective and strong. Sweet.

Vague.

This was all-out hunger, as if an intense maleness packed too tight for too long had burst through the first hairline crack in the dam that it found and was buffeting her in its force. This wasn't protection. This was utter greed.

"I've got to slow down," he said hoarsely into her hair, against her ear, against her throat, as his mouth slid over her, his hands gripped her everywhere, moving and squeezing and rubbing as if he had to touch all of her right now, all at once, *now*. "Please tell me to slow down."

"I've never—" She broke off. *Made love like this*, she couldn't say. He didn't want to hear comparisons to other men right now. But she hadn't ever made love like this. As if she was being consumed in an inferno of need. Her own need, too. She fought his to make space for herself, scrubbing her hands down his arms to feel all his muscles, gripping him through his T-shirt to make sure all of him was really there. "I'm so glad you're home." *So glad you're alive and here.*

"Anything I get right—just stop me and tell me. Grab my hand and hold it there. Whatever. And I'll keep doing it."

"You, too," she whispered. She had to live up to five years of a soldier's fantasies, after all. And everything about him was overwhelming her—bigger, more urgent, so much more *real* and *male* than she had ever imagined him in her head. "You tell me, too."

A groan that held something between despair and humor. "Célie, I'm way easier than you. As long as I can get inside you, everything is right for me."

It was kind of infuriatingly unfeminist how tempting it was to just yield to that need, to say, *Oh, if that's what you need so much then you can have it.* To just give up her own body to his demands. She caught herself. This was for her, too.

"I like this," she said, and felt shy to tell him. The man who had once been her friend, once been her hero. The man who had once been so infuriatingly trustworthy that she could test out all her fresh, teenage flirting skills on him, and he would never take advantage of her. She had to whisper what she wanted to that man, looking up at him. "I like it when you touch me all over a little rough like that, as if you're so hungry for me you can't stand it."

"I *can't* stand it." He kissed up her arm, this scrape of twenty-four hours without a shave and this stern silk of firm lips. "Sweetheart, if I screw this up, please be kind and let me try again. Please. I want you so damn bad."

"Okay."

He lifted his head, a little confused by the word even though he had made the request. "Okay?"

"Joss. You don't have to be perfect for me." She wrapped her arms around him and pressed her face into that chest that had a *scent.* Dreams never had scents, but the reality smelled of heat and a hint of sweat, of pine and strength and *him.* "I've always loved you just the way you were," she whispered into his chest.

A shudder ran through him. "Célie." He braced on his arms to look down at her. "Célie, you're so damn—*God.*" His hips thrust against hers, through denim and leather.

Her body softened at the pressure, in the desire to yield to it and let him in. She ran her hands over his chest again, flexing fingers into his muscles.

He stroked a hand over her stomach, down to her leather, bracing himself enough off her so that he could watch the path of his own hand. The warmth of it settled heavily over the waist of her pants. Her breathing deepened as she went very still, gazing up at him, suspended in desire for that hand to do anything it wanted. Slide a little farther down. Cup. Press. Open. Slip in—

"Oh, fuck." His head drooped suddenly, his fists clenching so that all the muscles on his arms stood out. "I don't have any—*fuck*." He lifted his head. "I wasn't—I've been living in *barracks*, and I didn't expect you to—"

"I've got some," Célie said without thinking, pulling open the drawer of her nightstand.

His face blanked. That deep dive into blankness that he did these days, whenever anything got to him too badly.

"I mean, they're not mine," Célie said quickly. "They're just leftover from—a—a"—*guy I dated.* She faltered to a stop, cringing as she realized exactly how much she shouldn't be saying any of this.

Joss reached into the drawer and took out the small, open box of condoms. His face, as he looked at it, went so completely devoid of expression it was scary.

"I didn't mean—" Célie broke off again, realizing she was starting to apologize. It was none of his damn business who had used condoms in her apartment. Joss was a friend of her brother who'd left for five years. She hadn't owed him any fidelity. She'd owed it to *herself* to try to make a good, new life on her own.

"I need a minute," Joss said abruptly, and thrust away from her, striding the one long stride it took to reach one of her casement windows. Célie sat up, wrapping her arms around her knees, still fighting that urge to apologize. She would *not* apologize, damn it.

"Joss, what did you expect?" she finally burst out, angry and desperate.

"I didn't expect anything," he said flatly without turning around. "I just didn't—think about that part." His fist opened, dropping the purple box to the floor. It had been crushed into a small ball.

"Of course not." She fisted handfuls of her sheet. "Because in your fantasies I was only what you needed me to be. Not what I actually was."

He threw her one dark, dangerous glance over his shoulder, like the throw of a knife blade, and abruptly jumped onto her balcony railing.

It was so sudden that she drew her breath to scream *Don't jump!* But she didn't have time to make a sound. His feet touched the railing just long enough to launch him upwards.

She ran forward, in a desperate urge to catch him back to safety, even as his body pulled upwards out of her sight. She got to the window and leaned out.

He was hauling himself over the edge of the roof.

"Joss!"

He paused to look down, leaning back over the edge of the roof. "I need a few minutes." It was flat and final.

"You have no right to be upset!"

"I know." His body disappeared.

"Joss!"

Just his head reappeared. He waited.

She sought for words. "Don't fall!"

He gave a brief nod and was gone.

Chapter 17

Joss sat on the zinc sheets of the rooftop, by a line of ceramic chimney tops, gazing down over Paris. Apparently this area where Célie lived had been built on higher land than the older, more central part of Paris, and from the rooftop, he had a clear view over those endless zinc-roofed mansards and chimney tops all the way to the Eiffel Tower. A pigeon came and pecked beside him, in the optimistic conviction that Joss must have climbed up here just to give it leftover baguette crumbs.

Grief tried to seize him in this gray, grim wave, that grief a man had to fight off in the Legion, because if you yielded to it, it was all over. You couldn't let yourself think about all you had given up, all you were missing out on, all the ways you might have screwed up by making this stupid, over-romantic choice to join the Legion because it sounded good from a distance. Heroic. So much better than being a barely adult mechanic who couldn't get another job because he'd lost the last one when his boss started thinking he must be in on the drug dealing, too, given the company he kept.

You couldn't think about how stupid you had been, once the choice was made, how much you wished you could undo that choice and just go home. You couldn't think about how the girl you wanted was probably dating other men, maybe even getting married, having babies. Legionnaires who let their thoughts go down those roads ended up killing themselves or deserting.

And a man who joined the Legion to make something of himself and then deserted halfway through because he couldn't handle it had nothing left of himself to hold on to, to believe in, at all.

So after that grim, bleak year two, Joss had learned mostly how not to think of anything but success, strength, getting through. When he imagined Célie, she was delighted to see him, she threw her arms around him, she kissed him, he kissed her, he nestled himself in those beautiful moments of her and never, ever let himself think about what the reality might be.

A half-full box of condoms.

None of his business.

Just his loss.

And that great, gray grief that he'd fought off for five years slumped down on him out of the gray-dark sky of Paris, pressing all its weight down on him until even his shoulders didn't want to bear up under it. And he'd formed those shoulders to bear up under anything.

***

Calvi, Corsica, three years before

Women were everywhere. Leaning against the bar, luring men into corners, glancing his way. Short-skirted, sweet-smelling, eager for fun.

Joss rubbed his thumb over the battered edge of the folded postcard in his wallet. Most of those cheerful postcards Célie had sent him the first six months he kept safe above his bunk, but he'd had to carry one with him. He'd chosen this one: *We miss you here, but I know you can do it! You can do anything. Bisous. Célie.* With a heart over the *I* in her name.

Uniforms mixed with all the scantily clad tourists in the bar around him. Back from Opération Serval and a successful nighttime drop over Timbuktu, the 2e REP was pretty full of itself. Back, covered in glory, by blue seas, where women wore bikinis, and no one was shooting at them.

Oh, yeah, those bikinis. Even in the bar, some of the women had only put on skirts with their bikini tops. They'd come to Calvi for one reason, those women, and the bar was full of exactly what they wanted: Legionnaires.

Joss pressed down harder on the edge of his postcard.

"That one's for you." Jefe shoved him in the ribs with his elbow. "She can't take her eyes off you."

Joss flicked a glance at the pretty blonde in a tight white skirt and lace-edged cami. No. That lace was the edge of her bra peeking over. *Hell.* "I've got a girl," he said flatly. Even if she'd stopped sending him postcards a year ago. He still had her. He did.

Jefe snorted. "Trust me, she's found some other guy by now. Come on. I'll take the redhead."

Joss's glance flicked to the redhead, and his heart stopped. Curves and athleticism, perky nose, braid down her back ... she turned her head.

He flattened. Not Célie. Of course not. What would she be doing in Corsica? Chasing him?

Ruthlessly, he crushed down that wish. *First,* he proved himself, that he could, indeed, *do anything.*

Then he got to go after his next goal, Célie. One goal at a time. *Like a horse with blinders on,* one of his instructors had told them during the six weeks in the green hell of jungle warfare training. *Keep focused on your one objective. Nothing else counts. Certainly not how much it hurts.*

But when morale was at its lowest, when a man was exhausted and bloodied and almost beaten, he always needed a thought, a dream, to save him. And Célie—she was such a bright, glowing dream. She shone through *everything.*

As long as he didn't, himself, tarnish her.

"I've got a girl," Joss said again.

The other men lounging at the table groaned. "Not that again." They all agreed with Jefe on this one. From Noah, with that geeky face of his and angular body that made him look like a surprisingly tanned hacker until he started moving, to Michael, whose altar boy eyes made him look as if he'd accidentally woken up in the wrong story, to Victor, the Ukrainian with whom Joss butted heads constantly—all of them thought he was crazy.

Beside him, Victor snorted. Victor had saved his life more than once, and Joss had saved his, but he still had a hard time not hitting the Ukrainian most days. "That girl you never go see on leave?"

"Fuck you." No sense wasting syllables on *it's none of your business* when two would do. Not with Victor.

Victor laughed. "The real question is who's fucking *her*?"

Joss shoved his chair back and shot to his feet. But before he could start a fight, their *adjudant*, Valdez, was there, gripping Joss's shoulder, making a *calm-down-boy* gesture of his hand toward Victor. Valdez tended to treat them all like cute and poorly behaved puppies—an attitude that worked surprisingly well on a band of ferocious wolves—and tonight was his send-off. Fifteen years and now he was done. He'd even told them his real name out there in the world, so they could look him up: Delesvaux. He'd promised to cook them meals that would make them cry, if they came to see him. Joss believed it. The man always cooked them a Christmas dinner that really had made some of the men cry.

A shift in the atmosphere, and Captain Fontaine was suddenly there. He'd been sitting at the bar, fending off or encouraging a pretty brunette—hard to tell sometimes with Captain Fontaine—but whatever else he might be doing, Captain Fontaine always looked after his men. He had the scars to prove it, too, and the fine lines of fatigue around his eyes despite the energy in his body even in repose. Scoured by sand and sun, until all of him, sand and skin, were that same faded brown. You could always tell a Legionnaire by the way he carried himself, tough as nylon rope but rough around the edges like hemp.

"Bar full of tourists, mostly women," Delesvaux told Joss, in that lazy, *easy-boy* tone he did so well, even in the midst of a firefight. "Not the send-off I'm looking for. Come on, guys, reassure me that you're going to survive without me."

"Cool it," Fontaine told Victor flatly. He, too, knew better than to waste syllables with Victor.

Victor subsided. One thing they had all learned fast was not to mess with Captain Fontaine. Unlike some of those namby pants they sent over as officers from the regular Army or fresh out of Saint-Cyr, Fontaine had worked his way up to captain from that same bare room of *what-the-hell-did-I-just-do engagés volontaires* that Joss and Victor and all the others had passed through. Joss knew almost nothing about Fontaine's past before that or his real name, per the usual Legionnaire silence on that subject, but he did know that the man who called himself Fontaine came from the south of France—that bouncing, drawling accent, strong on the *N*'s, made it obvious—that he had a lot of cousins in a family who worked in some kind of agriculture, and that once, after a nasty week in the Uzbin Valley, when they'd lost two of their men to fucking friendly fire because of a radio malfunction, Fontaine had actually gotten drunk, and drunk enough he'd gone along with the rest of them to get a tattoo. Exactly the kind of thing Legionnaires liked to do to assert themselves in a country where both alcohol and tattoos were illegal, at least for locals. Only instead of "Legio Patria Nostra" or "Honneur, Fidélité" or "March ou crève" or even the names of the dead, like most men got in those circumstances, Fontaine had gotten, of all things, a small rose.

He'd been pissed as hell the next day when he realized what he'd done, too. But he'd never had it removed. From time to time, when he was in a T-shirt, that olive green would slide up hard biceps and the rose would peek out again, surreal in that tough, harsh world of fighting men.

Maybe that rose was his own postcard, his own dream of another life. A woman he wished upon, like a star.

Joss had gotten "Honneur, Fidélité."

"I've got a girl," Joss told them all for the third time. "And just because you don't doesn't mean you get to fuck with me about mine."

Because when it came down to it, that was why they messed with him about this: jealousy. Because Joss had a girl he could carry with him back into whatever hell they got sent to. In dust and mud and falling mortar shells, she smiled at him, she told him he could do anything.

And all the others had to carry them through the same thing was the memory of their last fuck above a bar.

***

The pigeon gave Joss a disgusted look at his paucity with crumbs and flew off to find a park. The Eiffel Tower started to sparkle.

He lifted his head and looked at it. That was kind of annoying. Why did it do that? Sparkle like that. He'd heard about it, of course, but he couldn't remember ever seeing it before that evening on the bridge with Célie. Oh, yeah, once, he and Ludo and some other guys had hung out at Trocadéro getting drunk and pretending Paris was theirs until they missed the last RER home. It had been a long, cold night, waiting for the line to start running again at dawn, and the Eiffel Tower had gone black at one a.m., leaving them to endure those five bleak hours with no sparkles. Luring them in and leaving them out in the cold. *Suckers.*

But now, at a distance, the sparkling was much smaller.

It kind of reminded him of Célie, actually. That vibrancy she had, that resilient energy, that sparkle of toughness she let nothing extinguish. Not rain or cold or … anything really.

God damn it, he wanted to kill somebody. Anybody who had ever gotten his hands on that sparkle of hers.

He supposed he should be grateful that the jerks hadn't been worth her—if anyone had, she'd still be with him and not letting Joss up to her apartment instead—but it just enraged him further, to imagine some bastard who didn't deserve her getting his hands on her. Some lazy jerk who didn't even take her walking on the Seine.

Joss had done five years in the Foreign Legion, damn it, to deserve her, and meanwhile there were pieces of shit who thought they deserved to touch her just because, what, they existed? Assholes.

Fucking bastards.

It's your own fault.

Yeah, but that was what you couldn't start doing, as a paratrooper in the Foreign Legion: you couldn't start calling all you were killing yourself to accomplish a *fault*, a *mistake*, a decision that would *ruin your life*. You had to have all your courage, all your strength, all your belief in your goals, all the time.

It was a funny thing. He could climb a cliff barehanded with fifty kilos on his back. He could march two hundred kilometers over steep, mountainous terrain in four days or run thirty kilometers in under three hours, with a similar weight. Drop him off with only a handful of men in enemy territory, and it was the enemy who should be afraid.

Yes, he could take hurt.

Yes, he could persist.

Yes, he could crawl through a field of barbed wire for her.

But she wasn't hitting him, no matter how much she said she wanted to.

She wasn't asking him to crawl.

So he had to learn new skills.

He started to make his way down the steep slant of the zinc roof to her window and then remembered—he still needed to get some damn condoms. He wasn't using that other bastard's. The trapdoor onto the roof was locked, so he climbed down the inside, courtyard walls—helped drain some energy off—and let himself back out onto the street, walking down it until he came to the nearest white dispenser on the wall of a building and buying several. Then he realized he hadn't paid enough attention to her damn code, so he couldn't get back inside to the stairs or the courtyard. He checked the street. Kind of occupied but no police. Passersby probably wouldn't assume he was a thief at least, with this many people around.

He waved to a few people to make them believe he was doing some authorized stunt, and then just climbed back up the building to her little railing. At least it was entertainment. The lack of physical challenge in this city was making all his muscles frantic under his skin.

Be kind of fun to get in a fight with the police, to be honest, but since he was out of the Legion now, they might actually be able to arrest him, instead of just sending him back to his Colonel to get reamed out, put on some god-awful *corvée* duty, and then given a suspended sentence because the Colonel was secretly smug at how his police-defying wild Legionnaires enhanced the Legion reputation.

The casement window was still open—she hadn't locked him out at least—but for a second he thought Célie herself was gone.

Then he spotted her, curled up between her bed and the wall, her arms wrapped around herself as if she was trying to turn into a turtle and shrink into a shell.

Hell.

He swung into the room, and she sprang up, forgetting she still wore only her bra and leather pants, her hands going to her hips. "You have one hell of a nerve."

"I know." He stripped off his own T-shirt so they matched.

She gasped and then just went stock-still, staring at him.

Fine, maybe he did pause at that stare so he could drink it in, glad to have his muscles already pumped for her from the climbing.

She swallowed. Her hands left her hips to press to her lips. "Oh, wow," she whispered. "Oh, wow, you're ..." She looked dazed. "You're really, really hot."

Nice to know that part at least had worked out for him. He gestured to himself, to that feel of his muscles tightening still more to show off for her. "All for you."

She licked her lips.

Well, then. Some other assholes might have gotten a chance at her before he did, but he'd damn well make sure she never wanted anyone else.

He'd wipe them so far out of her mind she'd never again even *think* sex without thinking him.

He put one knee on her bed—it was true you could barely move in her apartment without falling onto the thing—and her eyes widened so much, he just went with that, dropping his hands to the mattress, too, and prowling across it to her. "Want to touch?"

"Jesus." She slipped one of her fingers into her mouth and bit it, hard.

He tsked and took it from her, slipping it into his own mouth and sucking on it soothingly. *There you go. Put yourself in my hands. They'll treat you far better than you do.*

She made a soft sound, and heat surged in that merciless wave through his body. But ... fuck it. It wouldn't be the first time he'd overcome his body and his mind and endured. He could do anything. He could take his time and make her lose her mind.

Make her lose all memory of anyone who had ever touched her before him.

"You can touch anything." He drew her hand from his mouth and pressed it to his shoulder. "Anything you want." He drew her hand down over his chest.

Her tongue touched her lips.

"Or that, too." His gaze zeroed in on her mouth. "I'd love for you to lick me."

"Joss ..." A dazed whisper. It had to be the most beautiful way his name had ever been pronounced in his life.

"I'll trade. You can have this." He gestured to himself. "If I can have all this." He reached for her, grazing his hand over her ribs to rest on her hip, tugging her gently toward him. "All for me, Célie." He looked up at her from his kneeling position on her low bed. "All mine."

"I—I—my body is actually mi-ine," she managed, but she was following his tug, swaying in closer to him until her shins hit the edge of the bed.

"You don't think it's a fair trade?" he coaxed. Her breasts were only a topple away from his face. All he had to do was tug a little more until she lost her balance and fell toward him. Soft, full breasts, pressed up by the black lace of her bra. In his fantasies, he'd tested all possible colors of bras out on Célie's body, depending on his mood. But his two favorites had included this one, the wannabe-tough sexy black from her Goth period, and a bright, hot pink like she really was inside.

"A fair trade for this?" she said incredulously, and her other hand came to rest on his other shoulder. "Have you ever looked at yourself in the mirror?"

Apparently not the same way she looked at him now.

"You're so pretty, Célie." His hand slid up to cup her breast. Soft and full, the lace getting in the way with its tantalizing extra texture. God, her breast felt so much better in real life than in his imagination.

"No, I'm not," she said warily, as if he'd just made himself suspicious by saying so.

"Cute. Full of life. Strong. Glowing." Darling. How to explain it? "Beautiful."

"You're delusional." But her face was crinkling up so funny, her eyes so wondering. "Joss, I think you really did turn me in your head into something I'm not."

"How'd you imagine me?" He pulled her closer, breathing on her lace bra. Her pulse throbbed in her throat, and he rose a little on his knees to open his mouth over it, touching it with just the tip of his tongue.

"Here," she said.

Damn it, he'd walked right into that one.

But when he pulled back, she didn't look like someone who was trying to stick another needle in him. She looked like he felt most of the time: as if finding the one word that expressed what she meant was a careful struggle.

"Here," he repeated, and drew her hand down his waist, over stomach muscles he tightened just to show off. "All right. I'm here. From now on."

"Joss." Her free hand flexed into his biceps. Then she lost track of whatever she had been going to say, her gaze going to her hand as she flexed again, and then again. "Wow."

"Unless I burn up right now. It's a possibility."

"Umm ... yeah. For me, too."

Hell, *that* felt good to hear. Heat surged through him, higher and more urgent.

"I knew I'd never manage to make you work for it," she said despairingly.

She had a really weird idea of working for it. Maybe he should show her some training videos from the Foreign Legion sometime. "I've worked. But I can work harder."

"It makes my tongue tingle just looking at you," she whispered. "You are *so hot*."

Hell, yeah, did he like the idea of her tingling tongue.

He liked it so much that his body wanted to explode.

"I'm not going to screw this up," he told her, flatly. He needed to approach this like any challenge in the Legion. Just because something was impossible was no excuse for failing.

"It does seem unlikely," Célie said wonderingly, her fingers running a line of fire up his biceps to his shoulder. "God, Joss." She squeezed his shoulder.

Sweet, small pressure against muscles that didn't know how to yield to it. His head tilted back, his eyes closed, as all of his being, more than five years of waiting, focused on that feel of her hands. "I like that. Célie. Please do it some more."

He opened his eyes to find her gazing down at his face, at her hands on his shoulders. Her eyes were so utterly fascinated with him that pride and hunger surged all through his body, beat in his dick and in his head, fogging thought. That fascination and admiration surpassed anything he'd ever come up with for her expression in his fantasies.

With one finger she traced slowly over the letters across his right biceps: *Honneur, Fidélité.* Her expression grew somber, focused. Then her hands stroked up, and she kneaded his shoulders again, strong, capable hands that were completely ineffective against the muscles of his shoulders. And yet it felt so good. "Yeah," he whispered. "Oh, hell, Célie, if you stop, I might die. I want you to touch me everywhere."

"Can I really?" she breathed, as if he was some kind of glorious present on offer that might still be yanked away from her.

Hell. The giddy arousal of her wonder in him was going to drive him out of his mind. It beat in him, trying to burst out of his skin.

He caught her hands, twisting her down onto the bed under him, one of his hands locking her wrists above her head. "A little bit at a time." His breathing was too fast and too rough, and he couldn't get it to slow down. "I'm so triggered." He pressed a kiss into her captured palms. His body was vibrating with arousal. It pulsed in his dick, this unbearable command.

"You let go of my wrists this second, Joss Castel. That's not fair. You can't look that hot and not let me touch."

"Shit." Joss released her reluctantly. "But then I will screw this up."

Célie drew her freed hands down his back, her expression so concentrated on the *feel* of him that it about drove him out of his mind. He'd never even imagined her sinking into him in this tactile, sensual way, as if he was something she had to greedily lap up. And he'd thought he'd imagined her every way possible by now.

"God, Joss." She pushed at his shoulders suddenly.

Hell, no. He did *not* want to be pushed back. But that was the thing about making himself so strong—the strength was to take care of her, not to control her. If he ever broke that rule, he lost everything. So he rolled away from her onto the mattress, trying not to let curses hiss through his teeth.

And she came on top of him.

His eyes widened, and he reached above his head to try to grab something, anything on her bed to help him out, but there were no bars on her headboard, nothing to hold on to. He grabbed a pillow and squeezed with all his might, and hell, that was flimsy, as Célie sat astride him, as her hands ran down his chest, her teeth sinking into her lower lip as if she was tasting him.

Yeah, taste me. Oh, hell.

Down, down, down went her hands, over his stomach that flinched even tauter at her touch, to the waist of his jeans, her fingers tracing delicately, curiously, shyly even, along the line of them, that space left by his tightened stomach muscles where she could have slipped deeper.

But didn't.

"Célie." His head arched back. He thrust his hips up into her before he could stop himself.

She brought one hand to her face and bit the side of it. "You're so hot," she whispered. "Joss, God."

"*Merde*, Célie."

"It's like you're half a stranger. This exotic fantasy lover. But then I say your name, and I remember I've known you so long. You were my friend, the man who was always there for me." *Until you weren't.*

But at least she didn't say it this time. He saw it flicker across her face, and his body tightened against the words, but she bit her lip and focused instead on her hands on his chest.

He, too, focused on her hands on his chest. And her pelvis pressed against his dick. Hell, but he would like to get these jeans off.

"Can I kiss you?" she breathed, staring at his chest and his arms bent behind his head.

This stupid, inadequate pillow. There was no way it could give a man anything to hold on to. "Anything," he said hoarsely. "Anything you want."

She ran her hands up his body again as she leaned down and kissed his chest.

"Sweetheart." The pillow lost. He curved his hands around that sweet, delicious ass, and *God* it felt perfect in his hands. He squeezed, pulling her hips in tight to his, rocking his up, fitting them to each other through their pants so he could rub them together.

She arched back up again, her spine flexing in a move that lifted her breasts beautifully and drove her hips down into his even better.

"Oh, yeah," he breathed. "Yeah. *Gorgeous.*" His fingers fumbled for the zip of her leather pants. *Too fast, you're going too fast,* he tried to tell himself, but his body fought his mind, trying to go even faster. Fingers that could strip and reassemble, in the dark, all the weapons most armies of the world had ever issued now fumbled over a zip.

But he got it undone. And not by ripping the thing open. He was pretty proud of that degree of self-control.

"Oh." Célie's eyes flew open as his fingers grazed against her panties. Her thighs tightened on his hips, knees pressing into his sides. "Oh." She covered her face with one hand.

He gazed at her half-hidden expression ... and then let his own fingers graze her panties again ... a little more deliberately, a stroke that slipped a little farther down over what was still half guarded by her pants. In fantasies, a man didn't have to worry too much about this part, because no matter what he did or how he did it, obviously Célie always came to pieces for him—it was his fantasy. But in real life, he figured he wanted to get it right.

She brought both hands over her face now, covering it completely.

Yeah?

"You like that, sweetheart?" He eased his fingers a little farther, using three fingers to stroke her broadly, watching her body, those hands over her face, for the spot she needed.

She was shivering now, her hips rocking into his involuntarily, and she wouldn't lower her hands.

"Yeah?" he murmured and rolled her over onto the mattress, so he could ease her pants down enough to give him more space.

She pulled his abandoned pillow over her face and locked it there with her arms.

Okay, hands were one thing, but a pillow was just cheating. He pulled it free from her and tossed it across the room.

Exposed, she stared up at him, face flushed, eyes dazed. So what did she need? She wanted to hide a little. She wanted to be in darkness.

So he laid one hand over her eyes, closing them for her. And holding her still for him.

And with the other he took up that searching, gentle rhythm over her panties.

"Joss." She clutched at him, at his butt through his jeans, and then, as he kept playing with the pretty, pretty texture of those lace panties, she pressed her hands down under his jeans, trying for his bare skin.

She couldn't get her fingers far enough, and she ran them up his back and down, and back up and down, and finally, finally, around to struggle with his button. But her hands were clumsy and losing focus, and he pushed that little bit of lace out of the way of his fingers and found all that soft lushness hiding behind it.

She made a little sound, her hips jerking. He threw one of his legs over her thighs, holding her still. Holding her for this mesmerizing exploration of her body there, of what made her react. She was trembling and twisting, and his fingers slid through curls and lush folds, slickened with moisture.

A tiny, muffled *oh.* She grabbed his hand and pressed it.

Well, hell. Maybe he wasn't going to screw this up.

Stunned at how much faster this had all happened than he had ever imagined it, how much more real it felt, how it had a *scent* and a texture and the sounds of her breathing, and how she wasn't doing one single thing the way he had imagined it but it was all *so much better because it was real,* he began to play with that spot where she had pressed his hand. Ah, yes, there it was, that tiny, sneaky part of her that hid like a secret treasure but that he had now found.

She'd let him. She'd helped him find it.

Her hand relaxed, so he must be getting something right. Her head tossed on the pillow, her breasts lifting and falling, her hips twisting. She clutched at him again, any random part of him she could reach, her hands sliding and gripping.

And he got to watch her. *See everything,* as she just lost it, her body jerking, her hands grabbing at him and falling away, as she shuddered and shuddered until she fell lax against the mattress again.

All her muscles seemed to abandon her, as if she was this breath away from falling into deep, pliant sleep. He eased his hand from between her legs and curved it gently around her thigh, almost afraid he'd lost her.

"Joss." She blinked her eyes open, dazedly, her hands coming back to stroke weakly over his arms and chest.

He braced his arms on either side of her, and she liked that, her hands came to his biceps and squeezed, making almost no impression on their tautness.

"Célie." His breathing had gone ragged, and all the tension he'd tried to slow down, tried to contain, gripped him, this too-tight, too-desperate hunger that was going to rend his muscles to shreds. "My turn now?"

"Yes," she murmured, running her hands over his back. They didn't grip the same as they had before, more lax, this sweet dreaminess to their stroking. "Definitely yes."

He pulled her leather pants and her panties off so fast. And her bra—oh, yeah, she took off her bra herself, and he buried his face in those soft breasts, his heart pounding out of control. She pushed at his jeans for him while he was buried there, tugging them down over his hips.

So he had to help her with that. Yes. Damn. Rearing up, getting the damn things out of the way. Oh, hell, he'd just thrown the condoms in the back pocket all the way across the room. He dove for his jeans as they landed on the edge of the window and jerked them back before they could slide off the other side and down into the street six floors below. Thank God. Although—"I think your pillow might be on the sidewalk down there."

Célie laughed a little.

He came back to stare down at her, naked and laughing, curves and strength, reddened, damp lips, the mark of his stubble on her breasts. Hell, she marked easily—all those little red prickles just from his kisses there.

He rubbed his jaw. But he didn't have a razor here in her apartment, and *hell* but he didn't want to stop.

"Okay?" he said, pulling the condom on. *Thank you,* his damn dick said at the feel of the latex tightening on him. *So that means this time is for real?*

"Yes. Joss, come here."

He was literally vibrating with tension as he came down over her, flicks all over his body. His muscles felt like elastic about to snap. He pressed his hands into the sheets on either side of her head, fisting handfuls of the soft cotton, staring down at her.

She bit her lip. She looked just a little scared.

"Tell me." God, his voice sounded hoarse. He sounded like an animal. He *was* an animal, reduced to absolute, primitive need. He had to keep some control. "If you need me to slow down. Or … stop."

Oh, hell, not stop, please.

"Okay." Her eyes had gone very wide. She stared up at him in a way that made him feel as if he was betraying years of her trust in him, years of being the guy she could count on not to take advantage of her.

I'm not taking advantage. I'm your hero now.

So I earned this.

Oh, hell.

"Joss," she whispered. "Are you *thinking*? Because this isn't a fantasy. You don't have to think this one through. You get to do it."

"I'm savoring. I've wanted this a really long time."

He lowered his hips enough that his penis grazed against her sex, and the touch jolted through him. Hell. Yes. This was happening.

"Me, too," she whispered. "But it's a lot more real and, and … bigger, in real life." She ran her hand over one of his taut arms, caressing the bulge of his biceps in a way that made him gloatingly proud of that bulge. "It's got sweat on it."

"Sorry," he managed.

"No, I … wanted you to become real. At least, I would have wanted that, if I ever thought it was possible."

"I'm real." His voice sounded almost like a growl, dragged out of his chest. "I don't think I've ever felt more real in my life." After five years of intensely physical demands, he knew exactly how to glory in his own body. And yet the moment was also so packed with fantasy come true that he was about to explode with it.

She stroked her hands down to his butt as she rocked her hips almost *shyly* up against his. "Joss. I'm not saying no."

Right. He'd picked that much up.

Her fingers kneaded into his butt muscles. "I'm not saying stop."

Arousal geysered through him, as he realized what she was repeating.

"I'm not raising a hand to push you back." Her fingers tugged on his hips.

He wet his lips.

She looked so damn ... sweet there, against her sheets, with her little uptilted nose and her wide mouth and her pointy chin and those brown eyes that were such a window into her warm, irrepressible, resilient soul.

"Joss. If I'm the stop button ... I say go." She wrapped her thighs around his hips.

"Oh, hell," he said, and just surged into her. *Way* too hard. Just like that.

She gasped, tightening around him, probably to try to squeeze him the hell out of her, and his brain just went black and hot and starry with pleasure.

"Célie," he tried. Her name, the only word with meaning that he could find amid the black hot stars in his brain, her name like *I'm sorry* or *Oh, my God, do that again, that feels so good.*

"Wow," she whispered, shifting her hips, trying to adjust, her fingers flexing into his butt again.

"I can't—I want—you're so—"

He couldn't think or speak. All his brain had zeroed in on that sensation of himself inside of her. This pounding, pulsing of himself, as if his entire being had packed into that one length of his body, trying to explode its way into hers.

"*Here*," he managed. "You're *here*. You're true. You feel so damn real."

"You don't," she whispered. "You feel incredible."

Yeah, *that* sounded like one of his fantasies, all right. Her telling him how incredible he was, while he moved in her. And he couldn't stop moving. Movement had taken over his brain, all he could think about, all he could focus on, just the slide of his body into hers, the way her muscles tightened on him and she tried to hold on. Shells could have started falling, the building could have crashed down around his ears, and he wouldn't have stopped.

"Mine," he might have said, tightening his hold on her too hard. "Mine at last." He had to ease off, he couldn't hold her this hard, he was too strong, she was too little, he had to—he had to—

Press into her as deep as he could.

Hell, that felt good. And out. Oh, yeah, and back in, this long drive of possession.

Her head tossed, and her hips flexed up. "Joss."

He slipped his hand between their bodies, in case his thumb against that favorite spot of hers would help him hear his name in just that tone again. But he couldn't keep track of that thumb. His mind was too utterly subjugated by the sensation of himself inside her, swirling down and down and down into it. Vaguely, he was conscious of her grabbing his hand and pressing it harder. Of her crying out again.

But when he felt her convulsing around him, muscles tightening and tightening, he lost himself.

He gave himself up to her.

And it was better than any fantasy he'd ever had.

It was worth the wait.

Chapter 18

"Célie?"

She started, tightening her arms around her knees, looking up at Joss as he came up onto his elbow in her bed.

"Célie, what are you doing?"

"Nothing." She kneaded her upper arms, feeling embarrassed and stupid. "I thought you were asleep." He'd seemed to be, when she came back from the bathroom and suddenly found herself too scared to climb back into the bed.

Joss stretched out a hand from the low bed to graze callused fingertips over her folded arms, gently. "I was faking it. Harder to kick a man out if you think he's asleep."

"I know," she said and winced. She probably shouldn't have said that. But she did know. The first time she had tried to be normal, to move along and have a healthy, happy love life and forget her stupid teenage crush, the guy had fallen asleep. She'd hated it, having him there in her bed all night. The whole thing had been awful.

"Damn you," she muttered.

Joss pulled his hand back, his expression closing.

"You made me try all this out on *other men*! Try and try to make it work and not really understand why it didn't work or why it always left me feeling like I had this big hole in my soul. You made me feel like there was something wrong with me! And all the time it was you!"

"Célie—"

"I needed *you*." She wanted to pound his chest in a flurry of stupid Scarlett O'Hara fists. "It was supposed to be with *you*." Wanted him to pull her into his chest while she pounded on it, like Rhett did, taking the blows and making it right.

"I loved *you.*" She covered her eyes with her hands. "Damn you, Joss. Couldn't you have at least told me before you left that you wanted me to wait?"

"No," he said flatly, obdurately, and she grabbed the spare pillow, crushing it between her knees and her face, and smothered another scream in it.

"I could ask you to wait for the man I am now," he said, "if I needed to be gone again."

She whipped her head up, shocked through with fear. "Joss, don't—"

"But I couldn't ask you to wait for the man I was then."

Her hands tightened on the pillow until she couldn't stand how damn yielding the thing was anymore and slammed it against the bed. Stupid, wimpy pillow. She needed a three-kilo pack of chocolate to slam right about now. She needed something *hard,* that made *noise,* that she could beat to smithereens. "I'm going to hit you, Joss. I swear I'm going to hit you."

"I'd prefer it. Over the words. But I suppose that's not fair, since you can't really hurt me with your fists, to ask you to use the thing you do the least damage with, instead of your strongest weapon."

Oh. Did her words hurt that much? She bit at her lip, unhappy. "I'd smack my head against yours instead, except it wouldn't work. I'd break my head open on you, and your skull would just stay there, as stubborn and unyielding as ever. It drives me *mad.*"

He gazed at her a moment, and then he lay on his side amid the sheets again. Maybe he was trying to make himself look yielding. It didn't work *at all.* It did make him look sexy, though, that hard body, brown from so much sun, the white sheet pulled across his hips and otherwise totally naked. Hers. In her bed.

"Damn you, Joss," she said weakly. She couldn't hit a man lying down. She could only touch him. Stroke him. Feel him.

Curl up next to him, that heat she had always dreamed of in her bed, and fall asleep, and not have to hide between her bed and the wall, not even in the darkest hours before dawn.

Until he disappeared again.

"I'm sorry about the words." She bent her head. "I just—" She broke off, unable to explain better than she already had.

"I'm sorry about the nights you curled up on the floor between your wall and your bed. I'm sorry about the other men. It's okay about the words, Célie. If you didn't care about me, they'd never come out of you that way."

"Joss." Célie clutched her knees. Her eyes tracked over him, up to his eyes watching her in the low, warm lamplight. She'd bought that lamp and that bulb so that she could have something that would gently diffuse the darkness, if a woman couldn't stand it anymore at three in the morning. She'd bought a night-light first, one that cast stars on the ceiling, but gazing at them, she'd imagined Joss out under some Afghanistan sky, and she'd started to cry.

She sighed that memory out, very slowly, and let herself focus just on him. The him he was now. That powerful body, the rugged strength and ability to do anything that he'd forged ... for her.

"You did something incredible." She touched his chest, carefully, trying to think past fear to concentrate on just what a precious treasure had been offered to her. Her hand slipped to his arm and stroked over the words *Honneur, fidélité*. "Utterly amazing. I'm proud of you. I'm sorry to keep making it all about me."

"Well, it was all about you," he started, and she closed her eyes tight and fisted her hand against his chest.

"But we can pretend otherwise," he corrected himself, expressionlessly. "If that's better for you."

She opened her eyes to stare at him, so gorgeous and so focused, there in her bed in the soft lamplight. God, he was beautiful. Just utterly beautiful, there and alive and in her bed and ... *there. I love you. I've always loved you.*

"Now why are you on the floor right now, Célie? You can't tell me you're *scared* of something with me right here?" Sheer incredulity in his tone, that there might be any fear she had that he couldn't kill with his pinky finger.

She tightened her arms on her knees again, foolish and stubborn. "It's all very well for you," she muttered. "Your fantasy was easy. An inflatable doll could have done that—"

Joss's lips tightened into a hard line, and his eyes blazed. He held up one finger, and that one gesture shut her up, her eyes widening. "Did you just say I treated you like an inflatable doll?"

"No! I just meant—*merde,* Joss, you know you're sex-starved, and that's the only reason you fixated on me! Your personal pin-up, you said. Anybody could have done! You just happened to focus on me!"

Joss's body did something she would have thought impossible—it got even harder. "That is the stupidest thing you've said yet," he said flatly, his lips thin. "I joined the Legion for you, and I did those five years for you, and if I focused my fantasies on you it was because *you're the person I always fantasized about, fucking hell, Célie!* Well the hell before you were even old enough for me to be doing that, and trust me, you were not my only damn option back then. And I'm pretty sure you aren't now, either. God damn it. My inflatable doll," he repeated bitterly, and threw himself onto his back on the bed, covering his eyes with his forearm.

Célie unfolded herself and knelt by the bed so that she could see his face again, stunned. "Don't be mad." She touched his chest.

He shifted his forearm just enough to glare at her. "What, you're the only person who gets to do that?"

"You never used to get mad at me before." Except a couple of times when he'd thought she'd done something stupidly dangerous. She felt completely disoriented by his anger, in fact.

"I was protecting you from me before, Célie. I was being your damn older brother, since your own was so crappy. I don't want to do that anymore. I want you to take all that I am."

"Oh," she breathed. That made her feel ... too full, overflowing, the thought of taking all that he was. But ... "I want that, too. That's exactly what I want."

"That's why I spent five years making myself into the best man I could, Célie. So when I asked you to do that, I wouldn't be ashamed."

Her eyes stung. "You ... you might be too big for me, Joss. I'm ... only me."

Joss touched her chin. "Well, look at that, you've managed to say something even stupider."

She frowned at him.

"Célie ... only you?"

Well ... she shrugged, embarrassed and annoyed. Sure, she was good with chocolate, but ... had he *looked* at himself, ever? "You could have, like, Gisele Bündchen now," she muttered hostilely. "Laetitia Casta."

He cupped her chin, fingers curving against her jaw, into her hair. "Where's my Célie? The girl who never puts herself down, who always has her chin up, defying the world to think less of her than who she is?"

Her eyes stung again.

"Besides, you know very well that you would punch Gisele Bündchen in the nose if she got near me."

Well ... yeah.

Joss smiled a little, tugging her gently closer. "And *think* of the lawsuit on that one. Her nose is probably insured for millions."

"Then she should keep it away from you," Célie muttered.

A leap of laughter in Joss's eyes. It still made pure joy light in her own heart, to see him laugh. On one elbow, he shifted forward to kiss her, slow and warm.

Oh.

The fact that *Joss Castel*, her hopeless crush, had just given her a casual, affectionate, possessive kiss kind of blew Célie's mind.

"You going to get up off that floor and get back in this bed and tell me why you were down there in the first place?" Joss's voice was so warm and firm. *Quit messing around, Célie.*

It was so exactly like Joss, such a familiar tone from when she was still a teenager.

He slid his hand around her back and urged her body toward the mattress.

She braced her hands against the edge to fight the pull, in a resurgence of panic. He stopped pulling and raised his eyebrows at her, waiting.

"It's all very well for you! Your fantasy was just ... just sex!" She knew better than to say the "inflatable doll" thing again. Joss got mad so rarely, she tended to respect it when he did. "But this is *my* fantasy. It's *hard*!"

"Célie, damn it." Joss abruptly picked her up and set her on the bed. She half sat, half knelt, awkward and stubborn, and he took her shoulders and forced her horizontal. "What's hard?" He propped himself above her to hold her eyes, exasperated.

"*This* is." She scowled at him, pissed off at her own ridiculousness and how he managed to make her even more ridiculous just by existing.

"Sleeping?"

"The cuddle!" she yelled.

His eyebrows went up again. "A ... cuddle?"

"Yes!"

"That's *hard*?"

"Not for you." She glared at him. "You just have to lie there."

He laughed, unexpectedly. It warmed her middle when he laughed, like drinking hot chocolate. "I guess you probably could have just lain there for my fantasy, too, Célie, but I appreciate it that you didn't." He grinned at her.

It was really not fair for him to grin. It made all her insides cozy and happy, as if she just wanted to hug him. As if this was real, as if it was going to work, as if they were *together.*

His fingers came up to sift gently through the feathered wings of her hair. "Why's it hard for you, sweetheart?"

"Because it's the thing I always dreamed about the most. The thing *I* fantasized every night, that you were here. It's what got *me* through. And I'm afraid if I believe in it, it will disappear. And then I'll never have it again." She closed her eyes a moment, ashamed and vulnerable and wishing she could hide under the sheet.

When she opened her eyes again, Joss's eyes were very intent. "You dreamed about me every night? Just about this? Me being here?"

"I tried not to," she muttered. "But ... it helped get me to sleep. It made me, you know ... fall asleep happy."

His eyes were somber. "I wish I had done some things differently. But I can't fix yesterday, Célie. I can only work on today and tomorrow." He shifted to the side and nestled her body in closer to his. "I can do this."

Breath moved through her, shaky and wanting, as his warmth wrapped around her. "You don't have to do anything," she whispered. "You just have to be there. That's all it takes for the cuddle."

"Seems as if I might be able to improve on it, beyond lying flat on my back to enjoy it." He nestled her more closely, turning her body so that her back was against his chest, his arm over her, his chin tucked against the top of her head, his body angling to envelope her in him without crushing her. "How about this?"

Her nose stung. "It's perfect."

"We have very different concepts of what is hard," he murmured to the top of her head. "This is the sweetest, easiest thing I have ever done, in my entire life."

"Is that bad?" Unease came back so quickly. "I know you thrive on challenge. You would never have gone off to the Legion, if you didn't need to seek out the most difficult challenges possible."

A little silence. "You don't trust me," he said suddenly, a note of realization. "It's not just that you're mad at me for before. You don't trust me now, not to let you down."

Of course she didn't! How could she? She scowled at the sheets in front of her.

He pressed a kiss to the top of her head. "I'm not going to go off to find another challenge, Célie. You're challenging enough just by existing."

"Hey."

"Shhhh." He jostled her gently, rocking her.

"I'm not as challenging as the Foreign Legion!"

"Maybe I have high standards for you. Maybe those are the challenge."

She frowned. That sounded far too close to the princess-on-a-glass-hill thing.

"It's not all about the challenge, Célie. You do that—you challenge me—but you do something else, too. You ... rest me."

Really? That made her feel so whole and centered and wonderful, to be his point of rest.

"Except that ... it's not that you're restful, exactly. Most of the time, you make me feel the opposite of rested. Full of energy. Wanting to do something, usually to you." He fell silent again.

Joss, searching for words. She waited, his quiet seriousness sinking into her as it always had, anchoring her. He made her bounce all over the place with energy and the need for his attention. And yet he was also the man she had curled up against to be able to fall asleep, in her head, night after night, for years. Before he even left, she would do that.

He closed his hand around hers and brought it behind her back, pressing it to his flat stomach. "You make me feel alive, down here."

Oh. Her fingers caressed that hard shield of muscle that protected all his soft essential organs.

"Sometimes it kicks up into a fire, and sometimes it's this low heat, but it's always what keeps me warm."

Her eyes prickled. She pulled his arm back around her, tucking his hand now against her belly, where it rode, firm and sure.

That warmth of him, the embrace, the sweetness, the happiness sank through her skin from his body stretching through her until it *became* her in a way that was terrifying. Because if this was her, and that happiness got taken away again, what *her* would there be left?

If so much solidity and security and warmth came from him, how precarious and vulnerable and cold would she feel when he was gone again?

"I can tell you a bedtime story," he murmured, his voice vibrating against her back.

"Mmm?"

"There once was a very young man who stood looking at tacky fake diamond rings in some stupid, low-class jewelry store window. Because he knew he had to leave, to become better, but ... there was this girl. And even though she didn't know it, and he shouldn't tell her, he really, really wanted her to promise to wait for him. He wanted it more than anything. But he hated how cheap those rings were so damn much, and he was so damn proud, and ... he couldn't. He just couldn't do it. He had to be able to offer her more."

A lone tear trembled over her lashes and snuck toward the mattress. “I would have been incandescent with joy, to wear your cheap fake diamond ring. People would have thought I was running around in sequins, so much happiness would have sparkled off me.”

“Yeah.” His arm tightened. “I know that now.”

She fell quiet. She could have said more—more regrets, more accusations, more ways their lives would have been happier, if only he had taken that step.

She let a slow, soft breath out, linked her fingers with his hand, and lifted it to her lips to kiss it.

“You’ve always sparkled to me, Célie.”

She nestled his hand close to her face as she let herself fall asleep.

Chapter 19

Joss rode with her to work and then gazed at her moped keys in some bemusement when she tossed them to him so he could use it during the day. She grinned. "It suits you."

"I think I need to get my own means of locomotion. Maybe a real motorcycle."

"I don't know. There's something to be said for having you squooshed up behind me on a moped," she said saucily.

His left eyebrow rose just a little, and heat washed through her, as she forgot how hilarious the vision of him on a moped was and remembered instead how tightly his hips fit against her butt.

"Didn't you always want a real motorcycle, Célie?"

She used to imagine herself all tough and sexy on some sleek, aggressive bike, yeah. Of course, that had been during her Goth period, when she was too young to legally drive one, only old enough to ride behind Joss if he ever fulfilled that fantasy of hers. She shrugged. "I've never passed my regular motorcycle license. This was what I could afford, when I first moved to Paris. And it suits me."

Except she still kind of regretted not getting it in pink. Maybe it was time for a new one. With flower decals.

He smiled. "Like your apartment," he teased. "That's all bed."

"It's a great apartment!" she declared, over her flush. "If you stand on tiptoe on the balcony railing, you can see a tip of the Eiffel Tower."

"Don't stand up on tiptoe on the railing unless I'm holding on to your waist." Joss put his hands on her waist to demonstrate and pulled her in for a kiss. "Ever think about getting a bigger one?"

"Apartments aren't cheap in Paris, Joss."

"Plus, you have such a great neighborhood. And only a couple of blocks away from that park."

She couldn't quite interpret the satisfaction in his eyes, like he was patting himself on the back. Maybe he was still telling himself he'd done the right thing in leaving, since she'd clearly done so well?

"You really are impossible, you know," she told him.

"So are you," Joss said. "Good thing I can do the impossible." He bent and kissed her, and her entire body lit with delight, to be kissed good-bye by him in the morning. It made the whole day turn into something marvelous, as if she'd been plodding her way through a gray morning, still yawning, and all of a sudden the sun lifted over the horizon in a burst of gold just as a bakery door opened and spilled the scent of fresh bread all over her. This golden, warm magic of his kiss.

He turned her and used both hands on her butt to push her firmly toward the glass doors. "Now go, before you're late."

***

Dom was late, for him, meaning Célie and Amand both arrived first. It also meant something else about Dom's private life, and while Célie preferred not to get a *detailed* picture, she nevertheless found it adorable. The man was kind of disgustingly happy these days.

So was she.

How she'd managed to get in before Dom considering the way she had spent her morning was a mystery to her.

Too full of herself to behave, she hopped up to sit on one of the marble counters so that she could grin at Dom as he came up the stairs and entered the *laboratoire*.

Dom stopped, looked at her butt on his counters, looked at her, and put his hands on his hips and raised an eyebrow.

Célie grinned and stuck her tongue out at him.

Dom sighed and rubbed his hands through his hair. "Why me? I can guarantee Sylvain does not have to put up with this shit."

"Aww," Célie cooed. "Are you jealous of Sylvain?"

Dom dropped his hands and glared at her.

She laughed, entirely full of herself.

Dom's eyes narrowed. "*Bordel de* ... I'm going to sock that *salaud* right on the nose. What are you, a damn pushover?"

Célie frowned at him. "You know, you didn't have to put it quite that way." She brought out the J-word. "And Jaime said no fighting. So you cannot hit Joss." She was pretty sure that no matter what her own personal J-word claimed about peaceful resolutions, he didn't have any qualms about violence, at least not where Dom was concerned. She didn't want to get anyone killed.

Dom sighed heavily, looking at his fist wistfully.

Célie grinned again involuntarily. "Can I tell you something?"

Dom looked wary. "Probably not."

"You're such a good guy."

Dom's jaw dropped. He took a step back, horrified.

"You made all the difference to me, giving me this safe, happy space, where I could grow big and, and"—she waved her arms wide to try to encompass it—"flourish."

Dom backed toward his tiny office, his expression one of confounded panic. "I've got to do some paperwork," he mumbled, grasping for the doorknob behind him.

"So thank you!" Célie called. "I appreciate you trying to look after me now!"

He dove inside. "Get to work!" his deep voice bellowed from his hiding spot. "And wipe that damn counter off!"

Célie grinned and hopped down. It was going to be a great day.

***

God, it felt good to use his muscles. What a fantastic day. Joss had always enjoyed building things, fixing things. Motorcycles and cars, as a mechanic before he joined the Legion. Bridges in Central Africa with mosquitoes buzzing all around, on humanitarian missions. Even just setting to and building their base, when all the other military forces around them were sleeping in miserable conditions waiting for their better conditions to drop out of the sky.

But this ... there was something about this. Building their *home*. Their place.

God, Célie was going to love this. It made him want to work even harder and faster, like a guy who just had to figure out a way to make Christmas come sooner, so he could see her face light up when he showed her his fantastic present.

We can't get much more real and together than a shared apartment. They'd be fighting over caps on the toothpaste and everything.

He grinned at the thought. Well, probably not. He'd probably just do whatever Célie wanted on that one. Save trouble. But he'd probably manage to do *something* that drove Célie crazy. And he'd get to haul her to him when she put her hands on her hips and narrowed her eyes at him, and he'd kiss her and drive her even crazier ...

He rolled his shoulders, after hauling the last of the crap down the six floors that were what gave it such a great view. It had been kind of ... weird to do it entirely by himself. Not that he minded—he'd done a lot more work than that in a day—but he'd gotten so used to having other men around him, working, too. The solidarity of it, the tempers and the humor and just the company. Doing things together.

Working on such a big job by himself was ... well, to be honest, fucking lonely.

But he'd get used to it. A man could handle anything he set his mind to. He checked his watch.

His first goal was to get the bathroom redone, because until he could insure uninterrupted access to facilities, he was going to be staying at a hotel or—hopefully—crashing at Célie's place. There was definitely something to be said for a space so little you couldn't help falling onto the bed.

Oh, yeah. Over and over and over. His body felt so damn good today, he was surprised his dick wasn't producing an aura of golden light around him for all to see.

He grinned, looking around to make up his mind what to attack next. The shower wouldn't be delivered until tomorrow, and he had some appointments this afternoon.

A couple more hours before he needed to clean up for those.

He started tearing out the old cabinets. He had a busy day ahead of him, getting started on his new life.

***

Joss sat still and big in Jaime's office in the Sixth. It was part of a floor of offices labeled *Corey* on the elevator button. His body felt restless. The morning's work in the apartment had barely made a dent in his energy. In the Legion, he'd be taking advantage of this rare opportunity to rest, but he didn't have anything now to rest up *for.* When he'd passed a construction site on the walk over here, men hauling down great sacks of stone from some top-floor apartment, it had been all he could do not to strip off his shirt and ask to help.

It kind of looked like more fun, working with them, than working on the apartment by himself.

He missed the physicality of his life, and he missed the camaraderie, too. Strong men, working hard together, taking risks together. Missed knowing that three words *A moi, Legion!* would bring every Legionnaire in earshot running to join in his fight.

"So your background checks out," Jaime said.

Joss raised his eyebrows a little. "The Legion gave you information on me?" What minister of France had they held hostage and tortured?

Jaime smiled faintly. "Hardly. But we were able to confirm that you were actually in it, as you said, and not in prison for the past five years."

Fair enough. Joss waited.

"I'm reticent toward private military companies," Jaime said.

Well, hell. Yeah. Who wouldn't be?

"But given the scale of our operations, and the detriment to Corey when local wars affect the cacao supply, we're under some pressure to employ at least some forces to protect our farmers. I resisted that in the past, but riding around on a moped trying to do good didn't work out that well for me."

Joss's eyebrows went up a little. He studied the slender, freckled woman across from him. "You rode around on a moped trying to create world peace or something?"

Jaime opened a hand wryly.

"Hell. That was stu—" He caught himself. Maybe she already knew that was stupid.

"At any rate, at this point we accept that we probably need to work with at least some private security forces," Jaime said.

"No," Joss said.

She paused. From the look on her face, people must not say no to her job offers all that often.

"I'm not interested in being a mercenary. Sorry. I'd rather have stayed in the Legion."

Jaime shook her head. "I wouldn't do that to Célie. I told you I was a friend of hers."

He was not entirely sure how female friendships worked. His past five years' experience was exclusively male—male solidarity, male enmity. He hadn't been the type to go to any of the brothels that always sprang up around military bases, particularly Legion ones now that the Legion no longer provided a brothel itself. Plus, he'd promised himself to Célie even if she didn't know it, so the only females he'd even chatted with in a friendly way had been the ones who worked the bars and cafés the Legionnaires frequented. Those women had seemed pretty isolated in a world of men, to him. Before that, Célie's teenage friends had never impressed him that much—catty, mostly, and often trying to hit on him when Célie's back was turned. But he'd liked Célie's friends the night before.

And Jaime Corey seemed ... kind of a good person for Célie to have at her back, actually.

"What I would like to have is an advisor," Jaime said. "Someone who can accurately assess a military situation and what it means when a country sends in this regiment or that one, but also someone who can assess the PMCs and help me work with them. Have you ever heard women complain about how mechanics and car salesmen treat women much worse than they treat other men? Well, that's nothing compared to how private military and security forces treat women. But they won't lie to *you*, a Legionnaire. They'd respect *you*."

"They should. Most of the ones I met couldn't survive a day in the Legion."

"Well, we can't hire the Legion," Jaime said wryly.

Joss gave her a dark, ironic glance. He'd had a cynical streak about politics even before he spent the past five years surrounded by profoundly cynical men—cynicism being that protective armor for, or perhaps the disillusioned flip side of, the crazy romanticism that would lead a man to join the Legion in the first place—and he had some pretty strong thoughts about how the billionaires in the world affected where he was deployed and what mud he was crawling through while they drank champagne or whatever the hell billionaires did while other men died for them.

"Well, it involves a lot of politics," Jaime corrected herself dryly. "It's hard to control. And it takes a really long time to get anything to happen. My dad always says getting what you want through the political system is like trying to thread a needle wearing boxing gloves. He says about the only good it does is that at least you're got something useful on your hands when you get ready to smack someone in the head. In other words, it's not really efficient or effective."

"That must be terrible for you," Joss said expressionlessly. "To have so much trouble perverting a democratic system to your ends." Goddamn billionaires.

Jaime paused a second. Then smiled. "I can't wait to introduce you to my father. Don't worry, he loves taking the gloves off with someone who can actually fight him."

Joss avoided rolling his eyes. That was one of the many things Legionnaire training came in handy for—control of expression.

"That." Jaime pointed at him. "That's what I need. Someone who can handle tough, strong men and not take any crap off them and make sure that *we*, Corey, and particularly *me*, my foundation, only use security forces that are doing the right thing."

"What kind of work are you doing? Besides exploiting cocoa farmers?"

A little pause. Jaime smiled again. "You know how I don't know nearly enough about the military to be hiring a company? You may not know nearly as much as you think about what we do, either."

"I know," Joss said. "I've never even tried caviar."

Jaime laughed. "We're working really hard to support and further the development of good, equitable, nonexploitative conditions on all cacao farms. Myself, I'm kind of an idealist, I guess, but my father, who claims to be a hardheaded pragmatist, will tell you it's in our own best interests, the same way it's in our interests to be moving heaven and earth to find a way to stop frosty pod rot. If you want a discussion with someone who can defend the capitalist system, you're probably better off with a different Corey. But let's just say we'd like not only our intentions but our actual actions to be good. A positive force in cocoa regions."

Fine, he probably should shut up now with the sarcastic comments. At least they were trying. That whole thing about manipulating the political system to get the military to serve the billionaires of the world had really gotten his back up.

"So would you be interested?" Jaime said. "You'd be based in Paris, but the position would involve a fair amount of travel, particularly to West Africa right now, but also somewhat to South America. We also work in the Pacific, but shouldn't need any military advising there. Your role might eventually develop to go beyond advising to making hiring decisions and solving any issue you see, but you won't be acting as a security force yourself. Although this is a new position we're creating, so you'd need to have the initiative and strength of character to form it into whatever would be the most effective."

That last sentence might have clinched the deal. He liked the idea of having control over his role, after five years in the Legion, when a man had to shut his mouth and obey orders, however insane. He'd achieved the rank of sergeant in his quest to have more power over his choices. But the military meant there was always someone higher in command. Here, he would make calls. Guide what happened.

"For a starting salary, we were looking at ..." Jaime said, and Joss went blank at the figure she named.

So that was why billionaires always got what they wanted. He'd be earning more in a month than he ever had in a whole year as a Legionnaire or a beginning mechanic in a poor suburb of Paris.

"Plus, bonuses and benefits, of course. Besides the benefits the French government requires we give here, there's a great educational benefit—all tuition paid for your kids at any accredited university in the U.S."

That was a weird benefit. He could pay for a complete education in France with only two weeks of the salary she had just named.

"And you're vested after only a year in your stock options, and then we'll contribute the equivalent of 13.6 percent of your salary into your private retirement funds as long as you put in three percent, and you get to keep that, no matter when you leave."

Joss stared at her. "I don't, ah, have kids." Good lord, *retirement*? He wanted to protest that he was only twenty-six, that he couldn't think that far ahead yet—that part of his brain hadn't turned on. And yet suddenly his own solidity struck him—that he'd become a *man*, someone who could raise kids, who could see them through to a successful adulthood and provide them an education, and ... he'd been hit by some pretty hard blows in the past five years, but this one took a minute to absorb. Struck by *himself*, the sheer mass of who he was now.

He'd gone into the Legion to create a much greater worth out of himself.

Apparently that had been successful.

What in the world did a man do with that much money? Ten times what he'd ever earned before. Take Célie on a nice trip somewhere she'd been dreaming of going? What else?

A motorcycle. A really nice motorcycle. Something he could soup up and customize and ... his palms itched with the desire to feel the hand grips.

"Remember, this is just a starting salary," Jaime said. "But I could go ten percent higher."

Joss didn't blink. Damn, but that Legionnaire training in a neutral expression was coming in handy. Apparently she'd misread his blank face as being unimpressed by the salary offer.

"Another ten percent," he said thoughtfully. "If you can push it to twenty, I think I might be tempted."

Jaime gazed at him a moment. And smiled again. "You know, you're going to do all right for yourself, Joss. And for your family."

He didn't have a family, he almost pointed out again. But he didn't say it, because ... it settled in him solid and centered, that he was the very opposite of a loser, now. He'd turned around his entire life and the lives of anyone in his care. He could even imagine how a loft bed would fit in that second room in the new apartment to maximize the kid's play space. He could kind of even imagine what a kid might *look* like, with Célie's brown eyes and vivid smile and ...

Whoa. This was getting scary.

"Twenty it is," Jaime said, and he kept his expression neutrally unimpressed, as if they were talking about the bare minimum a man like him could be expected to work for.

Jaime's smile deepened. "I should have made you negotiate salary with my dad or my sister. They're better at this game than I am."

"It's a game?" A man's salary? His life? "I might find being involved with billionaires a little bit challenging sometimes."

Jaime smiled wryly. "Don't worry, I find it challenging, too."

Chapter 20

"He's got flowers," Zoe hissed, poking Célie in the ribs. With her vintage black cat's-eye glasses and her ruler-straight brown hair pulled back in a ruthlessly smooth bun, Zoe looked as if she should be shushing people in a library, not mocking her chef chocolatier. Either looks were very deceiving, or Célie's and Amand's irreverence had worn off on her far too quickly. "No, Célie, I swear."

"He does," Amand called from where he was stirring caramel. "I can see them from here."

Célie abandoned the chocolate test batch she was tempering on the marble counter to peek through the window.

"See?" Zoe pointed. "He's trying to hide them, but you can see a couple peek out by his hips."

"I've got a good angle on them from here," Amand called, his loud voice mercilessly exposing Célie's private life to the whole *laboratoire*. Which, fine, *might* very well be payback for all the ways she had twitted Dom and Amand and everyone else about their dating lives, but still ...

Okay, fine, she liked it. But it made her blush.

She hugged herself, entirely baffled by how much happiness kept surging up in her. What did she *do* with it all? She'd always thought of herself as a happy person—well, a *tough* happy person who could wear black leather and cut aggressively through Paris traffic on the back of a ... not-pink moped—but this happiness was so, so ... bubbly. It was like being a bottle of champagne.

Dreams fizzed when they were coming true.

She turned back to her chocolate before she had to start the tempering all over. Joss would have to wait.

It drove her completely bonkers to wait. She paced, she bounced, she fidgeted. But Joss always stood patiently for her.

As if he would be there forever.

A very tricky, treacherous thing for him to do. She scowled at the ganache. But then she remembered his kiss good-bye that morning, and the scowl softened so as to be ready for more kissing. *I would wait more than five years for you.*

"I think they might be roses!" Amand called again across the whole damn *laboratoire*.

Heat trembled across her cheeks. No one in her whole life had ever brought her flowers. Certainly Joss hadn't. It would totally have blown his cover as her big brother's friend.

And roses?

He had brought her roses?

Across from her, Zoe gave her an amused-librarian look over her glasses and set a bowl of *praliné* on the scale. Célie looked down. In the chocolate Célie was supposed to be tempering, some idiot had written *Joss* and signed it with a graceful heart.

She sucked the chocolate off her guilty finger, flushing hot, and quickly scraped up the rest of the chocolate and finished the tempering. Good thing this chocolate was just for a small test batch and not for customers.

When she was ready to go, she hesitated over the selection of chocolates loose on the wire racks, unable to think which nine to choose for him. Not the bitter dark. Her fingertips flicked it away uneasily. There was the new idea she'd played with today, with just this hint of heat blushing through it so that the bite of it lingered on one's tongue as the chocolate melted. She and Dom had had an argument about it—whether anyone wanted anything but the chocolate flavor to linger on his tongue.

Or there was this ridiculous soft, sweet one, that had made Dom roll his eyes and object to having it in his cases, this softest, sweetest chocolate that didn't have a tough darkness in its entire chocolate being, an inexplicable experiment of hers that day ...

She finally put them side by side, to trick the palate—keep it guessing, unable to figure out what was coming next.

But *then*, she added the ones she knew already to be his favorites—the mint and the coffee and the plain dark, but not the extra bitter dark. She left that one on the wire rack.

"Uh-oh," Zoe said.

"Oh, no," Amand said.

"Where's Jaime?" Zoe asked.

Célie lunged back to the window. Dom was crossing the street. Joss straightened away from the wall at his approach, his hands loose and easy, his body ready for action. "Oh, crap," Célie said. And Jaime wasn't here. "Damn it, that can't be good."

She spun to run out of the *laboratoire*.

***

Joss felt a kick of hungry pleasure when he saw Dom Richard crossing the street to him, big and dark. That eagerness for aggressive action was immediately followed by resignation.

It was going to be up to him not to fight that bastard, wasn't it? To use the control and discipline and self-confidence he had developed in five years in one of the most elite regiments in the world to just refuse the fight.

Too many things on the line—Célie's job, his own new position and all it meant for them.

Damn. Sometimes it seemed as if a man had to spend his whole damn life exercising self-control over his aggressive urges.

The big, black-haired man stopped with a couple of meters still between them, clearly feeling that same frustrated buck of his aggressive tendencies against his own self-control. "You took a job with my wife?"

Joss's fingertips curled restlessly into his palms. This damn bastard had taken his place as Célie's hero. "If you want a woman to be your wife, I'm pretty sure you have to marry her. Little tip I learned from Célie last night."

Dom glared at him.

Joss smiled. "If you have the nerve."

Dom's eyes narrowed. "*You* are criticizing *me* for not having the nerve to go after the woman I want?"

Joss's smile pressed out. "You know, I'm getting pretty damn sick of having five years in the Foreign Legion dismissed as lack of nerve. I went after the woman I want. It just took me a while to get up to the standard I wanted for her."

The aggression eased unexpectedly out of Dom's stance. "They don't really get that, do they?" Dom glanced at the ring on his left hand. Joss couldn't quite figure that ring out. It looked like a wedding ring to him, but the two were only engaged? "That we might want to make sure we're worth them, before we ask for them."

Joss winced at the thought of trying to articulate that again to Célie and about what her reaction would be if he did. "God, it pisses them off," he muttered, heartfelt.

For a second, the two men exchanged a glance of complete understanding. That glance didn't feel so weird to Joss, after five years with tough men who fought each other when their great and incompatible prides clashed, but who fought side by side more often, and then went and played rugby to let off steam. But he had the impression that Dom found that moment of male understanding far more difficult to process.

Joss had known men like that, too, though. Men who had good reasons for never trusting other men near them, and who, when they came into the Legion, had to overcome their hostility toward other powerful males in order to form a unit.

"Women are funny," Dom said uneasily. "They don't really make that much sense."

Joss kept his lips sealed. No one was trapping *him* into saying anything sexist that Célie might later be pissed off about. No way.

"They're, like, this big." Dom brought his hand to a couple of centimeters below his shoulder. "And yet they want to go and trust a man just the way he is. That's so stupid."

Joss gave that some thought. "Not with me it isn't," he realized slowly. "Célie can trust me."

The moment of détente was broken. Dom's jaw set. "You seem very sure of that."

Joss nodded.

"You already hurt her once," Dom said grimly. "You're so sure you won't do it again?"

Joss hesitated. "I wouldn't do it on purpose. But ... doesn't life hurt sometimes?" He'd gone through a shit-hell of pain in the Legion. And ... Jaime Corey had talked about retirement and taking care of his *family*, and didn't creating a family hurt the hell out of the woman creating it, for example? His mind shied away from thoughts of childbirth, though, before he could break out in a cold sweat.

Dom's expression grew more menacing. "What hurts are you planning to inflict on her?"

Joss put a hand to his stomach. "Look, can we *not* keep harping on the childbirth thing right now? I'm only twenty-six!"

Dom blinked. And then that menacing expression disappeared before the flash of a grin, quickly contained. "You, ah ... got something on your mind?"

Joss rubbed his abs. "No," he said firmly. "I don't. This is all *very* premature. Célie's only twenty-three."

Dom's grin escaped again, and he firmly bit it back in favor of a menacing glare. "I meant did you plan to dump her and break her heart again?"

"I didn't mean to do it the first time," Joss said between his teeth. "I thought—it was just a teenage crush! I didn't know she..." ... *would keep existing when I wasn't there, and that I would make such a hole in that existence.* "I was stupid, okay?"

"How smart are you now?"

"Now," Joss said flatly, "I'm the man I need to be. To be worth her."

Dom stared at him. "What, you think your job is *done*? At twenty-six? That you don't have any growing left to do, to be as big as she needs?"

Joss hesitated.

"If you're not going to dump her, you're asking her to commit her fucking life to you! And you don't think that will require you to get any better, ever? Or maybe even day by day?"

Joss stared at him. He rubbed the buzzed hair at the back of his head, trying to think. "I—"

"Grow the fuck up!" Dom said.

Grow up? After all the things he'd done to become a man?

Joss's teeth bared. It took a lot to push him to rage. In the first months of Legion training, they tried to push every button a man could possibly have, and that man had to learn how not to break for it. But this attack on his potential worthiness of Célie surged rage all through him. "*I know I'll always have to work to be the best for her!* I like always striving to be my best."

Dom scowled at him, but that scowl slowly eased. "You might have to do something else for her besides strive to be your best," he said slowly, as if he was trying to digest his own words even as he produced them. "You might have to adapt to what *she* needs from you. Which might be something different."

Joss drew back in visceral rejection. "Something less than my best?"

"Something ... different," Dom said slowly. He looked down at that ring on his finger, eyebrows drawn together.

Joss frowned, disturbed in ways he couldn't explain. As if parts of him he'd thought he'd made solid were melting under a sneak attack of rain.

"Talk to her," Dom said. "See what she says she needs from you." He rubbed the ring on his finger.

Oh, crap. Talk to her. What if she said what she needed wasn't what Joss knew how to give?

"You ever had sex with Célie?" Joss challenged abruptly.

"What?" Dom jerked back, his expression crunching as if Joss had asked if he'd eaten worms. "*No.* She works for me, *merde.* What the hell?"

"You wanted to, though, didn't you?"

Dom shook his head. "Trust me, I didn't go out with women like her before I met Jaime. She's more like a … I don't know … a kid sister? A really impudent kid sister." He looked grumpy. "A *brat* of a kid sister."

Joss's fists tightened. "*I was her big brother.* Not you."

"Well, that would make you pretty fucking incestuous, wouldn't it? You're not her big brother when you can't even look at her without thinking about sex. When you've got it so bad you think every other man must obsess the same way. I'll give you credit for trying to do the honorable thing by her, though." An odd expression crossed Dom's face. "Honor … and fidelity," he said thoughtfully.

Honneur, fidélité. Just the reference to the Legion motto tightened Joss's belly, as if he'd heard a call to arms.

"Well, hell," Dom said slowly. "You really are a damn knight, aren't you? *That's* why you went into the Legion. It spoke to everything you were."

Everything he wanted to be, Joss would have said, rather than what he already was back then, but before he could argue, the doors on the other side of the street slid open, and Célie ran straight toward them without even glancing for traffic.

Joss jerked spasmodically toward her, his heart slamming, and then caught himself. *Fuck*, he needed to get over that reaction.

He found Dom giving him an odd look, as he took a deep breath and shoved the flowers behind his back before she spotted them. "No snipers here," Dom said quietly. "She's been safe."

Right. Safe with Dominique Richard. He struggled with it, his fist clenching on the roses behind his back. But ... she really was happy. Safe. He really did owe that to the fact that Dom Richard had been a good guy. To the fact that when Joss, at twenty-one, had been clueless as to the effects his actions might have on Célie, at least one other man in the world had been decent and honorable, too.

"Thanks," he said suddenly, low. "Thanks for that."

Dom took his own long breath, releasing it slowly out. "So you'll help keep my wife safe for me, too, then, is that it?"

"Yeah," Joss said quietly. "I will."

The two men faced each other.

"Although that thing about calling her your wife will work better if you actually marry her," Joss couldn't resist adding as he lifted his hand.

"Stop!" Célie yelled, throwing herself toward the space between them, just as their hands met. She bounced against the solid clasp of their hands. "Don't—fight." She grabbed both their arms, her words fumbling as she looked down at their steady grip. She looked back up, confused. "Are you two fighting?"

"Just working some things out." Joss loosed Dom's hand.

Dom raised his eyebrow at Célie. "What were you going to do to stop us if we were? Stamp your foot?"

Célie stuck her tongue out at him. "Take a picture and send it to Jaime."

Dom's eyes narrowed. "Somebody wants to lose her day off tomorrow, doesn't she?"

"Somebody wants me to form a union and organize a strike."

Dom sighed and gazed heavenward a moment, muttering something that sounded suspiciously like, "Why me?"

Célie grinned, and he rolled his eyes and stomped back toward the shop, grumbling.

***

Célie turned toward Joss, her grin fading slowly before solemnity. She stared up at him, again stuck in that choice—between kisses on each cheek, as if he was still the big brother-friend who looked after her, and a kiss on the lips, and all that meant.

"Célie," he said quietly, and her name shivered through her. He had a way of saying it as if it encapsulated her whole existence and reaffirmed it.

Which was why life hurt so much when that affirmation disappeared and you had to remember how to affirm *yourself*.

"Joss," she said defiantly. She'd like to see his name from her lips have as much power over *him*.

Oh, wait. Wasn't she the first person to say it in five years? The person he had sought out to be the first to say it? Maybe it did have power over him.

"What was that all about?" she demanded. "You and Dom?"

He shook his head and shrugged a little. "Just working a few things out," he repeated. Joss's communication skills drove her completely nuts sometimes.

Like that evening when he had kissed her good-bye very slowly on each cheek, four times instead of two, and then stood a long time looking down at her, and lifted his hand to cup her cheek, and tugged her hair. And *she'd* thought that expression in his eyes meant he was falling for her, waking up to the idea of her as something more than a friend, and she'd gone to sleep hugging herself in hopeful excitement. And the next morning, she found out it was instead his way of saying, *Good-bye, I'm off to join the Foreign Legion.*

He lifted a hand and rubbed a firm thumb over her cheek, then up over her eyebrow. His thumb left a path of heat over her skin and woke all the other heat trails he had left on her body the night before, until she felt as if an infrared camera would pick out the pattern of his hands on her. He brought his thumb to his mouth and slowly sucked it, his eyes holding hers. Her brain melted. "What's the flavor of that chocolate, Célie? The chocolate that gets stuck on your skin?"

"It's—it's probably—it—that is, it might be—" What had she been working on today?

He bent his head and brought his lips to just under the curve of her jaw, parting them to suck gently and thoroughly.

Her lips fumbled and stopped working. Her head fell back.

He smiled, rubbing the moist spot on her throat with his thumb as he lifted his head. "I think it tastes a little bit like you. Hot. Spicy. Sweet."

She stared up at him, blind to everything but the green in his eyes and the lingering sensation of his lips sucking her skin.

His thumb trailed over her chin. "You know how I'm always the quiet one, and you're always the one who talks? You don't know how much I like flipping that around, just by doing this."

She swallowed, and his palm rode gently against the motion of her throat.

"I brought you something." He pulled his hand out from behind his back to show the sweetest, most beautiful bouquet of roses—soft pink and variegated red and white, carefully arranged by one of the many expert florists who filled the Paris streets. "You can have it if you give me a kiss, like my girlfriend. Remember how we're dating?"

Every single other bouquet Célie had ever held in her hands, she had bought for herself, on the way home from work. She reached for it, forgetting the kiss, and found herself blocked by the box of chocolates she held. "I brought you something, too." She lifted it to him.

"In that case, maybe I'm the one who owes you a kiss." He bent his head again, and she parted her lips for him, so utterly, terrifyingly happy at the heat of his, at the reality of this fantasy, that she felt lost in it.

He got lost, too, his arm sliding around her, the bouquet pressing against her back as he deepened the kiss, until a wolf whistle sounded from one of the casement windows above. Joss lifted his head and raised an eyebrow in the direction of the window, and Célie twisted around to try the extra-mean-Foreign Legion look on Amand.

Amand laughed and blew her a kiss. Then his expression grew just a tad more careful, and he withdrew.

Célie twisted back toward Joss, gazing at him suspiciously. "Don't threaten my friends."

"What?" Joss asked, surprised. "I only looked at him."

She narrowed her eyes and tried to give him that Legionnaire look.

"God, you're cute." He pressed the bouquet into her hand, taking the chocolate box. "Let's trade."

So Célie found herself gazing down at the sweetest, most beautiful, most romantic bouquet, and her lips trembled again.

"Do you like them? There were so many beautiful ones I had a hard time making up my mind. All those flowers," Joss said, rather wonderingly.

She stroked the flowers, thinking of Joss without chocolates, without softness, for five years. "Not so many flowers in the Foreign Legion?"

He shook his head.

"Tell me about it." She took his hand as they walked toward her moped. Dom's big black motorbike was parked beside it, and somebody had parked another aggressive, built-for-speed motorcycle on the other side, but her little moped was refusing to be intimidated.

"Not sure what to tell. It was … challenging. And interesting. And sometimes hideously boring." He fell silent. "Tough a few times, too," he finally allowed.

She waited, but by the time they got to her moped, it was pretty obvious he wasn't going to elaborate.

"Joss!"

He shrugged.

"Where were you posted?"

"Afghanistan, quite a bit. Mali." He shrugged again.

She stood by her moped, waiting.

He ate a chocolate, his lips softening around the flavor.

"Joss!"

"Ah, *this* is where you got that chocolate on your skin." His gaze moved over her face and lingered on her lips. "There's a kick to it."

She put her hands on her hips. "You never, ever talk to me."

He studied her that way he always had when he wasn't going to let her get away with any melodramatic bullshit. "Never, Célie?"

See? And right there, she remembered all the times they'd talked, all the times she'd bounced around him while he sat on a wall listening to her and occasionally sharing something quiet and true about his own thoughts. "Not about anything important!" she said defiantly.

Hazel eyes just held hers, stubborn and green and gold. "None of those things were important to you?"

Darn it! Joss always did that to her. Won arguments just by highlighting the truth and putting her on the spot with it. "You didn't tell me you were thinking about joining the Foreign Legion!"

"Nobody ever tells his family and friends he's going to join the Foreign Legion. Too damn independent-minded and proud, I guess. Plus, you can't do something like that, if you give someone you care about the chance to talk you out of it."

"You think I could have talked you out of it?" Célie immediately fantasized a time machine, just jumping into it and catching Joss before he stepped onto the train south and ...

"You would have cried. I always wanted to hit someone when you cried."

She gaped at him. "Oh, so it's fine if you're making me cry *by myself behind my bed* but not if you have to see it?"

His gaze lowered.

She knuckled her forehead. "I'm sorry. I'm sorry. I know I have to let that go." She rested her hand on his chest, taking a deep breath.

He covered her hand with his. "I didn't ... imagine any of that, when I was thinking about it. I imagined me coming home covered in glory, that kind of thing. I guess you're right that despite how well I thought I knew you, I never really imagined what it was like for you at all."

Her lips twisted, this rueful blend of pain and a genuine desire to forgive.

His fingers tightened gently over hers. "And you imagined what it was like for me all the time, didn't you?"

She shrugged, her mouth turning down.

He lifted her hand to his lips and kissed her palm.

Oh.

Oh.

The incredible sweetness of that.

"But I don't really know what it was like," she whispered. "I can see a little bit of it." Her fingers traced lightly over his biceps, the muscles of his forearms, his ridged abs. He'd always been in great shape, always determined to be one of the strongest guys in their *cité*, but he was so much harder now, with this mean leanness to all that muscled strength, as if he hadn't always gotten enough food to support all the effort his body was making.

Her fingers drifted back up to graze against the hardness of his face, the way his lips defaulted to this firm, you-can't-read-me line whenever he wasn't actively smiling at her. "But I don't really know. Was it brutal?"

"Sometimes."

She gazed up at him.

He gazed back, somewhere between stubborn and helpless. "Célie. I don't even know where to start."

"Start with the diamond ring. Start with when you didn't buy that and walked away. What happened next?"

He was silent another moment. "Right here? Or can we go somewhere more comfortable?"

"A park? The Seine?"

A tiny pause. "Sure."

Her face flamed as she thought about what other option he must have been considering—her apartment that was *all bed*. He lifted a thumb and stroked the blush gently, maybe a tiny touch of color in his cheeks, too.

He pulled her keys out of his pocket and held them up by a single key, around which he wrapped her fingers when he handed them to her. She started to put it in the ignition of her moped, and it didn't fit.

She looked down at it, puzzled. That didn't look like one of her keys. She looked back up at Joss, who was smiling.

"I got you a present."

She stopped smiling. A present that involved a *key*?

"You know how you always wanted to drive my motorcycle, but I wouldn't let you, because you were too young?"

"You wouldn't even let me ride behind you, most of the time."

"That was for an entirely different reason. It kind of got to me, having you squeeze up behind me and wrap your arms around me to hold on."

So he'd only let her ride with him if it was either that or ride behind Ludo or another of his friends. He'd *never* wanted her to ride behind any of them. Ludo was reckless as hell.

"Well." Joss patted the seat of the aggressive-looking motorcycle parked beside her moped. "I wanted to make up for that."

Good lord, that bike was for *her*? She stared at the beautiful machine, all muscle and dark attitude. Part of her leapt in excitement, as if she was some teenager whose parents had given her a car. But she hadn't had that kind of parents—she hadn't had a dad at all—and part of her thought, *But he's not my parent.*

And ... and I bought that moped for myself. With my own money, from my own achievements, to create my own independence.

When I had no one to count on but me.

"You got me a motorcycle?"

"Like it?" Joss looked so pleased with himself.

She rested her hand on the seat of her moped. She didn't want to throw his gift back in his face. But, but ... "I don't have a license for a motorcycle."

"I'll pay for the courses. It's part of the present."

"I can afford the courses," she said, a little indignant. She could afford a motorcycle, too, these days. It was just that she'd gotten attached to her little moped. It was cute, and it made her feel cheerful, and she'd always been able to count on it.

"It's a present, Célie." Joss reached out and caught her hand, bringing it to rest on that black leather seat. "I want to do it for you. I wasn't there to help you as you set out, just as you said."

Had she said that? She wasn't sure that was quite what she had *meant*. Or it certainly wasn't what she meant now, at twenty-three, grown-up and independent. "I was trying to say something about mutual help, Joss. Doing things together."

Like ... shopping for a motorcycle. Or deciding on the purchase of one.

Of course, they *weren't* married or even living together and had barely started dating. As when he had left to join the Legion without talking to her about it, it wasn't as if he *owed* her any input into his decisions.

No matter how much they affected her?

"Not just me clinging to you," she said.

"So you won't be clinging on behind me." Joss pushed her hand, still holding the keys, toward the ignition. "You'll be driving yourself."

Right. It was a really nice present. Generous, special. Big. Kind of a guy thing to do, really—to give her a beautiful muscle machine, convinced that was the best present any human on the planet could ever want. And she always had liked motorcycles, as he knew.

"Didn't *you* need a motorcycle?" she asked.

He shrugged. "I can't drive two at once. I wanted to get you one first."

Aww. Wow. Joss loved motorcycles. He rebuilt them. He loved the speed and power and control. And the first bike he bought, once he was free of the Legion, hadn't been for himself but for her?

Her heart melted. No man she had ever met would have been willing to get his girlfriend an impressive muscle machine in priority over himself. The sweetness of it. Her fingers stroked over the leather seat.

"You don't like it."

She looked up quickly. Joss's face had fallen so low, but at her glance, he immediately schooled it into that neutral expression again.

"Yes, I do!" she said quickly.

He just looked at her, not buying it, his mouth that firm *I-can-take-anything* line.

"It's gorgeous. Wow, Joss."

He searched her face.

"It's a *beast*," she said with delight. "All sleek and aggressive. Driving this thing must be amazing."

Except that she really didn't want to give up her moped and change into that girl again. The one who depended on him.

He started to smile a little bit. "It is. I tested it out. You're going to love it."

"I'm sure I will!" And she was sure. She'd have liked to be involved in the decision, but ... she could kind of get used to the idea of herself, all sleek and sexy on a bike instead of cute and determined on a moped. She might have to get a sexier leather jacket.

"Hop on it." Eagerness slipped back out from behind his neutral shield. "I'll hold it to make sure you can balance."

So she straddled it while he held it for her. The weight compared to her moped and the sleek power between her legs gave her an exciting sense of slipping into some other role—Black Widow, maybe. *Ha! No one will mess with me* now. Maybe she should take martial arts. Whatever Black Widow did to get so tough.

Of course, Black Widow probably never needed any man to hold her bike to make sure she could handle it. She looked up at Joss. A grin had escaped that control he kept on his expression. He looked like a boy.

Actually, she kind of felt like a girl, receiving from that excited, proud boy his precious present of a snake.

Something she wasn't sure how to handle, and he *really* should have checked with her, but ... the intention was so sweet.

She smiled at him, her resistance melting. "Thank you."

"You really like it?" he checked, the doubt her initial reticence had instilled not quite ready to fade.

"It's beautiful. Do you think I look like Black Widow?" She leaned into the handgrips, trying to make herself look lethal.

He smiled and touched her flyaway pixie cut. "Maybe with a helmet. One without flowers all over it."

Yeah, but ... "I *like* the flowers."

He smiled, petting her hair. "Me, too, sweetheart. Maybe Célie is already the perfect, amazing person for you to be."

Aww. Damn it. She hopped off the bike and hugged him, hard. "Thank you."

"You really like it?"

"I love it," she said firmly. And she swallowed her deep reluctance when she added: "But I think for now you'll have to drive."

***

"Joss."

Joss startled out of a daydream in which his fingers were slick and deep inside Célie, and she was twisting naked under him, her breasts lifting toward him in pleasure, and ... he shook his head. "Sorry," he said, incredulous. He never really lost his alertness in public these days. "God, your world is peaceful. Great park. Also, riding behind you on a motorcycle is really not that much better than riding behind you on a moped, in terms of its effect on my ... what did you call it?.. Sexual starvation."

"You can't still be sex-starved!" Célie said indignantly. "After last night!"

"Oh, you have no idea." He tucked his hands behind his head to make them behave and tilted his head back against the tree, gazing at the sky.

She knelt on the grass and put her hands on her hips. "What would it take to make you *not* sex-starved?"

"Uh ..." His brain fused at all the possibilities that shot awake in it, all at once. They could ... and she could ... and he could ... or she could ... he finally managed to shake a couple of his synapses back to the purpose of producing speech. "I'm not sure that's possible?"

She tried to give him one of her minatory looks, but the blush on her cheeks and the way her eyes flicked over his body gave him a little bit of hope that she didn't mind his sex obsession nearly as much as she wanted to pretend. So he smiled at her and blew her a kiss. *Hell*, that was fun. To finally be able to flirt with Célie, to tease her and stir her up.

Thank God Dom Richard had stepped in to be her damn big brother instead of him.

"How's Ludo?" he asked suddenly. "In America? How's he doing?"

Célie's face closed. She shrugged her shoulders sullenly. "I don't know. He did the same thing you did, just went off without warning and never wrote."

Shit. That was pretty fucking crappy, to have betrayed her as badly as her real shit of a brother had. Actually, *merde*, he'd probably *inspired* Ludo to run off dramatically, like he had.

Personally, he thought Célie was way better off without Ludo, but still ... it was going to be a real damn trick, to teach Célie that she could depend on him again, like teaching a person who had spent her entire life walking on shifting sands that there was such a thing as rock.

He itched to get back to work on the apartment. He could see its building from here. *That* would help convince Célie. A man who bought a home for them, who built it into the best possible space for them ... that was solid. That was permanent.

That was what she most wanted, right? Permanence from him.

He reached out and caught her hand, putting it on his chest in lieu of the still-in-process apartment, just so she could get an idea of how solid and rocklike he was these days.

She leaned enough into him to rest a little of her weight on that hand, and he smiled.

"Were you going to start talking any time soon?" Célie asked.

Talk to her. See what she says she needs from you.

"Sex is really a much more compelling subject for me."

"Joss!"

He grinned at her. And blew her another kiss.

She tried that squinty-eyed look on him that was so cute, but those squinty eyes lingered on his lips, and the squint softened out of them. He let his lips part just faintly, invitingly.

"Damn it," Célie said helplessly, and leaned far enough down to kiss him, nearly all her weight pressing for a moment into that hand on his chest.

He toppled her all the way onto him and wrapped his arms around her.

"Joss, you're cheating."

He shrugged, enjoying the way that shifted his muscles under the weight of her body. "Can't figure out how." They were in a public park, a little out of the way of main traffic but not invisible, so he kept it subtle as he shifted the position of his thigh enough that it slid between hers and pressed against the seam of her jeans.

She didn't move away from that.

He smiled, rubbing her back and maybe occasionally shifting that thigh.

"About that *communication*," Célie said.

He sighed. "Célie ... I just did it, all right? I just ... I didn't have a single doubt, I was absolutely determined, until I was sitting in that room after I signed the contract, surrounded by all the other potential *engagés*, and I started to think, 'What the hell have I done?' But I didn't ... you don't have *time* for doubt. You'll *fail* if you take time to doubt. You have to give it your all, all the time. So I did. And Célie ... I just didn't realize you would miss me that much. I knew you had a crush on me. That was one of the things I was trying to protect you from. But ... I guess I was just that self-absorbed. I didn't understand that I would actually make a hole in your life."

"Self-absorption?" Célie asked his chest suddenly. "Or not understanding your own worth?"

Yeah. Maybe being too proud for his own actual worth, so proud he was ashamed to not be more, could really lead a man to let the girl he loved down.

"I understand it now," Joss said firmly. Or he thought he did. He just had to resist her anger and blame and doubts. The blame that *wasn't* like his mother's, because he *wasn't* like his father, but sometimes it got to him anyway.

She braced on her elbows on his lounging body to smile at him in approval.

Something about that relaxed a smile out of him, too—that a statement of his worth didn't make her react against bragging but made her glad.

She might be angry with him, and she might blame him, but she still ... believed in him. Believed that he had worth, that he was trying.

"And it's hard to think about anything else, once you're in it," he said. "You don't get any sleep. For four damn months. There were weeks when we might have gotten seven hours of sleep total, the whole week, and all of that while we were spending our days scaling fortresses, crawling through mud under barbed wire, marching fifty kilometers with fifty kilos of equipment.

They try to push you past all possible breaking points, and then they only keep the men who don't break. Only about one in five make it through, and then, if you want to become a paratrooper, you go straight down to Corsica for even worse. Or better, depending on your attitude toward that intense a level of training and what it teaches you about what you can do."

"Did any crazy sergeant ever make you do two hundred push-ups in the hot sun with rocks in your mouth?" Célie's fingers kneaded into his chest.

Hell, they'd done way worse than that. He smiled at her. "The rocks in your mouth thing is for speaking a language other than French. For the twenty percent or so of us who actually were French, that wasn't that big of a risk."

Her hand shifted to knead his biceps suspiciously. God, that felt good. He hardened his biceps just to show off. "And the push-up part?" she insisted.

"There might have been a few push-up drills in there," he allowed, amused. If she only knew. The guy he'd bought the motorcycle from—an old Legionnaire who liked to customize them—had warned him that civilians could never even begin to imagine it, the demands that a man's mind and body could meet and surpass. *Just get used to it,* the other former Legionnaire had said. *No one is going to ever really understand you and what you've done.*

"Josselin Castel," Célie said sternly, and his full name just kind of silked all through him, erotically. "You're supposed to be telling me about it. *Communicating.*"

"I missed you." He kneaded her butt. "That part was really hard."

She thunked her head against his chest in frustration, which surprised him.

"Really. It was one of the hardest parts of the whole five years. That and ..." He fell silent.

She lifted her head. "And ... ?"

His silence hardened on him like a shell, this need not to talk, not to let any of this out.

"Joss." Her eyes were anxious.

He closed his a moment.

She laid her head on his chest and began to stroke up and down his biceps. Even to show off his muscles, he couldn't keep them tense under that gentleness and slowly let them relax.

"It's kind of sexy to be shot at," he said suddenly, and she flinched against him. "There's this buzz to being in a firefight. Especially early on, when you don't really know what death looks like yet. It's not hard to kill enemies. It's actually quite easy, especially with the training we had. You don't think of them as people, you think of them as guns that you have to take out before they take you. But afterward, when the adrenaline dies down, it kind of ... weighs in your belly." He tried to knead his, reflexively, but her body covered it, so that he kneaded her lower back instead. "Like all the bullets you fired were swallowed instead and just lodged there, down in your gut, forever."

He was silent for a moment, and then said simply: "That's hard. That's really, really hard."

Her arms slid around him and tightened, holding on as well as she could.

Damn it.

Joss stared at the sky. Shit, was she *pitying* him now? "You know what's really hard?" he said suddenly. "Doing all that and coming back and realizing I'm still not your hero. I'm just the guy who screwed up with you when I was barely twenty-one."

Célie's head shot up from his chest. He watched his words shock across her face, and then the shock slowly subside into something very serious as she stared at him.

He made himself shrug. "But I've done plenty of hard things. I told you. I don't really know how to quit just because it's hard. You're the only stop button I've got."

Célie's forehead crinkled slowly, her fingers worrying at his chest. "I'm sorry, Joss. I think you're amazing. I always have."

Frustration tightened in him. "But I'm *different* now. Can't you tell that? I couldn't be amazing then *and* now. The word doesn't even mean anything, if you can use it for both men. You're just patting me on the head." The incredible frustration, to pack himself with so much power and accomplishment and come back and find himself patted on the head while she wished for the man he'd been before. To be *blamed* for it. Hell, the only person who'd seemed to recognize what he'd made of himself was Jaime Corey. And maybe, a little bit, the damn big- brother substitute Célie had replaced him with, Dom Richard.

Couldn't Célie even tell that the man she'd had a crush on at eighteen had been the raw version? *That* was the man who'd walked off on her. This man, the man he'd forged himself into, would never have to do that.

Célie was silent for a moment. "Joss. Remember all those pastries I would give you, when I was training at the bakery? Did you think those were amazing?"

Just the thought of them made his mouth water, all those warm, buttery, delicious things offered to him, her eyes so bright with the pleasure of giving him pleasure. There had been times out on maneuvers with only rations when he'd missed those flaky, beautiful pastries and the look in her eyes so bad that if he'd been a dog he would have howled. "Oh, yeah," he said softly.

"And what about these?" Célie picked up his box of chocolates and pried off the metal lid. "Do you think these are amazing?"

He looked at their exquisite, perfect delicacy. "Yeah." His face softened into a smile. He touched the edge of a chocolate, almost the same tingle running through his thumb as when he touched her cheek. "You did good, Célie."

"But what I'm doing now is much higher quality than what I was doing then. From an average baker *en banlieue* to the top chocolatier in Paris—that's a big climb, Joss."

He smiled at her, pressing his thumb now into her full lower lip. "You did very, very good, Célie."

Her face suffused with pride and pleasure just at the words from him. But she persisted: "So you thought I was amazing both times? As an eighteen-year-old apprentice and working as one of the top chocolatiers in Paris?"

"Oh, hell, yeah." He slid his hand behind her head to sink his fingers into that wild pixie hair. He was so damn glad he got to kiss her when he wanted now. Or at least half the times he wanted. Fine, maybe one-one-hundredth. He bent his head to do it.

"Did you even think about what you just said at all?" Célie asked.

"Yeah." His mouth closed over all that warm sweetness of hers. "God, I miss those pastries, though. Do you think you could make me some more sometime, just for me?" He spoke against her lips, too hungry to back off, shifting his head to kiss from more angles. Now *this* was amazing. As much as he loved having her run out of her bakery or her chocolate shop with something special and delicious to offer him, he'd take the deliciousness of her mouth over any other option, if he had to choose.

But knowing Célie, if she got in the habit of letting him have her mouth, she'd never make him choose just that, over all the other ways she liked to lavish pleasure on him.

"Joss." Célie pulled away enough to thunk her forehead against his. "That was supposed to make your brain wake up to an important moment of understanding."

He rolled her under him on the grass, claiming her mouth again. Mmm, yes, the hot and the sweet of that ... "Célie. I love everything you make. But God, I'd take this any day."

Célie twisted her face away, about driving him crazy. "Take what?"

"You." He sought her mouth again. "Just like this."

"Just me," Célie said against his lips. Damn, she liked to chatter at inopportune moments sometimes. He parted her lips with his, tasting her gently with his tongue. And she yielded, falling into the kiss. But as soon as he lifted his head for a breath, she got her next word in edgewise: "No accomplishments, just me. You think I'm amazing just like this."

"Yeah." He pressed his hands in the grass to keep from doing things in public he'd get arrested for. "Hell, yeah." He sought her mouth again.

She locked her hands against his chest to hold him back, making his teeth snap together in frustration. "Joss. If you're really so sex-starved that you still haven't figured out what I'm saying, maybe we should work some of that starvation out so your brain can turn on again."

"Oh, that sounds like a really, really good idea to me," he said, just before his peripheral vision caught feet striding toward them.

He was on his feet between Célie and the man approaching, faster than a blink. The park guardian stopped in his tracks, rocking back on his heels.

Joss eased his stance, calming himself down. *There aren't that many real threats here, you idiot. Just...easy, okay?* He tried to change his expression and posture into something that wouldn't scare the park guardian even more, keeping his hands loose by his sides. "Yes?"

"There ... there are children present," the guardian said stiffly.

Oh, for God's sake. Because he'd been kissing his girlfriend in the grass? Like he was the first man to ever do that in a Paris park. Joss reached down and caught Célie's hand, pulling her to her feet. "You're right," he told the other man evenly. "We'll take it indoors."

It was all he could do to lead her straight past their new apartment to her own little one and not spoil the surprise. But he managed it. He had to save that for her, until it was the best it could be.

Chapter 21

I wish you hadn't … Célie stroked the thought down over biceps and sinewy forearm. *You never should have …* She traced her thumb over the strength of a wrist, over the hairs on the back of Joss's hand and the scars across his knuckles that he hadn't had before. *If only you had …* She caressed her fingers against the toughness of his palm, drawing her fingertips up the length of his, lingering on the calluses and the lines of the underside of his knuckles.

He shivered and grabbed at her pillow with his other arm, tightening his hold on it as his eyes closed.

I'm so mad at you for going. Her hand teased through the curls of hair on his chest, pressed into the hard muscle of his shoulders.

But you are gorgeous.

Her warrior returned, who had done it all for her.

You are amazing.

The way his head tilted back at her touch, his throat exposed to her, the only vulnerable spot on that hard, unyielding body.

No. That wasn't right. It might be the only vulnerable spot to anyone *else*, but every single place on that ruthless body seemed to be vulnerable to her. The tough skin at his elbow, from crouching in low cover or dragging himself through it on his forearms. He drew a rough rush of breath, when she stroked him there. The stubborn chin that had a small scar on it now, from sparring practice maybe, or a fall during training, or shrapnel. He licked his lips and bit into the lower one, when she stroked her fingers over that chin.

Why did you do it? Expose yourself to shrapnel, to explosives and bullets. You idiot. Why? You don't have to be this amazing for me. I loved you just the way you were.

Those words that she had to learn how to swallow and release from her heart unspoken. Because he had said it clearly to her: He had done something amazing, incredible, impossible, and she, instead of understanding and admiring, kept tearing it down.

And she couldn't do that to him. She had to care for him for who he really was and what he'd chosen to do. Even if he thought he was doing it all for her when really, in great part, he had been doing it to fulfill a need in himself, she had to respect and understand that, too.

Such a profoundly incomprehensible need in him. She'd hero-worshiped him so much, and he'd gone off on an impossible quest to make her worship him even more? Without even quite understanding that the quest deprived her for five years of the hero himself?

Yet he'd done it. And he'd come back to lay all that incredible, brutal quest for glory at her feet.

"I love you," she whispered and bit the rest of it back. *I always have. You never should have ...*

Breathed that away, turning it into a caress of those so hard-earned muscles.

"Célie." He shivered, his eyes opening to stare at her in the late afternoon light filtering through her windows, his face half shadowed by the pillow he clutched. "What are you doing? I can't ..."

"You're beautiful," she said, and his face crinkled in incredulous confusion.

She caressed her fingers down his body, over the bone of his hip, to the muscled thigh.

"This is too much," he whispered, squeezing the pillow almost anxiously. "I can't handle the way you're ... touching me, Célie." But he didn't stop her. He didn't grab her hand or roll them over on the mattress so he could take over. He swallowed and shoved the pillow over his face a second, his body lifting toward her touch.

"You're incredible." She kneaded her fingers into his thigh.

He pulled the pillow aside enough to show his face again. "I'm not *incredible.* I'm just—"

She put her fingers over his mouth. "You shut up. I get to be the judge of how incredible you are. You clearly have no freaking clue."

Where did it come from, this will to drive oneself past all limits, to never believe you were good enough unless you were the absolute best any human being could ever be? She knew it very well. Dom had it, too, after all—the man who had driven himself to be the best chocolatier in Paris, and who, whenever he showed up on some random list written by an idiot with no proper understanding of chocolate as only the *second* best or the *third* best in the whole entire world, ripped the paper and went to the gym to box to the point of exhaustion or threw himself on his motorcycle to cut through traffic in suicidal aggressiveness. (Although he'd calmed down about the motorcycle business now that he had Jaime, as if the desire to keep his happiness had trumped his aggressive recklessness.)

She even had it, the little pastry apprentice from the *banlieue* who had come to work for the rising star chocolatier in Paris and made herself into his right-hand woman, someone who could produce that best of the best of the best. When *she* saw their chocolates appear as only second or third best in the world instead of *the* best, she drew faces of the guilty journalists on craft sticks and gave them yarn hair and suspended them over her chocolate as if she was going to drown them in it—and then left them there, just shy of actually tasting that chocolate, like Tantalus. Okay, fine, she'd only done that once, in great ceremony in the middle of the *laboratoire* for a particularly idiotic critic who had put them all the way down at number *six,* but it had made even Dom laugh.

Célie Clément did not do second best.

Striving for the best was kind of her way of being worthy of herself. And of Joss.

Too proud to be small, Joss. Too proud to give her a cheap diamond ring.

And I was too proud to be just a little baker en banlieue *if you were going to be a glorious Legionnaire.*

His dad had been a decent dad when Joss was little, based on the things Joss used to let slip in their easy conversations as teenagers. Then he had gone rapidly downhill after he lost his job when Joss was twelve, descending into alcohol, no longer there for his son. Had that been part of what pushed Joss? His mom was a bitter woman, blaming her husband, blaming her son, blaming even Célie after Joss left, claiming it must have been her fault.

Was that part of why he'd never given Célie a chance to have a say? He'd been afraid she would try to reduce him, just like his mother did?

Was a refusal to be his father part of what drove him?

Was it nature or nurture, really, that kind of drive? Or both? All these circumstances and choices that had fused Joss into the hardened, determined warrior who was now shivering under her hand.

He stuffed the pillow back over his face.

"Hey." She pulled it off. "Don't make me throw this one out of the window, too. It's the last one. Your chest might make a great pillow in fantasies, but in real life, it's actually pretty hard to punch into just that right shape under my ear." She smiled at him.

"Célie. I just—I need the pillow." He reached for it again.

She dropped it on the floor. "No, you don't." She framed his face in her hands as if he was a fragile chocolate she had to touch just right and lowered her head toward his. "You're just fine, Joss," she whispered between his lips and let her own close gently over his and then slide away, stroking him with her lips, lingering at the corners of his, exploring the bow of his upper lip, the way she could make that firm line relax and yield to her. "You're just about perfect."

"'About'?" he asked, like a man ready to jump down and do a few more push-ups right then to fix any possible flaw.

"Well, you've got this." She caressed her fingertips over that square jaw and followed with her mouth, lingering over the tiny scar. "That's not perfect. It's too stubborn. So stubborn you'll let it get hurt, rather than give up or give in."

"Célie." The corners of his lips trembled in such a vulnerable start to a smile. "You—"

"And this." She brought his big hand to her lips and turned it over to kiss all along the thick calluses at the base of his fingers. "Look at this hand. You've been getting it into trouble. You need cocoa butter."

He shook his head. "I need the calluses. Soft skin just gets ripped to shreds when you want to do anything."

"Oh." She considered her own hands, kept soft by constant exposure to cocoa butter. She'd taken to weight training when Joss had shown her as a teenager how to get started—taken to it at first because of the erotic sweetness of having him adjust her arms or hover ready to catch a weight—and she was extremely proud of herself to be able to do a pull-up, these days, but she wore gloves for that and hadn't a single callus to her name. "So soft hands aren't perfect?" She ran her palm slowly down his arm.

He shivered. "They're perfect. Célie—"

"Are they *both* perfect?" she asked in pretend surprise. "Yours and mine? But they're so different." She drew his hand over her own arm, rubbing his calluses against her skin, and a shiver chased through her, too, her eyes closing into the pleasure of it. "Oh, yeah. I think, after all, yours are definitely perfect."

"You like them?" He caressed her bare back, rubbing those calluses up her sensitive skin to her bra strap.

She arched into the touch, erotic delight spreading out from it all through her body. *"Yes."*

He smiled a little, watching her, playing with the textures he could bring to her back, stroking his callused fingertips up her spine and down, then walking them out in little pressures that made her muscles flinch and her back arch and relax again into the pleasure.

"Remember when I was teaching you how to lift weights?" he asked suddenly. Sometimes Joss picked thoughts straight out of her brain, she swore. "God, that killed me. Your little muscles straining, and the sheen of sweat on your skin, and me just barely touching you to adjust your form and not ever being able to touch you for real. The way you would strain so hard to get strong."

"You wouldn't go dancing with me back then. So I had to do something physical around you."

"I'll do anything physical you want with you now." He rolled them over, bracing himself above her on the bed.

Such a glorious body to have braced above hers. But that wasn't what hit her the most. It was this purity in his eyes, this truth and fidelity through everything he had been and seen. "I love you," she whispered suddenly. "Not ... not like a brother."

He drew a sharp breath. In the slanting late light through her windows, his eyes were gorgeous.

"You're amazing. And"—her voice dropped very soft, and shy—"you're my hero."

That brilliance in his eyes, as if she'd crowned him king after an impossible quest.

"You always have been. And you still are. Even more." Her hands ran over his arms. "If you asked me to, *I* would wait more than five years for you. I would be *proud* to."

"Célie," he breathed, luminous in that light that turned all his hard, sun-darkened body to gold.

"But don't leave me again." She wrapped her arms around him abruptly. "Don't take me up on that. Promise not to."

"I won't leave you," he said, low and final.

The promise vibrated through her, as if a seal had been stamped down on her, of ownership, of home.

"Célie," he said suddenly, combing his fingers through the tufts of her hair. "You know I love you, don't you? You figured that out?"

"I—I—" It was too beautiful to believe or even think about straight on, and she almost couldn't say it. "You seem to."

"I *seem* to." He shook his head. "You're a hard woman to convince."

Stay with me. Include me. That convinces me. But she had to take what he offered. She ran her hand over the muscles of his arms, one manifestation of all his efforts.

"Célie. I think you're my heroine."

It sounded beautiful, at first, and yet she hesitated. "Like ... the heroine tied to the train tracks? Who needs saving? The princess in a tower?"

He ran his thumb over her cheekbone in a delicate stroke of callus. "Like Wonder Woman. The woman I look up to. The woman I think is amazing. I can be what's-his-name, the Air Force pilot."

Her nose crinkled against the sting in it. "Really?"

He looked up to *her*?

"All that life and courage in you, Célie. That way you stick your chin up and challenge the world and tease it. The way you ... sparkle. You're like the Eiffel Tower. You don't even *notice* all the rain and the cold and the gray skies, you just sparkle away and refuse to let them put you out."

Her fingers stroked their way to his shoulder, kneading it like a cat might a very hard pillow. "You know, when it's cold and rainy in Paris," she murmured, feeling silly and shy again, "it's just exactly perfect weather for curling up with someone. And, and ... maybe making him hot chocolate."

His face broke into the most brilliant grin. "*God*, I love you." He rolled them over so that she was on top of him. "Hell, you make me actually wish it was winter." He ran his hands up her arms. "Maybe with a fireplace." A little gleam in his eyes that she couldn't interpret. "I bet you'd like that."

Hard to find an apartment with a fireplace these days. She shrugged funnily. "S ... summer's nice, too. You can go skating along the Seine. Stay out late. Maybe ... maybe go somewhere on vacation in August and explore a whole new world together."

"I bet the whole year is nice," he said softly. "I bet every day of the year, with you in it, would be beautiful."

Oh. She wanted to hug herself, to hug the words to her, but their bodies were so close she could only hug him.

He stroked her hair. "Célie. I don't 'seem to' love you. I really do. I would do anything for you."

As long as that "anything" demanded he grow bigger, meet hard challenges, and didn't demand he shrink, she thought, with sudden insight. He had a compulsive need to be better, never lesser.

But that was okay. As long as he included her, as long as he trusted her, she could be that person, who had a big enough heart to let him grow as big as he needed and still fit in it.

"I would, too." She pushed herself up to hold his eyes. "Do anything for you. Except ask you to be less than you are."

His face broke into that rare, brilliant smile. "I knew there was a reason I loved you."

"Only one?" She tried to put her chin up. But sometimes she wondered how there could even be that many. She was so quick-tempered, and she flew off the handle. She knew he was amazing, but somehow she beat her head against him anyway, wishing he would be a little less amazing in exchange for letting her in.

His face softened, his eyes so true. "Célie. There are so many reasons I love you. As many sparkles as there are on that Eiffel Tower. But that one, that you won't ask me to be less for you … that one's like the whole iron frame that holds those sparkling lights up."

Yeah. It did kind of feel as if she was trying to grow as strong as the iron of the Eiffel Tower, in order to be strong enough to honor the best that he could be. She took a deep breath, stretching herself, trying to get her heart used to being that big and strong.

It felt kind of … natural, actually. As if that was what her heart had always wanted to be.

"You're sure it's not just sex starvation?" She tried to make her voice sound teasing, but a part of her still worried about that.

He grinned, his eyes lighting. "I don't know." He checked her clock. "We'd better test it. Let's see if I still love you in … oh, about an hour."

Chapter 22

Célie was so happy she couldn't get over it. She felt like walking around with her arms wrapped around her own body in a hug instead of working. Whenever she tried to concentrate on her chocolate, she ended up rocking on her toes, dreamy, and would blink awake at some teasing comment from the rest of the team to discover she'd been drawing hearts in chocolate again.

Then she would try to get back to work and instead find herself rising on tiptoe to see if she could spot Joss in the street below.

Dom sighed. "I suppose this will wear off and you'll turn back into a halfway decent chocolatier one day."

He should talk. He *still* mooned over Jaime. Célie stuck her tongue out at him. And then the full impact of his statement hit her. "A—*halfway decent*? Did you just say—" She started for him as Dom grinned and ducked into his office.

Just then, Jaime ran up the stairs and pushed the glass doors of the *laboratoire* open, and Dom reappeared immediately.

Those two were so mushy. Célie smiled a little as she turned away from their kiss to peek out the window again.

Hey! There he was. Coming down the street. Happiness lilted through her, this crazy chirp of it that was like being caught in a hiccup of joy. It was almost too much. It shook her too hard.

And yet she loved it. She hugged herself, watching that long, strong, steady walk. Joss really wasn't in the least pushy with all that power, politely shifting to one side well before he reached someone coming the other way on the sidewalk, and yet she could see the normally assertive Parisian pedestrians part and flow around him like boats giving a very wide berth to an iceberg.

Jaime leaned in the open window beside her, smiling. "How's it going?"

Célie shrugged happily and hugged herself.

"You guys are so cute," Jaime said.

"Hey, we're not as mushy as you and Dom."

Over setting some trays of fresh-made chocolates on the wire racks, Zoe made a choked sound of amusement.

"What?" Célie asked indignantly. "Nobody's as mushy as these two!"

Zoe smothered a grin and turned away.

Hmm. Célie glanced sideways at Jaime, who seemed to be smothering amusement, too. Heat touched her cheeks, but she hugged herself anyway. It was kind of ... nice to be mushy.

"Try not to draw hearts and Js over *every* surface while I'm gone," Dom drawled. "I'm a little worried about you leaving you running the show."

Célie stuck her tongue out at him, too happy to let him get much of a rise out of her. As *if* she couldn't run this show. Ha! The only problem was that she was jealous. *She* wanted to go see the cocoa farms in Côte d'Ivoire with him and Jaime, too. She'd been curious about visiting an actual cocoa farm for ages. But the thought of not having to leave Joss for a week right at that moment made it easier to be left behind this time. Maybe next time she could come.

"You don't mind me stealing Joss?" Jaime asked.

Hunh?

"I feel bad to do it so soon, but we need him to get started. I could *really* use his insight in West Africa."

Célie turned her head and stared at Jaime. Her diaphragm hurt suddenly, as if one of those hiccups of joy had frozen right in the middle and wouldn't release her.

Below, Joss lifted a hand to her, smiling, and glanced up and down all the buildings around him with that quick Legionnaire glance before he started to cross the street.

"What are you talking about?" Célie's lips felt funny around the words, bee-stung.

Jaime blinked. And straightened from the window, her expression going wary. She glanced toward Dom, who was dipping a finger in the ganache to taste what Célie had come up with, and Dom lifted his eyebrows at the glance and shifted toward them.

"You don't ... know anything about it?" Jaime said. "Didn't you guys spend the weekend together?" The Sunday–Monday weekend of those in the restaurant business.

Yeah. They'd gone out to Rambouillet on the new bike—Joss driving them out of Paris, just like some teenage fantasy of wrapping her arms around him on a motorcycle while he broke them free of their childhood—and picnicked in the woods and then Joss had rolled her under him on that picnic blanket and...

"Tell me what you're talking about," Célie said between her teeth.

"Just the ... trip down to Côte d'Ivoire with us tomorrow."

Célie's brain buzzed. Joss reached the sidewalk below them and stood with his head tilted back, waiting for her to look at him. "What are you *talking about*?"

"The, the ..." Jaime looked from Dom to Joss below. "Did nobody mention to you that I'd *hired* him? That he's going to be advising Corey on security issues? That he's going down to Côte d'Ivoire with me tomorrow?"

Breath hissed between Célie's teeth. She felt as if she'd just been hit in the stomach. Almost as hard a punch as that morning when she'd learned that Joss had gone off without a word to join the Foreign Legion. "No. Nobody mentioned that."

"Oh." Jaime put a hand to her lips, glancing worriedly at Dom. "Uh-oh."

Below, Joss lifted an inquiring palm, asking maybe, *Will you be long?* Or, *Why aren't you smiling at me?*

Célie stared down at him. Her brain hurt, swelling against her skull as if it was trying to get out. That damn clutch in her diaphragm still hadn't released, the pressure of that interrupted hiccup of joy growing unbearable.

Joss raised his eyebrows at her in smiling inquiry, no clue in his head what might be wrong. Because, yeah, it would never even occur to him to have told her any of this himself.

And all of a sudden, all that pressure burst. "Joss Castel!"

His smile faded at her tone. He searched her eyes from the distance of a floor below.

"You—you—you—" On a surge of pure rage, Célie grabbed up the bowl of ganache Dom had just tasted and dumped its entire contents out the window, down onto his head below.

That would teach him to try to treat her like a princess in a tower who had nothing whatsoever to do but be his object. She knew how to defend her ramparts, if that was the way he wanted to be.

The ganache splattered all over his hair and face in this giant slosh of chocolate. Several customers leaving the shop stopped dead. Then they pulled out their cameras.

Jaime clapped both hands to her mouth, twilight blue eyes enormous.

"Nice shot." Dom leaned in the window beside her. "That one's going to be all over the blogs. Good job on the publicity, Célie." He held up a hand to give her a high five. Célie ignored him, glaring at Joss below.

Joss shook himself, scraping chocolate off his face until he could open his eyes again. "Okay, what the hell?"

"You—*aargh*!" Célie grabbed up the nearest ammunition she could find—chocolates—and threw whole handfuls that bounced off his shoulders and head.

"Hell, Célie." Dom grabbed her wrists. "Now you're getting expensive."

"You go to hell, Joss Castel!" Célie yelled through the window. "I—you—" She pulled her wrists free and grabbed her hair, yanking it as she strangled her scream. One of these days, she was going to take a rowboat out into the middle of the ocean for the pure purpose of being able to scream as loud as she possibly could over Joss Castel.

"Célie," Joss said, in that firm, warning note that always ran a little jolt of eroticism through her. *You are over the line*, that note said.

And her body responded: *Oh, yeah? What you gonna do about it?*

"I—I—" Célie grabbed another chocolate and threw it at him.

"Damn it, Célie!" Dom grabbed for her wrist again.

Joss caught the chocolate and looked at it a second, his eyes narrowing. Then he looked up at her.

A frisson of expectation ran through her body. It was the Legionnaire look. And it was turned on her. Very deliberately, holding her eyes, he ate the chocolate.

She licked her lips.

He launched himself straight toward her—one powerful lunge of his body upward, a catch of some point in the wall she hadn't even known existed as a possible hold. Involuntarily, she stretched through the window to try to follow what he was doing—and his body surged into her vision, both hands gripping the edge of the window as he pulled himself into it.

Chocolate coated most of his face and shoulders, except for the smeared somewhat-clear spot where he'd wiped it off his eyes and nose. His eyes locked with hers.

She took two steps back before she caught herself and braced her feet, putting her hands on her hips.

"Can I just *push* him?" Dom asked Jaime. "This is *my territory*, damn it."

Jaime grabbed Dom's hand and pulled him toward the door of the ganache room. When he stopped at the doorway itself, she shifted behind him, put both hands on his butt, and shoved him. It was a considerable tribute to Dom's utter adoration of Jaime that he actually let that move him.

"Good chocolate," Joss said meditatively, rubbing his fingers across his chocolate-smeared mouth. "You want to tell me what the hell, Célie?"

"I'm—going—to—*kill you*!" Célie gripped her chef's jacket to give her hands something to strangle. He couldn't even *guess* what the hell?

Joss came away from the window in one easy, lethal move and caught her, lifting her up and pressing his face right between her breasts, holding her there while he rubbed his face clean against her chef's jacket.

More or less clean. When he lifted it—still holding her off the ground—liberal smears still decorated it and his military short hair, but at least half his skin was visible in random streaks and stripes of chocolate.

He looked kind of yummy that way, actually. He made her mouth tingle.

And if his hair had been even a centimeter longer, she probably would have yanked *his* instead of her own.

"You—you—you—I can't believe you *haven't learned one damn thing*!"

"I've learned plenty. But apparently not about you."

"You're still acting as if I *don't even have anything to do with your life*! You don't even tell me! And you just go off—" Her voice choked her. She struggled to get her breathing to calm down but it kept coming more and more hysterically. "You're *leaving me* again. And you said—you said—you—" An onslaught of ugly sobs bottled up in her, and she fought to keep them contained.

He pushed her back against the wall, between two shelving sets of chocolates, capturing her inside a cage made of her own rich-scented work and him, still half covered in chocolate.

"I had a plan." He pushed the words through her incipient hysteria. "Calm down."

Her breath hitched at the command ... and then came in with one long, deep pull and held a second, and then slowly released. The threat of raging sobs eased at that long breath. She stared up at him. God, he looked hot like that. She wanted to lick that chocolate off him so bad. And she was so mad at him.

"I've got something for you." Those hazel eyes held hers. *Behave, Célie.* And, *Listen to me.* She hiccupped a little, staring up at him, taking another deep breath. He smelled so good, too, the chocolate and that scent of sand and sun and wild herbs. She needed to make a chocolate that captured sand and sun and wild herbs ... "It's in my pocket."

But his arms stayed braced on either side of her to keep her captured.

She looked at his shirt. He was wearing, actually, what was a pretty nice shirt for Joss, a dress shirt, pressed, unbuttoned at the collar, rolled up at the sleeves, and now thoroughly stained in chocolate. And there was a small square box in the front pocket.

Her breath hitched in again. She stared at him until his stubborn, beautiful eyes seemed to fill her whole world.

"You want to get it out?" he asked.

Her lips pressed together vulnerably. She shook her head.

His eyebrows drew together faintly. He didn't release her, but he pushed his body a little farther back from hers. "You don't want it?"

"Not ... not like this. This isn't a good idea. You'll—this is really not a good idea right now, Joss."

"I had a *plan*," he insisted, adamantly, pressing the words into her.

Oh, God, of course he had. That he'd decided on all by himself.

"Remember that night I said good-bye to you? And you didn't know you wouldn't see me again, and I didn't tell you? I didn't offer you that ring?"

She nodded, struggling not to cry.

The hardness in his body gentled. His hand framed her face, and his thumb grazed gently under her damp eyes. "I wanted to undo that. I wanted to do that night exactly the opposite way."

Oh. A tear spilled out. He caught it, rubbing it carefully against her cheek.

"I wanted to tell you," he said quietly, full of all that intensity that Joss packed into him, "that I had to leave for a few days, but that I was going to be back. I wanted to talk to you about this job I'd taken and reassure you, if you had worries about it."

He couldn't have talked to her *about the decision*? Like, *before* he made it? As if she was part of it? Was he still so convinced that she would hold him back?

"And I wanted to ask you"—he reached into his pocket—"if you would wear this."

He opened the box. Light sparkled off the diamond ring, like sunlight off a glass mountain. She had never thought she liked diamonds, had never been the girl who fantasized about receiving one. But this one sparkled like joy.

Célie covered her face with her hands. But she kept her fingers parted, so she could see that ring, and how utterly beautiful it looked when held in that callused hand. She'd never even *noticed* diamond rings before. It was the frame of that strong, male hand that set it off. Made it beautiful.

"Because it would make me so proud," Joss said. "Incandescent with happiness. People would think I was running around in sequins, if you were wearing my ring."

The utter wonder of Joss sparkling ... over her. Tears streamed down her cheeks.

"I'd probably look ridiculous, I'd glow so much," Joss said. "But I wouldn't care. If you were wearing my ring."

Célie couldn't stop crying.

"Maybe everyone would know we went together," Joss said. "If you were sparkling that much, too. We'd match."

She pressed her fingers against her tears, but they wouldn't stop.

"And you say I'm terrible at communicating," Joss muttered. "What does that mean, Célie?" He touched her tears through her fingers. "Is that a ... yes?" This pause and hush on the last word, as if it held worlds of wonder.

Oh, God, this was so hard. This was killing her, it was so hard. As if great giant claws had sunk into her body and were ripping her asunder. "No," she whispered.

"What?" He bent deep to hear her, his face close to hers, his eyes so pure and true and intent.

"No." The word was so soft it was almost no more than a shape of her lips, all the sound choked out of it.

"What?" He gave his head a tiny shake and pulled back, staring at her lips as if they didn't make sense, and then into her eyes.

She swallowed, like swallowing a mountain, cramming all of it down her too small throat. And shook her head. "I can't, Joss."

From the vicinity of the doorway past him came a sharp sound of protest. Everyone in the *laboratoire* must be jammed into the door of the ganache room, watching this show.

Oh, God, she was rejecting him before all of them. Shaming him.

"But—" Joss looked down at the ring and then back up at her. "I thought that was what you said you wanted. I thought you said you would have been incandescent with joy."

"I *would have*, Joss. When I was eighteen. God, I would have been so happy. But now … now I know how crappy it is to be the princess in a tower. Now I want someone who will include me. I'm not very good at waiting up in my tower for the prince to get back. I want to be part of the life I live. And of the life you live, too. I want us to live *together*."

"I'm *working* on that, Célie," he said in a rush. "I've got an apartment for us and everything. I just—it's not ready for you yet."

"You *got us an apartment*?"

He drew back, dumbfounded, alarm flaring. "Célie—"

"Without even—without even—" She pressed her hands to either side of her skull, hard, trying to hold it in. *"Without even talking to me about it?"*

"It's not *ready*. I want it to be perfect first."

She stared at him. Her fingers dug into her hair and slowly started to pull. "Good enough for me?"

"Exactly," Joss said, relieved. "You really don't want to see it in the state it's in now. It—"

"And you figured that out all by yourself? What I needed? What would be good enough for me?"

He hesitated. And then he fell silent, staring at her.

"For us?"

His lips pressed together. That look, that dive-deep neutral look he got when he knew things were going to get really bad.

"There are two people in an *us*, Joss. One of them is me."

"It's *for* you, Célie. It's all—"

"No." Célie's hands fell slowly from her hair. She straightened from the wall.

Joss's hand shot out and covered her mouth. "Célie, don't—"

She jerked her head away. "*No,* Joss. The answer is *no.* I'm not who you think I am, and I can't and I won't ever be that person again. But you—you're *still* the man who would walk off on me because you thought I deserved better and *never think to ask me what I really wanted.* In case it obliged you to change your mind. Or bend your pride."

He stood stock-still, staring at her.

"No," she said again, even though he had chocolate smeared across his face and mouth and across his shirt and she wanted to take him home and *lick* him, even though his eyes were so beautiful and stubborn and true, even though he had the hottest body a woman could ever dream of. And even though he'd done it all for her. "No, Joss. You're destroying all the happiness I ever built for myself. Please go away and leave me alone."

Chapter 23

Joss stood dully in the middle of the apartment. God, he felt tired. As if he'd been through one of those training weeks with only an hour of sleep a night, and gotten nearly all the way to the end of the White Képi March, and then just sat down and given up, without ever earning the *képi*. Utter exhaustion. All coated and weighed down with unforgivable failure.

Finally he just lay down on the stained and rotting floorboards, half of which needed to be replaced and all of which needed to be sanded down and refinished. Hell, he'd probably best just rip out the whole thing, get some proper hardwoods in here.

Except who cared?

None of it mattered now.

Not the view on Célie's favorite park.

Not the shower that sat there, delivered and uninstalled, where she was supposed to have stood caught in sprays at the end of the day, washing the chocolate scent off her and maybe smiling at him through the glass or even wiggling her naked butt saucily, when he came in pretending he needed to brush his teeth, just so he could eye her.

Not the measurements for the marble counters, so that her own home kitchen could be a place that gave her as much pleasure to work in as that beautiful *laboratoire*. So that it became a place where they could maybe make supper … what was that word of hers? … *together*.

Not the wall-to-wall closet that he had been going to set into one bedroom wall, to maximize the space, so that her clothes and his clothes both fit in the bedroom. Together.

Definitely not the damn bed.

He slowly pulled out the little box. God, he'd loved the fancy jeweler's name on it. Loved standing in front of the shop on the Faubourg Saint-Honoré and thinking, *Yeah. Now I can get her* this.

His chest ached.

His throat resisted all his efforts to swallow.

He rolled over and pulled his old battered duffle to him from the corner of the room, unzipping and unzipping, until he found what he wanted.

He pulled it out.

A cheap, slim ring with a stone so big because it was fake, cubic zirconium. The kind of ring a man bought when the words swam in front of him all the time at school, and the teachers thought he was stupid, and he had to take the mechanic track instead of anything that would let him go to university. When he was a *good* mechanic, he was good at it, he liked it, and he thought that was worth something, but then he got fired from his job because his closest friends were fucking drug dealers. When his father was a bumbling alcoholic who once, long ago, had seemed like a decent dad, and his mother was a bitter woman whose every word focused on how her husband or her son was failing or going to fail.

When the only bright spot in his whole world was the girl who ran out of her bakery apprenticeship with her eyes lighting up at the sight of him and some box held up filled with some precious pastry she had made and saved because she wanted to see his eyes light up, too.

When he would do anything, anything in the world, rather than become her failure. The man who didn't live up to that bright hope in her eyes.

Anything, rather than become the man who sank into grimy nothingness and weighed down all her hope and let his kids grow up to the same gray, dull lack of future.

It was the kind of ring a man bought just before he said: *No. No. I can't give her this crap. I have to be more.*

And if he was just turned twenty-one, and at heart desperately wanted to be the great romantic hero, went off and joined the Foreign Legion.

His throat hurt so bad. His hand fisted around the ring, and the damn thing was so cheap, he bent the setting of the fake diamond.

Anybody could see the other was better, right?

Anybody in the world could see that he'd done the right thing.

Except Célie.

And she was the only one who mattered.

He closed his eyes.

Five years of brutal effort and unstoppableness seemed to crash down on him all at once, and he turned his head into his arm, with the rings still clutched in either hand, there on the rotting, stained floor, and fell so solidly asleep it was like crashing into dark water.

Chapter 24

"I'll never have the cuddle now," Célie told the water dully. Not crying. She'd cried more the past week in public than in the past twenty-three years combined. Now grief weighed so heavy it had crushed even her tear ducts closed.

"I'm really sorry." Jaime sat astride the wall of the canal, one foot dangling just above the water next to Célie's. "I didn't mean to create problems."

"It's not the job. It wasn't the Foreign Legion either. He doesn't have to stay smaller for *me*. But … he thinks he does. He thinks if he talks to me about it before he does anything, I'll shrink him."

Jaime grimaced, failing to find words. Yeah, because what words were there? No one wanted to be a guy's idea of shrink-wrap on his dreams. "The cuddle?" she asked finally.

"You know." Célie's mouth drooped. She stared at the black water. "So you don't have to hide behind your bed at night. So you can just relax into someone's arms and be happy. It's gone now. I'll never have it."

Jaime put her hand on Célie's shoulder and squeezed gently.

Which was nice, but it wasn't the same as a Joss squeeze. Not as big, not as strong, not as longed-for.

"I was so happy before he showed back up," Célie said. "I was *over* him. I only ever even thought of him maybe a couple of times a day."

A rueful, sympathetic glance from Jaime that seemed to suggest a couple of times a day was still a lot. Little did Jaime know.

"And now it's going to be so hard." Célie's throat tried to strangle her, it tightened so much. Anger had given her the strength to shove him away so that she could go back to the cheerful, strong life she had built for herself. But now that the anger had subsided, she felt like a girl who had gotten rid of everything but spinach in her house in a determination to lose five kilos. Who the hell cared about five kilos? She didn't want a life of spinach. She wanted chocolate.

"Célie," Jaime said. "You're underestimating that man of yours. He's going to analyze his failure and then come about and get it right the next time. You'll see."

Weight settled down on Célie, heavier and heavier grief. Because even if she'd needed anger to give her the strength to make this purge, something much more serious than five kilos was at stake here.

"Don't you get it? That just makes me the object of his plans again. I want to be the person who *takes part in them.* You know ... *together.*"

***

The first postcard arrived at the shop the day Dom and Jaime came back. A stamp with a plumeria flower was on the corner of the envelope, inscribed *République de Côte d'Ivoire,* its postmark a week old. The address was in precise, square, careful handwriting, her name, c/o the shop address.

The card she pulled out of the envelope was of a palm tree over a sunset beach.

Célie. The long pause could almost be felt in the paper, in the heart that had been drawn over the *I* in her name, thickly layered with ink from a pen that had repeated it over and over, as its owner sought words. And then, *I'm terrible at this. Joss.*

A smile kicked through her despite everything. She stroked the deep impressions of the pen, made by a man who fought with pen and paper to get it to say what he wanted.

Dom, who had handed her the envelope with her name on it, eyed her a second, warily.

"I'm fine," she lied. And, unable to resist, "How did it go?" For once, she could actually know something about what Joss did on those adventures he sought out without her.

"He's got this covered." It was clear by Dom's expression that his impressions of Joss had undergone a radical transformation. "The way he moves. The way he assesses every situation and every person constantly and reacts exactly as fast as a situation needs, handling it immediately or taking his time to see what is developing. That control and steadiness coupled with instant reflexes and no energy spared to do what needs to be done. And he speaks the military language. They listen to him, and he gets their respect. My wife and all those cocoa farmers she cares about so much are all going to be safer because he's there."

So much pride swelled in her, to hear her much-loved, big-brother boss praise her boyfriend, that Célie bounced on her toes with it before it burst her.

Then she remembered he wasn't her boyfriend.

Shit.

"Your wife?" she asked Dom, as saucily as she could manage.

He pointed a big finger at her. "Don't you start."

"What?" she exclaimed, and maybe Dom couldn't tell how fake and forced the teasing sounded over her own empty heart. "It's been a week! Didn't you miss me?"

"I had your damn boyfriend to keep me company. Trust me, I've heard enough out of him about putting a ring on somebody's finger. I think my own method is working out better for me in my relationship, thank you."

Hey. If Dom and Joss were in a contest, Célie kind of wanted Joss to win. Except, of course ... she stared at her bare left ring finger.

Damn it.

She went to make chocolates. Mint. Joss's favorite.

Merde.

And maybe she did keep glancing out the casement window. But Joss never showed up to stand in his usual spot.

Leaning on the railing of her apartment window that night, gazing out at all the other millions of people in Paris, some of whom must have screwed up their chances of happiness, too, she thought for a moment she spotted him, leaning against a building down the street, looking up at her apartment. But he made no sign to her if it was him, and when the male body shifted from that spot and walked down the street away from her, she decided she must have imagined it.

Still the sight of that broad back leaving her farther and farther behind broke her heart.

The second card came the next day. A view of Abidjan at night, glowing glamorously against the water. *Célie.* The ink on the heart over the *I* in her name was so thick it almost couldn't be recognized as a heart. Then, *I miss you. Joss.*

She stared at it a long time, that emotion that he had pulled out of himself and put down onto vulnerable paper. Then she hugged it to herself and placed it very carefully in a line at the back of the marble counter by the casement window. *I would wait more than five years for you. I am terrible at this. I miss you. Joss.*

But he still didn't show up at the end of the day, and the next day, no cards came at all.

Her stomach knotted until even chocolate couldn't sit in it. When she left work, she stared at the motorcycle, still parked where Joss had left it ten days ago, and then drove her little moped home. In the middle of the night, she had to sit between her bed and the wall again, arms wrapped around herself as tightly as she could hold.

Dom tossed two envelopes to her as soon as the mail came late the next afternoon. She grabbed them and carried them into the currently empty ganache room, opening them in order of postmark.

Célie. No heart over her name, the usually square handwriting angled, as if he'd written quickly. *I know you told me to leave you alone. The thing is, you also made me promise not to do that ever again. So I … here's my phone number. Just to make sure you have it. Joss.*

She swallowed, around so many things stuck in her throat that she couldn't get down.

She opened the fourth one. *Célie.* Her name underlined three times, a heart drawn over her name just once. *Je t'aime. Joss.*

She pressed the postcard to her chest and stood at the casement window, staring down at the empty street. It took her a long time to release that postcard and set it in the line with the others. *I would wait more than five years for you. I am terrible at this. I miss you. Here's my phone number. I love you. Joss.*

Her fingers stroked that first postcard from Côte d'Ivoire, the words, *I am terrible at this.* It had made her smile over the deep twist of her heart, because it was so true. He *was* terrible at writing his thoughts and feelings down. It was just exactly like him. His true offer of himself: *I am terrible at this. But I am going to try for you anyway.*

Exactly like him.

Like, *I'm going to screw this up,* when she let him up into her apartment. This thing deep inside him, this conviction, that he would fail. A belief he shoved aside ruthlessly, refusing to allow it power over him: *I* won't *screw this up. I* will *get it right.*

The mixed-up determination of a man who couldn't offer the girl who was crazy about him a fake diamond ring.

She went to the window again.

And … there he was. She almost didn't recognize him seated, his forearms braced on his knees, his shoulders slumped, his head bent. He didn't look like her Joss at all.

***

Joss sat waiting again, a man they were probably going to arrest as a stalker. He didn't stand in his usual spot but sat on some crates piled outside a store, gazing down at his linked hands, his thumbs pushing and catching at each other like miniature martial artists.

For the past two weeks, he'd done his job. That was what a Legionnaire did, after all—his job, no matter what. He'd gone to Côte d'Ivoire, with Jaime Corey and her overprotective boyfriend. Just watching Dom lay his arm over Jaime's shoulders possessively felt as if Dom was carefully dropping stupid, sparkly flakes of that precious sea salt Célie liked so much into every single wound Joss had. And smiling in self-satisfaction at a job well done, when Joss clamped his jaw together to hide the agony.

But, in fact, Dom was probably just too damn blissfully content to think about his effect on Joss. Although he and Jaime *both* slipped Joss little bits of advice at every opportunity.

Most of which was probably good. A few of the officers in the Legion had good marriages, but he mostly only saw those when they were being performed—when the men were invited over for tea, for example. For *real* relationships, his most positive model had always been his own with Célie.

And given that they had been teenagers and he'd been trying to play the role of her brother's friend instead of her lover, it was possible that he still had a lot to learn about relationships before he could get his own right.

God, he missed Célie. Like his own heart ripped out of his chest. Just as he always had.

When he'd ripped her heart out of her chest, five years ago, she'd still written him postcards. A dozen postcards, until she gave up. Cards. Writing. His worst possible form of communication.

He'd stared down at the first card he'd bought in Abidjan as if blank paper was a sleeping cobra. And then, as he had that day in the *salon de chocolat*, grabbed on to the one thing he knew was true: *Célie*.

Funny how, once that one word was set down on the paper and the paper failed to bite him, the rest of it came more easily. After only, say, twenty minutes of searching for the next word.

Stick with the truth. Even if it's not good enough.

He wondered if she'd ever spent as long as he had, trying to figure out what to write to *him.* Skipping over all those other options like, *You bastard* and *Why did you leave me?* to a cheerful, encouraging *We miss you here, but I know you can do it!*

Postcards that were half a lie—she'd missed him far more than the cheerful little cards that so quickly dried up had ever let him understand—and half the truth—she truly wished the best for him, even so.

Célie came out slowly and hesitated a long time before she crossed the street to him. She looked as tired as he felt, as if someone had finally managed to put out the sparkles on the Eiffel Tower.

And that someone would be him.

"Hi," he said to his thumbs, without trying for anything—not a kiss on the lips, not kisses on each cheek, nothing.

Célie sighed and braced. And then abruptly shoved a little metal box into his hands and folded her arms across her chest protectively.

He held the little flat box in his palm, staring down at it. It hurt so damn much, that gift of chocolates despite everything. And yet it made him breathe again. As if maybe there was still a little bit of life left in the world.

"Did you ... get—"

Célie nodded, tightening her arms around herself.

He looked down at the chocolates again. He didn't want to eat them. They might have to last him for a very long time. He looked up at her. "You, ah—you want to go for a walk?"

She kneaded her fingers into her arms.

"Just, you know—together. I'm working on the communicating."

She swallowed and turned. But she only took a step down the sidewalk before she stopped and waited. So that must be an okay.

He stood and fell into step beside her. They walked through République to the canal. He flexed his hand a couple of times, uncertainly, and then extended it just a little.

She shoved her hands into the pockets of her leather jacket.

His hand fell back to his side, hope deflating.

They walked until they could climb one of the footbridges. He leaned his forearms against the railing, locking his fingers together again. His thumbs fought with each other. Relentlessly, neither one willing to give up.

"It's a good job," he said finally, low. "It pays … a lot. And it's something I'm interested in, and I can use my skills."

She nodded and didn't look at him.

"I—like that. I like knowing I can be good at what I need to do. I guess you were too much younger than me to know how crappy I was at school, when I couldn't ever figure out what the texts said fast enough or what the teachers wanted from me. I like being *good*."

"You're good, Joss."

She didn't look at him when she said it, but the words still mattered. He took a breath. "But I'm sorry I didn't talk to you about it. It seemed a straightforward decision. And I had, you know … that plan."

Célie sighed, her own forearms on the railing, staring at the water. The fitted leather that was supposed to protect her on the moped and make her look tougher only served somehow to emphasize the smallness of her forearms, compared to the power carried so easily in his own, bare just beside hers. And yet she was very strong—

those arms could knead bread all day, could whisk and mix and spread ganaches.

"It will take a while to get that apartment in shape. Maybe ... you could take a look at it. See if you'd be interested in us working on it ... together."

She looked at him without turning her head. His right thumb slayed his left one, and then the left one popped back from the grave and wrestled his right one down.

"It's important to you?" she said finally. "That I see it?"

He nodded, staring at his thumbs.

"All right," Célie said slowly, straightening from the railing.

He didn't ask about the motorcycle, when she led the way back to her moped. He didn't knead her hips when he rode behind her. He just balanced with the grip of his thighs.

Sickness grew in his stomach as he entered the code for the building, and he entered it wrong twice, a last-ditch subconscious effort to stop this self-humiliation. He swallowed the sickness down, but the bones of it lodged in his throat and even poked through in odd places in his chest, spiny shame.

That shame grew bigger as he opened the door, this acute, puncturing pressure from his belly out all through him. He stepped to the side and pressed his back to the wall, bracing himself so that he didn't leap forward and start blocking her way to the worst rooms.

The rotten floorboards were right there for her to see. The stains from God-knew-what on the walls. The half-ripped-out bathroom. The old, cheap, yellowed linoleum counters in the kitchen, and the ugly, rusty, chipped white sink. He drove himself back against the wall with all the strength of his legs and closed his eyes, listening to her move around the place. God, he didn't want to see her expression.

"It, ah, needs a lot of work," she said finally, coming back from her solitary exploration of the rooms.

"I know," he said between his teeth, staring at the floor.

She stopped in front of the windows. "Oh, wow. What a view."

He lifted his head a little.

She opened one of the windows and leaned out. "You can see most of the park! And the Eiffel Tower!"

He watched her silhouette against the light outside. "And you, ah, like the neighborhood, right?"

"It's funky. Diverse. Not so—" She did a snobby thing with her nose and waved toward the horizon, apparently indicating other possible quarters in Paris. "Wow," she said after a moment. "I can't believe you found a place right on the park." She snuck a quick glance at him. "No wonder you grabbed it."

He opened his hands, palm up. *See? I thought I was doing the best thing.*

She pulled her phone out of her jacket pocket and showed it to him. "Maybe you could have texted me. Sent me a photo. Called and said, 'Célie, I found this awesome place, but I have to grab it fast. What do you think?'"

"I had a plan." He rested his head against the wall behind him. *Go all out for your goals.* He'd already waited at least eight years for Célie, which seemed a long courtship. And he'd forgotten what she told him, that she hadn't been waiting for him.

Because he'd been too proud to ask her to.

She turned away from the window to look at him. "What was your plan, Joss?" she asked, her tone so much gentler than it had been last time this came up.

"To turn it into something beautiful before you saw it. So that your face would light up, you'd think it was so wonderful, and you'd, you know ... cover me in kisses." His cheeks heated. That same old stupid dream. "I didn't want you to see it like *this*."

"Joss." She came toward him. A little shock ran through him when she slipped her hands around his waist and leaned back to look into his face. His cheeks grew hotter under her look, but he stared down at her, caught by the fact that she had touched him again. "I'm never going to think of you as a failure. You know that, don't you?"

He swallowed, and then tried to harden his jaw. He'd learned young to shut out shame and blame—his teachers', and later his mother's. A psychopathic corporal on a power trip could dress him down during training and try to shame him and his fellow *engagés* into giving up and quitting, and he just let it wash off him, water off a duck's back.

But Célie ... she mattered.

"Never." She lifted her hands to rest them on his shoulders. "Not then and not now. That's not who you *are.*"

It was who he had been refusing to be since ... maybe since he was twelve. When his dad lost his job and everything started to go so wrong.

Maybe he'd been drawn to the military because he, too, needed a strong big brother or father figure. To help him figure out how to be the man he was trying to be.

Célie gave his shoulders a gentle squeeze. "You've always sparkled to me, Joss."

His blush swept up so deep he could feel it burning in his forehead.

She stroked it, from his forehead down to his cheeks, which she framed.

He took a deep breath, trying to absorb the coolness of her hands.

"*Sparkle* is maybe not the right word," she admitted. "You're so steady and deep and true. And you try so hard. Joss, I just ... you have to trust me with you enough to let me in. Because otherwise it's always you going off on your own to make sure everything's good enough, and leaving me alone."

"I'm trying," he said.

She looked around, at the wreck of an apartment in its perfect location. "Joss. Maybe there are men who were born perfect, born rich, born princes. But I don't give a crap about them. I like the ... *work* of you. The heart. The effort. I like that if you walk into a dump like this, you immediately see that all it will take to make it magnificent is you." She ran her palms down his arms to take his hands and lift them. "Your own hands."

His cheeks just refused to cool. His fingers wanted to link with hers and clutch, like a drowning man. And he was supposed to be stronger than all this. *He* was supposed to be saving *her.*

"But I like to work, too, Joss. I like to build, and make things better, and put my stamp on the world. If this is supposed to be *our* home, I'd like to be right in here with you, from the very beginning, scraping plaster off brick and painting walls and doing whatever else needs doing, to make it a perfect place for us."

"It's filthy work, Célie."

She shook her head. "I'd way rather crawl through the mud beside you to get to a goal than sit somewhere in a tower wondering what you're doing and if you'll succeed."

"I'll succeed," he said immediately. "I won't fa—"

She put her hand over his lips. "Maybe you will fail, sometimc, Joss. Maybe you'll screw up again. Most of us *do,* don't you get that? It's what we do with our failures, and how we pick ourselves back up and grow, that shows our worth. Just because something might not succeed as well as you want it doesn't make *you* a failure, as if that one effort defines your whole worth."

His breathing grew slower and deeper at her steady, firm voice, that sickness starting to calm. That warmth she brought him was growing in his middle, quieting the rest. "I should ... talk with you about this more," he said.

She smiled wryly, but her eyes were such a rich, welcoming brown.

"You—make sense." He rested his hands on her shoulders. God, they felt good under his hands. Small and strong. Her own kind of strength.

"See? If you help make sense of me, and I help make sense of you ... you see how that works? But for it to work properly, you have to let me know when you feel weak or wrong. So I can, you know, help get your head back on straight."

"Center me."

A surprised smile kicked across her face. "That's what you do for me," she protested.

He ran his hands down from her shoulders, squeezing her upper arms gently. "I guess you're saying that we can do it for each other."

The surprise faded from her smile, and she looked so happy. But she grew solemn again. "And if you're doing something hard that I can't help you with, that I can't do, too, I'd like to be around to support you. I would have done that, you know. Finished up my baker's apprenticeship and come to join you in Corsica, maybe opened up my own little bakery there. I bet I could have made a killing off all those hungry soldiers. But you would have had to trust me enough to risk letting me see you fail."

Trust her not to think of him as a failure, not to *make* him a failure by that very loss of belief in him, if she saw him struggle with or even fail at one of the thousands of impossible challenges thrown at men who wanted to become paratroopers in the Foreign Legion.

"I'm not your mother," Célie said.

He stiffened. "I know that, Célie." For God's sake, he was twenty-six years old, a paratrooper in the Foreign Legion, and she assumed he was still confusing his girlfriend with his mother? What the hell did a man have to do to prove himself as strong, free of his parents, above all that?

Besides, Célie wasn't anything like his mother.

Not ... anything.

No matter how mad she got, she never shamed, she never reduced, she never called a man a failure. *You're amazing.* Actually, half the time when she got mad at him, it seemed to be because he didn't think he was amazing *enough.* The very opposite of shame.

Célie smiled ruefully. "I know you know that here." She rested her hand on his heart. "But sometimes you forget it here." She touched her other hand to the back of his head.

He raised his eyebrows at her.

"Is that where the subconscious part of the brain is?" she whispered. "The back of the mind?"

So he had to laugh a little. Damn, he loved her. He pulled her in closer.

She held his gaze. "I won't ever try to make you smaller. I won't ever look down at you for not being good enough."

She was so fierce, as if the princess in the tower had always really been a dragon who happened to have long, curly eyelashes. No wonder that, eight years in, he still hadn't managed to win her. He'd been trying to court the wrong damn species.

"I think I always knew that here." He covered her hand on his heart. "But maybe I sometimes forgot it here." He covered her hand on the back of his head. "Or wherever that idiot part of the brain is."

She smiled a little. "And you know," she said quietly. "*I* might do something hard. I might like to have you around to support *me*, too, in *my* quests. When I'm, I don't know ... working forty-eight hours straight the week before Valentine's and would maybe, when I can finally stop, like someone who can just pick me up and take me home and feed me something besides chocolate and put me to bed, instead of having to make it home on my own."

Oh, *yeah,* he could do that. He liked the thought of it so much. Carrying her home—in his head, it was literally in his arms, through the streets, up the stairs—

putting her to bed, giving her that cuddle. He wanted to be her source of cuddles more than anything in the world.

He took another slow breath, long and clean, relaxing tension. “I like this communication of yours. Just talking it out. I like it this way, kind of ... calm, you know? When you’re not angry or accusing or blaming, I can ... hear you better.” Instead of his whole being bracing against it.

She squeezed his face very gently. “I could maybe improve my communication style, too.”

That made him smile. “I don’t know. The chocolate take on boiling oil from the castle walls had a certain flair.” Or maybe that had been a chocolatier-dragon’s version of fire-breathing.

She laughed a bit and rose on her tiptoes suddenly to wrap her arms around his shoulders. “I can cover you in chocolate again sometime,” she murmured teasingly into his neck. “It’s a cute look on you.”

Laughter. His arms closed around her. If she could tease him, then she had let him back in.

“Trust me, I’ve been covered in worse.” He boosted her up, urging her thighs around his hips so he could fit them better together. That brought her face nearly level with his, and he kissed her quickly, unable to help himself.

She kissed him back. It was supposed to be a quick, stolen kiss, but it turned into something else—slow and careful on both sides, tender and gentle, checking out all the angles. *Are you still here? I can still do this? This way, too? And this way? Are we going to be okay?*

She leaned back to take a breath, her eyes a little shy.

“Do you, ah ... think we could go back to dating?” he asked. “Like girlfriend and boyfriend?”

Her smile lit her whole face. “I would like that.”

"And ... would you consider taking on this dump of an apartment with me? Maybe we could beat it into shape?"

She squeezed him in happiness and tucked her face into the side of his neck again, kissing his jaw.

So that was what it felt like to get covered in kisses.

Not quite how he had imagined it, but definitely good enough for him.

"You *don't* make any sense, though," he mentioned, involuntarily. "I mean—you'd rather break your back and rub your fingers raw on this dump than have the apartment handed to you shiny and beautiful, with nothing for you to do?"

"I don't know, Joss. How would you feel if you found out I was working my butt off by myself trying to beat an apartment into shape to hand to *you*?"

He hesitated a very long moment. His eyebrows drew together suspiciously. "That can't be the same thing."

She nipped his neck very delicately. "Just chalk me up as weird, then." She jumped down and spun around to look at the place and stopped before the wall covered with peeling, stained old wallpaper, her eyes narrowing. "What do you want to bet there's a brick wall under there? It's going to be a *bitch* to get off all the plaster and reveal it, though."

"Did you see the fireplace?"

She looked back over her shoulder to give him a slow smile. "Nice, cozy rug right here?" She gestured to the space in front of the fireplace. "Couch here?" Another gesture.

And she was right. It *was* so much nicer to work on it together.

***

"I really do like this apartment that's *all bed*," Joss said that night, with that low, deep vibration of his voice through her back. His breath tickled her hair, his arm heavy and warm over her, that callused palm gently stroking her forearm. She smiled into the fold of white sheets that half blocked her view of the window. "I'm glad it's going to take us six months to get that other apartment into shape. I'm sorry I take up so much of your space here, though."

Her smile deepened. "No, you're not. You like taking up as much space as you do."

His thumb rubbed her forearm, and he kissed the top of her head.

"I like this cuddle," she whispered. "I like it so much."

"Yeah. I like it, too."

Yet another thing that made it better than all her vague imaginings—the sand-rasped depth of his voice, the way she could feel it in her own body, because he lay so close and warm against her. That warmth and sweetness that seemed to sink all through her and become her in some essential way.

Maybe it was a good warmth and sweetness to let herself become.

"I could tell you a bedtime story," that low, deep voice said against her back.

She linked her fingers with his big ones and waited.

"There was once a man nobody believed in. Not one person. Except you. And he'd do anything, anything in the world, not to lose that belief in him. But he felt like this unfired clay standing out there in the rain, slowly dissolving, while she kept looking up at him like he was a marble statue. And one day, he thought: I will go get fired in a kiln at least. I will become that man, so nothing and nobody can melt me into mud at her feet instead of the hero she thinks I am. He thought it was a fair trade—to take away the clay and mud for a while so that he could come back as the real thing."

Her fingers tightened on his, pressing his hand to her belly. *Oh, Joss.*

"But ... he was just a stupid kid. And kind of screwed up. He didn't know how long five years was, or that *his* girl couldn't possibly wait in a tower that long—she'd climb down her own hair and cut it off to get free and go make her*self* into someone she could admire, since she had to have someone. He's proud of her that she did that, though." His arm squeezed her. "He's sorry that he wasn't there, but he's very, very proud."

She brought their linked hands to her lips and kissed the calluses on his palm. "She's proud of him, too," she whispered. "She's very, very proud."

Chapter 25

"I love this rug." Célie petted the plush, soft white thing. Joss watched her, a profound peace and satisfaction stretching through his body, like the warmth from the fire.

Their motorcycle leathers hung by the door, drops of rain still clinging to them, and the light from the fire flickered over them. They'd finally been able to move in three weeks ago. Just in time for the Christmas season, when Célie was utterly swamped.

She'd worked until ten yet again, and Joss had swung by to pick her up. Mostly Célie preferred to drive herself. In fact, he'd kind of created a monster with that gift of a motorcycle, because she drove *way* the hell too fast, he was *always* having to fight with her to slow down, and she'd decided to let her hair grow to shoulder-length so she could see if that and the motorcycle leathers made her look like Black Widow.

She teased him about being Captain America, too, but Joss just shook his head at her. No offense to Captain America, but that man did not need to wait around eight years respecting Black Widow and not making his move on her. Just a little tip Joss could give him.

Plus ... Captain America was a superhero, serum-enhanced. And Joss ... Joss was human. All the impossible tasks Joss and his fellow Legionnaires had accomplished, all the buildings they'd jumped from and cliffs they'd scaled and weights they'd carried, all the wounds they'd survived, they'd had to do it with their own base human bodies.

With the clay of them, that they fired in a kiln of their own will.

He liked the hardness of his human body. Liked the way it felt, when he picked Célie up on his own motorcycle because she'd worked so hard and so late that she ... maybe didn't *need* him. Maybe that wasn't the right word. But it helped her, that he was there when she could finally get off, those nights when she was too tired to play at Black Widow. It helped her that she could slide exhausted on the bike behind him and wrap her arms around him and let him handle the traffic in the dark and the rain. It helped her that he made sure she put some actual decent rations into her body besides just chocolate, to get her ready again for another tough day tomorrow, and the next day, and all the way through until after New Year's.

He liked being her strength when she needed it. He liked it a lot.

"I love this hot chocolate," he said, because even as tired as she was, she'd made him some anyway, with a quick smile and sparkle of her eyes, whisking the chocolate into hot milk as he washed their plates.

He'd spent the hours between his quitting time and hers in the gym, working out, so he could use all the hot chocolate he could get.

His muscles were still a little pumped, in fact, which he was enjoying quite a bit because Célie's eyes kept lingering on his biceps whenever she glanced his way. He smiled at her.

She rolled on her back on the rug, gazing at the brick wall. God, the backbreaking, tedious hours she'd spent scraping plaster off that thing. And now she beamed every time she looked at it.

Kind of like he did, every time he looked at the gleaming hardwood floors or the elegant efficiency of the bathroom or the beautiful kitchen he'd built her, after consulting with her every step of the way—how she moved, what she reached for, what kind of things needed to go on the high shelves only he could reach for her, and what things in the cabinets she had to bend for. It meant that most of the things were slightly misplaced for him when he cooked, but that was okay. It was still way the hell better than anywhere he'd ever lived before.

On the wood mantle he had built for the fireplace sat photos Célie had framed. Them dressed up at Jaime's wedding—about damn time Dom got his guts up for that—and another of them a mess of sand and fun after helping build a sandcastle that same wedding weekend over in the U.S. Joss in Legion camouflage, with the men from his unit after they'd just finished cleaning out camps of drug dealers in Guyane. Herself, splattered with chocolate and beaming, holding up a trophy she'd won in a chocolate-making competition. Joss loved that one. It made him want to lean over and taste her for chocolate every time he looked at it.

She kept the postcards he had sent her in a drawer by her side of the bed, hidden, thank God, so that every friend who came over didn't have to see how bad he'd been at putting his heart down on paper. But sometimes, if they started snapping at each other over some minor thing, she would stomp off to the bedroom mad. He'd take a few minutes to calm down and want to make up, then follow to find her sitting on the bed looking through the postcards. And she'd smile at him, the irritation forgiven and forgotten in favor of what really mattered.

"I love this place," she said softly.

"I love you," he said.

She found his bare ankle and curved her hand around it, her thumb caressing his ankle bone as if even that part of his body had a texture she couldn't resist.

Hell, that felt good.

He set his chocolate on the hearth and pulled her up to nestle back against his body, her head tucked against the join of his thigh and hip.

"A lot. I mean ... really a lot."

He just didn't have the eloquence to tell her how much. "Really a lot," hell. Maybe he should have gone off for five years of poetry classes instead. He suspected Corey Chocolate wouldn't pay him nearly as well for an expertise in poetry, though.

She smiled at him. "I love you, too."

Maybe ... now would be a good time?

His stomach tightened. He tried to breathe through it. Hell, if Dom Richard could finally get up the nerve to propose to Jaime, *Joss* could risk a second rejection.

He could.

Damn it, he could.

Mostly because he just wanted it so damn bad.

Célie reached up from her position against his thigh to stroke his cheeks, and the coolness of her fingers made him realize how hot his skin was. Oh, fuck, was he blushing?

"How am I doing on the cuddles?" he asked.

She nestled her face into his thigh. "I'm so happy."

Sometimes he didn't know what to do with how much tenderness swamped him in moments like this. He almost couldn't breathe from it, as if it was his kryptonite or something. A force that could overwhelm a man no matter how strong he tried to be. He had to stroke her cheek and just sink into it.

"I wanted to ask you something." Heat burning in his cheeks, he rubbed one hand against the slate of the hearth. "I suppose now is a good time."

"Okay," she said quietly. She'd gotten so good at that—listening to him. She'd managed to breathe that anger out of her somehow and release it, in the way his mother had never been able to release her anger with his father, not even when she let it spill onto her son, too. Célie's quiet when he tried to talk to her now made him feel as if they were teenagers again—when they could talk about anything. When she had been his refuge, the person who made his thoughts feel whole and true and worthy of being shared.

Like teenagers, but ... bigger. Stronger. Even a little wiser.

Oh, hell, he just had to go for it. He cleared his throat and dug awkwardly into the pocket of the hip she wasn't lying on. Yes, he *had* been putting this item in his pocket every morning for the past six months, just in case his chances looked good that day. Just in case he could get his nerve up.

He got it free and took one deep breath, trying for the techniques he'd learned to deal with adrenaline in the Legion—fill your lungs. Hold it two seconds. Let it out long and slow. And go. "Do you ever think there might come a time again when people would think you were running around in sequins because it would make you so happy … to wear this?"

He held out the diamond ring she had once turned down.

And his stomach tightened to the point of implosion. The platinum burned against his fingers as if he'd pulled it straight out of a fire.

She drew in a breath, pressing her fist to her mouth.

Was that—oh, God, that was the exact same expression she'd had on her face just before she said *no* the other time.

His fist clenched around the ring. "Or, if you'd rather …" He had to clear his throat much harder this time. He fished in his pocket again. "There's this one."

God, this goddamn ring. Cheap, slim band, oversize fake diamond, bent setting. He had to breathe slowly to keep his hand open and the cheap thing resting on his palm, instead of hidden inside a fist.

But Célie … she lit up like, like … sequins. She sat up, grabbing his hand so she could look at it better. "Did you go back and buy me one just like the one you almost bought me before?" Her voice came out so hushed and wondering.

Damn, his throat felt rough. Five years in the Legion had ruined his voice. He tried to clear it anyway. "This is the one I bought before. Five and a half years ago, the night before I left." *See how pathetic it was? See why I couldn't offer it to you?*

Her hands tightened spasmodically on his. She jerked up her head so fast she almost hit him in the chin.

"You *bought* it? You actually had it in your pocket when you told me good-bye that night? And you lost your nerve?"

"I wanted to be better," he said low, a little helplessly.

"Oh, Joss." She threw her arms around him, holding on as tight as she could. Hell, that felt good. That was so much better than crying and telling him to go away. Oh, thank God. No matter how badly this proposal attempt turned out, at least it was already better than the last time. "I will strangle you one of these days, I swear."

He rubbed her back gently. "I've got a strong neck. I can risk it. For you."

"I love you so much," she whispered. "I always have."

Okay, so he was making progress. He was definitely getting better results this attempt than last one. But ...

Oh, fuck, would she just *say* it? Yes or no? The fucking suspense was killing him. What if she was letting him down gently? Or *what if she was going to say yes?*

He set both rings into the same hand and held them out to her on his palm. "You can have either one you want."

His pinky finger curled surreptitiously over the cheap one, trying to hide it.

Célie peeled his pinky finger back, looking at it. Oh, hell.

She looked back and forth between the two rings for a long time, the one that he was so proud of, that showed all that he had been able to accomplish, and the one of which he was ashamed, that showed where he came from. When she looked up at him, her eyes were shimmering. *Fuck*, not the tears. That had ended so badly for him last time.

And then she said, "Can I have both?"

He blinked, not quite able to absorb what she had just said. He felt kind of ... dizzy. As if all his world had just turned into this mass of swirling sequins under a disco ball.

"Because I love both those parts of you. Who you were and who you drove yourself to become. I love that you loved me then, and I love that you love me now," Célie said.

He snatched her into him, hugging her hard as he buried his face in her hair. "You can have either one you want." His voice hurt, coming through his throat. "As long as you say yes this time."

"*Yes*," she whispered.

Yes. His arms tightened on her so hard that she made a muffled sound of protest, and he eased his hold, but his empty hand kept petting her too deeply, over her back, her arm, up to frame her face. Yes, she was still there. It was the real Célie. She wasn't disappearing before his over-urgent fantasies. "Really? Hell, Célie, *really*?"

She opened the fist he'd made over the rings when he grabbed her and eased the tip of her ring finger into the cheap ring on his palm.

Damn that cheap one. But he took her hand and eased it on properly, then followed it with the other, much finer one.

Which looked ridiculous. "Célie." He covered the cheap one with his finger. There now. That expensive one on her finger—*that* looked beautiful.

"Maybe one on each hand." She pulled them off, and Joss quickly pre-empted her choice and slid the expensive one on her left ring finger, leaving the right ring finger for the cheap one.

She held out both hands. "Okay, that looks kind of ... excessive."

Joss frowned at the cheap ring. But ... it still did look kind of pretty on her hand. Way, way better than leaving that hand bare. He rubbed it, an almost wistful affection brushing him, as if he was honoring a fallen, difficult comrade.

"I'm going to have a jeweler frame it in gold," she decided. "So that it makes a pendant, the ring in its little frame. And wear it here." She placed her hand over her breast, right near her heart.

Because she valued everything about him. His accomplishments and his failures. Who he was and who he had been.

"You really have always loved me," he said low. "And I've always wanted to be good enough for that love."

"And you always have been good enough, Joss. Always."

He petted the wisps of hair on her forehead and stroked down her cheeks. "You make my life light up, you know."

She linked her hands behind his head. "You, too."

He shook his head, a little bemused. "Hard to imagine myself as lighting things up."

"It's all those sparkles off you," she teased gently. "Now that I'm wearing your ring."

A slow smile seemed to grow deep down in his belly and blush all the way through his body. He thought this might be what happiness felt like. Just this utter, blissful security of accepting and believing in love. "Think I should get us costumes made out of sequins?"

She shook her head, nestling into him. "It would be redundant."

Joss snuggled her in more closely. A deep, profound wonder filled him, a warmth and surety he never could have believed possible, once upon a time.

"You know, you were right all along," he said softly. "Together is a really good way to be."

***

FIN

THANK YOU!

Thank you so much for reading! I hope you enjoyed Célie and Joss's story. And don't miss Vi's story, coming up next in the Paris Hearts series! Sign up for Laura's newsletter (www.lauraflorand.com/newsletter) to be emailed the moment it's released.

Working on Célie's story inspired me to write a short story about Dom and Jaime (it involves sandcastles and courage) that I want to offer free to readers who love those two. If you are signed up for the newsletter, you'll be emailed a copy as soon as it's released.

(If you're new to my books and would love to read Dom and Jaime's full story, it is in *The Chocolate Touch.*)

All for You is the first in the Paris Hearts series. If you enjoyed the Paris and chocolate of the setting, you can find more of it in the Amour et Chocolat series. Or head south to a world of sun and flowers with the Vie en Roses series. (Keep reading for glimpses.)

Thank you so much for sharing this world with me! For some behind-the-scenes glimpses of the research with top chefs and chocolatiers, check out my website (www.lauraflorand.com) and Facebook (www.facebook.com/LauraFlorandAuthor). I hope to meet up with you there!

Thank you and all the best,

Laura Florand

Website: www.lauraflorand.com

Twitter: @LauraFlorand

Facebook: www.facebook.com/LauraFlorandAuthor

Newsletter: http://lauraflorand.com/newsletter

OTHER BOOKS BY LAURA FLORAND

Paris Hearts Series

All for You

Amour et Chocolat Series

All's Fair in Love and Chocolate, a novella in *Kiss the Bride*

The Chocolate Thief

The Chocolate Kiss

The Chocolate Rose (also a prequel to La Vie en Roses series)

The Chocolate Touch

The Chocolate Heart

The Chocolate Temptation

Sun-Kissed (also a sequel to *Snow-Kissed*)

Shadowed Heart (a sequel to *The Chocolate Heart*)

La Vie en Roses Series

Turning Up the Heat (a novella prequel)

The Chocolate Rose (also part of the Amour et Chocolat series)

A Rose in Winter, a novella in *No Place Like Home*

Once Upon a Rose

Snow Queen Duology

Snow-Kissed (a novella)

Sun-Kissed (also part of the Amour et Chocolat series)

Memoir

Blame It on Paris

ALL FOR YOU

ONCE UPON A ROSE

Book 1 in La Vie en Roses series: Excerpt

Burlap slid against Matt's shoulder, rough and clinging to the dampness of his skin as he dumped the sack onto the truck bed. The rose scent puffed up thickly, like a silk sheet thrown over his face. He took a step back from the truck, flexing, trying to clear his pounding head and sick stomach.

The sounds of the workers and of his cousins and grandfather rode against his skin, easing him. Raoul was back. That meant they were all here but Lucien, and Pépé was still stubborn and strong enough to insist on overseeing part of the harvest himself before he went to sit under a tree. Meaning Matt still had a few more years before he had to be the family patriarch all by himself, thank God. He'd copied every technique in his grandfather's book, then layered on his own when those failed him, but that whole job of taking charge of his cousins and getting them to listen to him was *still* not working out for him.

But his grandfather was still here for now. His cousins were here, held by Pépé and this valley at their heart, and not scattered to the four winds as they might be one day soon, when Matt became the heart and that heart just couldn't hold them.

All that loss was for later. Today was a good day. It could be. Matt had a hangover, and he had made an utter fool of himself the night before, but this could still be a good day. The rose harvest. The valley spreading around him.

J'y suis. J'y reste.

I am here and here I'll stay.

He stretched, easing his body into the good of this day, and even though it wasn't that hot yet, went ahead and reached for the hem of his shirt, so he could feel the scent of roses all over his skin.

"Show-off," Allegra's voice said, teasingly, and he grinned into the shirt as it passed his head, flexing his muscles a little more, because it would be pretty damn fun if Allegra was ogling him enough to piss Raoul off.

He turned so he could see the expression on Raoul's face as he bundled the T-shirt, half-tempted to toss it to Allegra and see what Raoul did—

And looked straight into the leaf-green eyes of Bouclettes.

Oh, shit. He jerked the T-shirt back over his head, tangling himself in the bundle of it as the holes proved impossible to find, and then he stuck his arm through the neck hole and his head didn't fit and he wrenched it around and tried to get himself straight and dressed somehow and—oh, *fuck.*

He stared at her, all the blood cells in his body rushing to his cheeks.

Damn you, stop, stop, stop, he tried to tell the blood cells, but as usual they ignored him. Thank God for dark Mediterranean skin. It had to help hide some of the color, right? Right? As he remembered carrying her around the party the night before, heat beat in his cheeks until he felt sunburned from the inside out.

Bouclettes was staring at him, mouth open as if he had punched her. Or as if he needed to kiss her again and—*behave!* She was probably thinking what a total jerk he was, first slobbering all over her drunk and now so full of himself he was stripping for her. And getting stuck in his own damn T-shirt.

Somewhere beyond her, between the rows of pink, Raoul had a fist stuffed into his mouth and was trying so hard not to laugh out loud that his body was bending into it, going into convulsions. Tristan was grinning, all right with his world. And Damien had his eyebrows up, making him look all controlled and princely, like someone who would *never* make a fool of himself in front of a woman.

Damn T-shirt. Matt yanked it off his head and threw it. But, of course, the air friction stopped it, so that instead of sailing gloriously across the field, it fell across the rose bush not too far from Bouclettes, a humiliated flag of surrender.

Could his introduction to this woman conceivably get any worse?

He glared at her, about ready to hit one of his damn cousins.

She stared back, her eyes enormous.

"Well, *what*?" he growled. "What do you want now? Why are you still here?" *I was drunk. I'm sorry. Just shoot me now, all right?*

She blinked and took a step back, frowning.

"Matt," Allegra said reproachfully, but with a ripple disturbing his name, as if she was trying not to laugh. "She was curious about the rose harvest. And she needs directions."

Directions. Hey, really? He was *good* with directions. He could get an ant across this valley and tell it the best route, too. He could crouch down with bunnies and have conversations about the best way to get their *petits* through the hills for a little day at the beach.

Of course, all his cousins could, too. He got ready to leap in first before his cousins grabbed the moment from him, like they were always trying to do. "Where do you need to go?" His voice came out rougher than the damn burlap. He struggled to smooth it without audibly clearing his throat. God, he felt naked. Would it look too stupid if he sidled up to that T-shirt and tried getting it over his head again?

"It's this house I inherited here," Bouclettes said. She had the cutest little accent. It made him want to squoosh all her curls in his big fists again and kiss that accent straight on her mouth, as if it was his, when he had so ruined that chance. "113, rue des Rosiers."

The valley did one great beat, a giant heart that had just faltered in its rhythm, and every Rosier in earshot focused on her. His grandfather barely moved, but then he'd probably barely moved back in the war when he'd spotted a swastika up in the *maquis* either. Just gently squeezed the trigger.

That finger-on-the-trigger alertness ran through every one of his cousins now.

Matt was the one who felt clumsy.

"Rue des Rosiers?" he said dumbly. Another beat, harder this time, adrenaline surging. "113, *rue des Rosiers*?" He looked up at a stone house, on the fourth terrace rising into the hills, where it got too steep to be practical to grow roses for harvest at their current market value. "Wait, *inherited?*"

Bouclettes looked at him warily.

"How could you *inherit* it?"

"I don't know exactly," she said slowly. "I had a letter from Antoine Vallier."

Tante Colette's lawyer. Oh, hell. An ominous feeling grew in the pit of Matt's stomach.

"On behalf of a Colette Delatour. He said he was tracking down the descendants of Élise Dubois."

What? Matt twisted toward his grandfather. Pépé stood very still, with this strange, tense blazing look of a fighter who'd just been struck on the face and couldn't strike back without drawing retaliation down on his entire village.

Matt turned back to the curly-haired enemy invader who had sprung up out of the blue. Looking so damn cute and innocent like that, too. He'd *kissed* her. "You can't—Tante Colette gave that house to *you*?"

Bouclettes took a step back.

Had he roared that last word? His voice echoed back at him, as if the valley held it, would squeeze it in a tight fist and never let it free. The air constricted, merciless bands around his sick head and stomach.

"After all that?" He'd just spent the last five months working on that house. Five months. *Oh, could you fix the plumbing, Matthieu? Matthieu, that garden wall needs mending. Matthieu, I think the septic tank might need to be replaced.* Because she was ninety-six and putting her life in order, and she was planning to pass it on to him, right? Because she understood that it was part of his valley and meant to leave this valley whole. Wasn't that the tacit promise there, when she asked him to take care of it? "*You*? Colette gave it to *you*?"

Bouclettes stared at him, a flash of hurt across her face, and then her arms tightened, and her chin went up. "Look, I don't know much more than you. My grandfather didn't stick around for my father's childhood, apparently. All we knew was that he came from France. We never knew we had any heritage here."

Could Tante Colette have had a child they didn't even know about? He twisted to look at his grandfather again, the one man still alive today who would surely have noticed a burgeoning belly on his stepsister. Pépé was frowning, not saying a word.

So—"To *you*?" Tante Colette knew it was his valley. You didn't just rip a chunk out of a man's heart and give it to, to…to whom exactly?

"To *you*?" Definitely he had roared that, he could hear his own voice booming back at him, see the way she braced herself. But—who the hell was she? And what the *hell* was he supposed to do about this? Fight a girl half his size? Strangle his ninety-six-year-old aunt? How did he crush his enemies and defend this valley? His enemy was…she was so *cute*. He didn't want her for an enemy, he wanted to figure out how to overcome last night's handicap and get her to think he was cute, too. Damn it, he hadn't even found out yet what those curls felt like against his palms.

And it was *his valley*.

Bouclettes' chin angled high, her arms tight. "You seemed to like me last night."

Oh, God. Embarrassment, a hangover, and being knifed in the back by his own aunt made for a perfectly horrible combination. "I was *drunk*."

Her mouth set, this stubborn, defiant rosebud. "I never thought I'd say this to a man, but I think I actually liked you better drunk." Turning on her heel, she stalked back to her car.

Matt stared after her, trying desperately not to be sick in the nearest rose bush. Family patriarchs didn't get to do that in front of the members of their family.

"I told my father he should never let my stepsister have some of this valley," his grandfather said tightly. "I told him she couldn't be trusted with it. It takes proper family to understand how important it is to keep it intact. Colette *never* respected that."

His cousins glanced at his grandfather and away, out over the valley, their faces gone neutral. They all knew this about the valley: It couldn't be broken up. It was their *patrimoine*, a world heritage really, in their hearts they knew it even if the world didn't, and so, no matter how much they, too, loved it, they could never really have any of it. It had to be kept intact. It had to go to Matt.

The others could have the company. They could have one hell of a lot more money, when it came down to liquid assets, they could have the right to run off to Africa and have adventures. But the valley was his.

He knew the way their jaws set. He knew the way his cousins looked without comment over the valley, full of roses they had come to help harvest because all their lives they had harvested these roses, grown up playing among them and working for them, in the service of them. He knew the way they didn't look at him again.

So he didn't look at them again, either. It *was* his valley, damn it. He'd tried last year to spend some time at their Paris office, to change who he was, to test out just one of all those many other dreams he had had as a kid, dreams his role as heir had never allowed him to pursue. His glamorous Paris girlfriend hadn't been able to stand the way the valley still held him, even in Paris. How fast he would catch a train back if something happened that he had to take care of. And in the end, he hadn't been able to stand how appalled she would get at the state of his hands when he came back, dramatically calling her manicurist and shoving him in that direction. Because he'd always liked his hands before then—they were strong and they were capable, and wasn't that a good thing for hands to be? A little dirt ground in sometimes—didn't that just prove their worth?

In the end, that one effort to be someone else had made his identity the clearest: The valley was who he was.

He stared after Bouclettes, as she slammed her car door and then pressed her forehead into her steering wheel.

"Who the hell is Élise Dubois?" Damien asked finally, a slice of a question. Damien did not like to be taken by surprise. "Why should Tante Colette be seeking out her heirs *over her own*?"

Matt looked again at Pépé, but Pépé's mouth was a thin line, and he wasn't talking.

Matt's head throbbed in great hard pulses. How could Tante Colette do this?

Without even warning him. Without giving him one single chance to argue her out of it or at least go strangle Antoine Vallier before that idiot even thought about sending that letter. Matt should have known something was up when she'd hired such an inexperienced, fresh-out-of-school lawyer. She wanted someone stupid enough to piss off the Rosiers.

Except—unlike his grandfather—he'd always trusted Tante Colette. She was the one who stitched up his wounds, fed him tea and soups, let him come take refuge in her gardens when all the pressures of his family got to be too much.

She'd loved him, he thought. Enough not to give a chunk of his valley to a stranger.

"It's that house," Raoul told Allegra, pointing to it, there a little up the hillside, only a couple of hundred yards from Matt's own house. If Matt knew Raoul, his cousin was probably already seeing a window—a way he could end up owning a part of this valley. If Raoul could negotiate with rebel warlords with a bullet hole in him, he could probably negotiate a curly-haired stranger into selling an unexpected inheritance.

Especially with Allegra on his side to make friends with her. While Matt alienated her irreparably.

Allegra ran after Bouclettes and knocked on her window, then bent down to speak to her when Bouclettes rolled it down. They were too far away for Matt to hear what they said. "Pépé." Matt struggled to speak. The valley thumped in his chest in one giant, echoing beat. It hurt his head, it was so big. It banged against the inside of his skull.

Possibly the presence of the valley inside him was being exacerbated by a hangover. Damn it. He pressed the heels of his palms into his pounding skull. What the hell had just happened?

Pépé just stood there, lips still pressed tight, a bleak, intense look on his face.

Allegra straightened from the car, and Bouclettes pulled away, heading up the dirt road that cut through the field of roses toward the house that Tante Colette had just torn out of Matt's valley and handed to a stranger.

Allegra came back and planted herself in front of him, fists on her hips. "Way to charm the girls, Matt," she said very dryly.

"F—" He caught himself, horrified. He could not possibly tell a woman to fuck off, no matter how bad his hangover and the shock of the moment. Plus, the last thing his skull needed right now was a jolt from Raoul's fist. So he just made a low, growling sound.

"She thinks you're hot, you know," Allegra said, in that friendly conversational tone torturers used in movies as they did something horrible to the hero.

"I...she...what?" The valley packed inside him fled in confusion before the *man* who wanted to take its place, surging up. Matt flushed dark again, even as his entire will scrambled after that flush, trying to get the color to die down.

"She said so." Allegra's sweet torturer's tone. "One of the first things she asked me after she got up this morning: 'Who's the hot one?'"

Damn blood cells, stay away from my cheeks. The boss did not flush. Pépé never flushed. You held your own in this crowd by being the roughest and the toughest. A man who blushed might as well paint a target on his chest and hand his cousins bows and arrows to practice their aim. "No, she did not."

"Probably talking about me." Amusement curled under Tristan's voice as he made himself the conversation's red herring. Was his youngest cousin taking pity on him? How had Tristan turned out so nice like that? After they made him use the purple paint when they used to pretend to be aliens, too.

"*And* she said you had a great body." Allegra drove another needle in, watching Matt squirm. He couldn't even stand himself now. His body felt too big for him. As if all his muscles were trying to get his attention, figure out if they were actually *great.*

"And she was definitely talking about Matt, Tristan," Allegra added. "You guys are impossible."

"I'm sorry, but I can hardly assume the phrase 'the hot one' means Matt," Tristan said cheerfully. "Be my last choice, really. I mean, there's me. Then there's—well, me, again, I really don't see how she would look at any of the other choices." He widened his teasing to Damien and Raoul, spreading the joking and provocation around to dissipate the focus on Matt.

"I was there, Tristan. She was talking about Matt," said Allegra, who either didn't get it, about letting the focus shift off Matt, or wasn't nearly as sweet as Raoul thought she was. "She thinks you're hot," she repeated to Matt, while his flush climbed back up into his cheeks and *beat* there.

Not in front of my cousins, Allegra! Oh, wow, really? Does she really?

Because his valley invader had hair like a wild bramble brush, and an absurdly princess-like face, all piquant chin and rosebud mouth and wary green eyes, and it made him want to surge through all those brambles and wake up the princess. And he so could not admit that he had thoughts like those in front of his cousins and his grandfather.

He was thirty years old, for God's sake. He worked in dirt and rose petals, in burlap and machinery and rough men he had to control. He wasn't supposed to fantasize about being a prince, as if he were still twelve.

Hadn't he made the determination, when he came back from Paris, to stay *grounded* from now on, real? Not to get lost in some ridiculous fantasy about a woman, a fantasy that had no relationship to reality?

"Or she *did*," Allegra said, ripping the last fingernail off. "Before you yelled at her because of something that is hardly her fault."

See, that was why a man needed to keep his feet on the ground. You'd think, as close a relationship as he had with the earth, he would know by now how much it hurt when he crashed into it. Yeah, did. Past tense.

But she'd stolen his land from him. How was he supposed to have taken that calmly? He stared up at the house, at the small figure in the distance climbing out of her car.

Pépé came to stand beside him, eyeing the little house up on the terraces as if it was a German supply depot he was about to take out. "I want that land back in the family," he said, in that crisp, firm way that meant, *explosives it is and tough luck for anyone who might be caught in them.* "This land is yours to defend for this family, Matthieu. What are you going to do about this threat?”

Available now!

LAURA FLORAND

THE CHOCOLATE TEMPTATION

Amour et Chocolat series: Excerpt

She hated him.

Tossing around dessert elements as if they were juggling balls he had picked up to idle away the time and, first try, had dozens flying around his body in multiple figure eights.

Patrick Chevalier.

Sarah hated him with every minute painstaking movement with which she made sure a nut crumb lay exactly the way Chef Leroi wanted it on a financier. She hated him with every flex of tendons and muscles in her aching hands in the evening, all alone in her tiny Paris apartment at the approach to Montmartre, knowing someone else was probably letting him work the tension out of his own hands any way he wanted.

She hated him because she knew he probably didn't even have any tension in his hands. That after fifteen or more brutal hours in one of the most mercilessly perfectionistic pastry kitchens in the world, he was still as relaxed as if he'd been sunning all day on a beach, occasionally catching a wave.

She hated him because five thousand times a day, his body brushed hers, his hand caught her shoulder or touched her back to guide their bodies around each other, in that constant dance of sixteen bodies in a space much too small for so many people working at blinding speeds. She hated him because every time his body controlled hers so easily, she felt all the lean, fluid muscles from his fingertips to his toes – and knew that however lazy he looked, those muscles knew tension.

She hated him because most times when he touched her he didn't even notice, and once in a while, when he did, those vivid blue eyes laughed into hers or winked at her as if she was gobble-up delicious, and then he was gone, leaving her heart this messy, unthawed lump that had just tried to throw itself into his hands and ended up instead all gooey over her own shoes.

Fortunately black kitchen shoes were used to receiving a lot of gooey messes on them over the course of a day.

"Sarabelle," he called laughingly, and she hated him for that, too. The way her ordinary, serious American name turned so exotic and caressing with those French Rs and dulcet Ahs, like a sigh of rich silk all over her skin. The way he added *belle* onto it, whenever it struck his fancy, as if that couldn't break someone's heart, to be convinced someone like him thought she was *belle* and then realize he thought everybody was *belle*. He probably called his dog *belle*, and his four-year-old niece *belle* when he ruffled her hair.

And they both probably looked up at him with helpless melting, too.

She hated him because she knew he couldn't even have a dog, given his working hours, and that somehow her entire vision of Patrick Chevalier, which was all of him he let her have, could not possibly be true.

Available now!

ACKNOWLEDGMENTS

First of all, a huge thank you to author Virginia Kantra for her patience reading the original drafts of the manuscript and offering advice in terms of pacing and story. She is one generous, classy, insightful woman, and I can't say enough in her praise. A huge thank you also to author Stephanie Burgis for her early feedback and her wonderful support.

And thank you also to my wonderful beta readers for this story, Mercy and Dale Anderson, Lisa Chinn, and Nikki Cheah, who have been so generous with their time and support. Having that early feedback was invaluable!

And, of course, since we are back in Dominique Richard's salon de chocolat for this book, I must again thank the amazing Jacques Genin, who patiently allowed me to research in his laboratoire and whose beautiful salon and chocolates were the inspiration for this setting. I also want to thank Sophie Vidal, Jacques Genin's chef chocolatier, who was equally patient with me in my research and who showed me what the role of a chef chocolatier in such an establishment consists of.

And a huge thank you, of course, to all my readers, as always, for all your support which has kept me motivated to write more books! Thank you all so much.

ABOUT LAURA FLORAND

Laura Florand burst on the contemporary romance scene in 2012 with her award-winning Amour et Chocolat series. Since then, her international bestselling books have appeared in ten languages, been named among the Best Books of the Year by *Romantic Times* and Barnes & Noble, received the RT Seal of Excellence and numerous starred reviews from *Publishers Weekly, Library Journal,* and *Booklist,* and been recommended by NPR, *USA Today,* and *The Wall Street Journal,* among others.

After a Fulbright year in Tahiti and backpacking everywhere from New Zealand to Greece, and several years living in Madrid and Paris, Laura now teaches Romance Studies at Duke University. Contrary to what the "Romance Studies" may imply, this means she primarily teaches French language and culture and does a great deal of research on French gastronomy, particularly chocolate.

COPYRIGHT

Cover by Sebastien Florand

ISBN-13: 978-1-943168-00-2

Made in the USA
Lexington, KY
07 August 2015